DANIELLE

Vivian Schurfranz

SCHOLASTIC INC.
New York Toronto London Auckland Sydney Tokyo

To Dad and Minnie

ISBN 0-590-33156-6

Copyright © 1984 by Vivian Schurfranz. All rights reserved. Published by Scholastic Inc.

12 11 10 9 8 7 6 5 4 3 2 1   8   4 5 6 7 8 9/8

Printed in the U.S.A.   06

DANIELLE

A *SUNFIRE*™ Book

SUNFIRE

Chapter One

DANIELLE Verlaine mounted her black
stallion, Ebony, and sat her saddle with ease.
"Let's go slowly, my beauty," she whispered,
"until we reach the banana grove."

Ebony's ears perked up in response to his
mistress' voice, and with a sedate gait he
moved along the trail away from the sugar
plantation. Danielle, in a dark riding dress
and leather boots, had braided her blond hair
in a coil around her head. She knew, despite
her fifteen years, that she appeared to be
quite the mature horsewoman, although she
had been considered immature by her mother
that morning.

Smiling, she recalled the scene. She had
stripped down to her pantaloons, leaving her
dress and petticoat on the banks of the
Mississippi River, and plunged into the flowing waters that were swift because of the

recently heavy rains. She had been the only swimmer for miles, and except for a water snake or two, she had the whole river to herself.

When she'd come back to the plantation, dripping wet, her mother had shaken her head in disbelief. "Danielle!" she had scolded. "Don't you realize there are people all along the river — field hands, fishermen, washerwomen, and bargemen? You mustn't be so bold. You're no longer a child, and you should behave like a young lady."

Impulsively, Danielle gave her mother a kiss. "It was great fun, Mother, and by the Great River Spirit, no one saw me. Oh, wait." She paused to reflect, tapping her finger on her chin. "Maybe two or three flatboatmen!"

When she saw her mother's eyes widen, she laughed. "I'm just teasing. Don't worry. I have perfect manners in the right circumstances," and with these words she went up the steps, chin high, in a most dignified manner. As dignified as was possible, that is, in her wet undergarments.

Now the warm sunlight glinted over the pink oleanders, and a gentle breeze wafted through the low weeping willow branches. On such a glorious September afternoon in Louisiana in 1814, it was difficult to believe that a war was taking place. The British, who had already burned Washington, D.C., and forced President Madison and his wife, Dolley, to flee with the Declaration of Independence, had also pledged to burn New

Orleans. Danielle read constantly about the war and the military situation, even though such interest was considered unladylike. Danielle knew one of the main reasons for the conflict was that the British were boarding U.S. ships and taking American sailors off, declaring that they were British deserters. The Easterners had suffered from the war the most, but it looked as if it would soon be Louisiana's turn. If New Orleans were attacked, chances for survival would be slim, for the city's defense consisted of only a small militia force. Danielle pressed her lips together. The British needed to be taught another lesson. It seemed they still viewed the States as their colonies.

But at Cypress Manor everything was serene and peaceful. "Come, Ebony." Gently, Danielle prodded the horse forward. He responded eagerly to her slightest signal and broke into a canter.

A blue heron soared and dipped over the green, shimmering leaves of the banana trees, and a squirrel skittered across the dusty path. Danielle, happy to be alive, tried to put the war out of her mind, but she couldn't help thinking of her father, one of Governor Claiborne's chief military advisers, who would soon be called to defend the city of ten thousand. It was reported that the British had already set sail for the Gulf of Mexico, and Andrew Jackson, who was supposed to defend New Orleans, was still fighting Indians near Mobile. Well, Danielle could shoot and ride as well as any man, and if need be, she could defend herself.

Arriving in New Orleans, Danielle waved to a flower vendor who was almost hidden among his rich hibiscus blossoms on Dumaine Street. As she continued down the pretty thoroughfare, she passed raised cottages with ground floors of brick and the upper floors of cypress. Gardens and trees were abundant, with lush flowers overflowing on the balconies. Turning onto Royal Street and the fancier houses with their beautiful courtyards, Ebony's hooves clattered by cast-iron balconies, and once in a while, Danielle was able to glimpse a well in the center of an exquisite patio or a circular wrought-iron staircase. Some mansions had wide carriageways that could be seen through an arch; and one had a towering wall, covered with bougainvillaea on one side and a row of arches on the other. On St. Philip Street, she passed the pillared mansion of the pirate Jean Lafitte and his brother, Pierre. Oh, the parties those two buccaneers gave! How she'd love to have an invitation to one of their sumptuous dinners.

Farther along, the sight of a cool fountain splashing in a shady patio looked so inviting that she was ready to relax over a cup of coffee with Paul. As she neared the harbor and came upon Tchoupitoulas Street, she spurred Ebony a little faster, for this street was where the flatboatmen lived, and they were known for their brawls and gambling.

She wrinkled her nose at the odors, strong and pungent. Crabs and shrimp were kept in wooden vats, and fishermen had brought in catfish this morning, still wrapped in leaves to shield them from the sun. Others were cleaning great pompano fish on long tables.

Turning down a narrow cobblestone street, she pulled on Ebony's reins before the Inn of the Red Parrot. Dismounting, she flung open the gate in the iron fence and entered the coffee house. Paul Milerand rose to his rangy six feet. Skirting the tables, Danielle lightly kissed the blond young man on the cheek and sat across from him, smiling secretly at her brazen behavior.

Her British mother, Adelaide, was cool and competent, keeping the records for the plantation's sugar output, and she had taught her daughter both self-reliance and etiquette. Danielle's freewheeling behavior might be frowned upon in London or Boston, but in New Orleans, young ladies grew up differently. At least if their parents were Adelaide and Antoine Verlaine! Nonetheless, Danielle's daredevil ways were too much even for them, and she had been admonished more than once to "act more like a lady."

Her father, a Creole, like so many Louisianians, had been born in the New World of original French settlers. He was a plantation owner who was fiercely independent and refused to allow any slaves in his sugarcane fields . . . only freemen who were paid a decent wage. He had reared Danielle to stand up for her rights but to respect the dignity and worth of every individual. He called her the brainiest girl in all Louisiana, and also the prettiest. Nonetheless, he was beginning to curb her headstrong ways now that she was becoming an adult, and she hated having the reins pulled.

"Young ladies don't do that," he would admonish. How she chafed under these new restraints. Why was being fifteen so much different from being thirteen or fourteen?

"Why are you smiling?" Paul asked.

"Oh, nothing . . . just something Father said." She didn't want to elaborate because she was certain Paul disapproved of her independent spirit.

The young midshipman ordered two demitasses, and as they waited, he placed his large hand over hers. "Danielle, I've saved over six hundred dollars this year by serving on the *Carolina*. With my father's help, I'll be able to own a schooner by the time I'm twenty-two."

Frowning slightly, Danielle replied, "You plan your life like other people plant gardens . . . everything in neat little rows."

The tiny coffee cups were brought, and she added a teaspoon of sugar and stirred it. "I can't believe that in four years' time you'll be a captain." She studied his handsome face. His nose was a little too crooked, but people overlooked this when they saw the warm, brown eyes that dominated his face. They were set wide apart and were ever so gentle, like Paul himself. He looked smartly handsome in his striped shirt with the large collar, red neckerchief, and dark blue jacket.

"Since your father is the captain of his own ship, I know he'll help his only son follow in his wake." Danielle smiled at Paul teasingly.

"Most of the money I will have earned by my own work," he countered resolutely. The sparkle in his large eyes vanished, and he set his cup firmly in the saucer.

"I believe you." She smiled impishly. "I love to tease you, Paul. You take everything so seriously."

She sipped the chicory-laced coffee, thinking he was indeed a special man. Paul's mother had died of yellow fever when he was only ten, but not before she had instilled in him her own sensitive qualities. His inner strength was attractive, although at times his lack of adventure proved exasperating.

"I admire you," she said simply.

"I'd rather you'd love me," he replied with a grin.

"You'll have my love when you're a rich and famous captain," she answered, teasing again. "I'm afraid, though, that the pirates will plunder your cargoes."

"I'm not worried. By the time I own my schooner, the United States government will have swept every pirate out of the Caribbean Sea."

Danielle shrugged. "Perhaps." The uncertainty in her voice mirrored her thoughts.

She doubted whether Jean Lafitte and his men would ever be captured. Maybe one here and one there like Pierre Lafitte, but not the thousand buccaneers loyal to Jean Lafitte.

"Pierre Lafitte's been in jail all summer," said Danielle. "How long do you think Jean Lafitte will permit his brother to lie in chains in a cell?"

"Not much longer, I'd guess, but Jean will need to be extra careful. The whole militia is waiting for his move to release Pierre. Who wouldn't want the five-hundred-dollar reward?"

"Remember when Governor Claiborne first posted a reward for the capture of Jean Lafitte?" Danielle laughed. "The next day all the posters had been torn down, and there were new posters offering a fifteen-hundred-dollar reward if any man would deliver Governor Claiborne to Jean Lafitte's island, Grand Terre. The governor was furious, and Father almost had an attack of apoplexy. Jean Lafitte is one bold, handsome pirate!"

"I wouldn't be so quick to admire his swaggering ways."

"Oh, Paul, why not? Most New Orleans citizens consider him dashing. Besides, he smuggles in luxury goods people are eager to buy."

"He'll get caught one of these days! He's still auctioning off slaves, and that's detestable! The way he spits in the eye of authority will catch up with him, you'll see. Then let's see how much strutting he'll do!"

She took another sip of the thick coffee but said nothing. Paul reminded her of her father; not as volatile, but neither of them could recognize Jean Lafitte's boldness. Just because he skirted the law a little was no reason to be so hostile toward him. Besides, she'd heard he no longer sold slaves.

"Let's forget the pirates." Paul shyly reached in his vest pocket and drew forth a velvet pouch. "I brought something to show you." He extracted an emerald ring and held it out for her. "This was my mother's, and one day soon, I want you to wear it."

The green jewel sparkled in the light, and Danielle reached for it, then withdrew her hand, empty. All at once she was the one that felt shy. She wasn't ready to accept this lovely ring set in a gold filigree mounting. Paul was the only boy she'd ever really known. She wanted to experience meeting other men — seeing places other than New Orleans.

"This is an engagement ring, and when the war is over, I'll talk to your father and hopefully slip it on your finger. If he approves, will you wear it?"

"I — I don't know," she stammered. She knew her father and mother liked Paul, and for a long time there had been a tacit agreement between their two families, but she wasn't ready for marriage! Everything had been prearranged when she was only six years old, and now that she was grown, she didn't like it. She didn't intend to marry Paul just yet, and maybe she never would.

Her father had taught her to be independent, and that's just what she meant to be. Besides, she yearned to have a man who would sweep her off her feet. That would never be Paul. Nonetheless, she would be tactful.

"Paul, you know I'm fond of you, but I'm not ready to talk about a wedding yet." She stood and abruptly changed the subject. "I need to buy *maman* some writing quills."

"Can I walk with you?"

"Of course . . . if you can keep up." She laughed sweetly.

Paul frowned at the jibe but rose gracefully. "Will you have time to look at the *Dolphin*? It's a schooner in from Boston and similar to one I want to buy."

"I'd love to see it."

He reached for her hand and they left, heading first for a shop where Danielle purchased six goose quills and then on to Decatur Street, which led to the wharves and the harbor.

The port was alive with sloops, frigates, and gunboats — and one beautiful two-masted schooner, riding at anchor. Her hull rode the waters delicately as if eagerly awaiting the wind and the sea. The ship was painted black with red trim. Its white sails were being hoisted.

"The *Dolphin*'s preparing to sail," said Paul. "I was hoping to be invited aboard, but she's already leaving for Boston."

"She's so graceful." Danielle watched breathlessly as one sail caught the breeze on the mainmast while one large sail and three smaller ones billowing in front on the foremast turned the ship toward the Gulf.

"You know, without our navy the British would have won the war already. They've won every land battle so far, but our ships, well, that's a different story!" He removed his wide-brimmed hat and ran his fingers through his thick hair, which the sun made even more golden. Pulling his eyeglass from his back pocket, he opened it to its full length and studied the moving ship. "It looks as if it's going to catch the west wind and be able to fly. Such a beautiful day for sailing." His voice sounded wistful.

"It sounds as if you're ready to reboard the *Carolina*."

"I love the sea, Danielle. I can't wait to take you on my schooner. You'll love it as much as I do." He gazed at her admiringly. "Your eyes match the sea's moods and change into as many colors. What a fine captain's lady you'll be!"

"Possibly," retorted Danielle, and hoisted herself up on a wide post used to secure boats. Shading her eyes, she watched a ship glide into the harbor and drop anchor.

"It's the *Pride*, Lafitte's ship," Paul murmured, studying the fine lines of the bow through his spyglass.

Within five minutes, a skiff had been lowered and a sailor and a gentleman disembarked.

Paul said sourly, "Surely Lafitte has more sense than to venture into town!"

Drumming her heels against the post, Danielle smiled broadly. "That's exactly what he's doing! He's daring Claiborne to arrest him. That's what I call courage."

Paul snorted. "Sometimes, Danielle, you don't seem to know right from wrong."

The burly pirate easily rowed the skiff through the water. Lafitte, his black hair ruffling in the breeze, sat straight, surveying the boats about him as if he owned the harbor.

As Lafitte stepped from the skiff to the dock, Danielle noticed his black, snapping eyes and black beard, which extended partway up his cheeks. He was dressed in a green velvet waistcoat, striped trousers with buttons down the side, and a silk cravat, all in the latest fashion.

Deftly, Lafitte reached down to his oarsman for his hat and cane, and with an assured gesture, fitted the tall beaver hat jauntily on his head and sauntered down the pier's length, stopping briefly in front of Danielle.

Danielle's eyes widened, and she sat as still as a deer sniffing the air when a wildcat is near.

With a flourish, Lafitte doffed his hat, sweeping it across his chest as he bowed low. "Mademoiselle Verlaine, *bonjour.*"

"Good day," she stammered, feeling like a bumpkin perched atop the post. "How did you know my name?" she asked lamely.

Lafitte threw back his head and laughed, showing even, white teeth against his rather pale skin. "I know all about my old enemy, Captain Verlaine. You are his only daughter and his joy. And this sailor, Paul"— he snapped his gloved fingers in frustration — "Paul?"

"Milerand is the name, Paul Milerand." Paul's tone was cool and self-possessed, not at all cowed before the most wanted criminal in Louisiana.

Lafitte turned to the buccaneer who had finished tying the skiff and was hurrying to catch up to his leader. "Gambi, do you hear? We have a brave American sailor here who is lucky enough to escort the loveliest girl in all the Americas and the West Indies!"

Gambi, slightly out of breath because of his bulk, came rushing up to Lafitte. His bowed legs, massive chest, and oversize head set on a thick neck made him appear like the formidable cutthroat he was. Gambi, bowed legs apart, tapping his fingers on his saber's hilt, glowered at Danielle.

"Well, Gambi?" Lafitte quizzically lifted his thick brows. "Don't you agree? Isn't she beautiful?"

Gambi only nodded, then said slowly, "She may be beautiful, but anything spawned by Antoine Verlaine has to be evil."

Paul stepped forward, only inches from Gambi's dark face with its bristling mustache. "Careful, pirate."

Lafitte stopped smiling. "No, no, my young

buck. My men are not pirates. Call him a privateer or my corsair but never a pirate." His cool tone lightened, and he continued, "Gambi is a rough, simple man who never understands the finer nuances of a subject. To him, people are either *for* Captain Lafitte or *against* him." He turned and grasped Gambi's massive arm. "Come, Gambi, it's time for a stroll down Royal Street."

Gambi grunted, shot Danielle an angry look, and went on ahead.

Lafitte gave Danielle a dazzling smile. "Good-bye, mademoiselle. I hope we meet again." Glancing in Paul's direction, he added, "And you, too, young man. It's good to know we have sailors like you to fight the British." Chuckling, he left them with his final words, "Now I intend to turn a few heads and to start a few tongues wagging."

Danielle, speechless, watched Lafitte's retreating back. Finally, she slid from the post and said, "What do you think of that, Paul?"

Paul shrugged. "What is different? Lafitte, the pirate"— he emphasized those last two words —"defies authority whenever he gets the chance."

"There you go again, Paul, always siding with the law. Sometimes the law is wrong, too."

"Of course, my love." He took her hand, eyes twinkling. "But not very often." Playfully, he lifted her over a broken plank in the pier. "You'll see that others can be as gallant as your precious Jean Lafitte and still not have a price on their heads."

When her boots touched the wood, she again slipped her hand into Paul's. His strength and loyalty would always be hers. She recalled Gambi, and with a shudder expressed her feelings, "I'd hate to meet Gambi alone. He is not as gallant as his chief." The words were thoughtfully said. Despite Lafitte's warning, Gambi was truly a pirate, and whenever that bully was near, she'd try to become as small as a river shrimp, for it was evident by the hatred in his eyes that her beauty held no fascination for him.

Chapter Two

At lunch the next day, Danielle ladled a serving of crab gumbo onto her pewter plate and asked, "Where's Father?"

Her mother dabbed the corner of her mouth with her napkin before replying. "He's on the veranda, talking to Tulci."

Danielle, staring at the yellow-paneled walls, pondered what this meant, for Tulci lived in the swamp and kept plantation owners abreast of what was happening along the Mississippi River. He was a good source of information, for no one knew the bayous like this old swamp man. The bayous, those long marshy fingers of water that extended out from the river, had caused more than one trapper or fisherman to disappear. "What do you suppose Tulci wants?"

"I don't think Tulci *wants* anything, Danielle. I think, for a price, he's giving your father information." Adelaide placed a cover

over her husband's plate to keep his food warm.

"You're probably right, as usual," Danielle said, gazing at her mother with admiration. Adelaide's high cheekbones, porcelain skin, and blond hair worn pulled back in a bun made her look shy and delicate. Nothing could be further from the truth. Adelaide's fragile air was deceiving, for she had a resilience few people possessed. From her British aristocratic background, Adelaide had inherited an even temper and was able to cope with almost any emergency — even her husband's volatile temper and passionate outbursts. She was his perfect counterpart, soothing him if he became upset. Danielle knew *she* had her father's strong emotions, but she also knew her fair complexion and more rational approach to problems was due to her mother's influence.

Danielle snapped back to attention at her mother's next words. "Tulci is probably telling your father about a new development in Barataria Bay."

She groaned inwardly. Barataria Bay, where the island of Grand Terre was located. Tulci must be reporting on Jean Lafitte and his men. Perhaps Lafitte was advertising another auction for the sale of smuggled goods, and that would send her father into a fine temper. Danielle finished eating the gumbo and rice, then sipped her coffee. Tulci was certainly filling Father's ear with news!

Finally the door slammed and her father's tread was heard, fast and heavy.

"Can you believe it?" The veins of Antoine Verlaine's neck throbbed prominently as he sat down hard and jerked his chair forward. He snapped his napkin open and spread it across his lap. "I always knew Lafitte was a slaver and a pirate, but I didn't think he would betray New Orleans to the English!"

Danielle set down her coffee cup, not daring to speak. Not Lafitte. She wouldn't believe he was a traitor!

"Why are you so certain that Lafitte and the British are in a conspiracy?" Adelaide inquired. "Do you have proof?"

"Proof! Who needs proof!? I always knew Lafitte would be a Judas and sell us out, but this time it's not for a paltry thirty silver pieces. No! Lafitte's price is thirty thousand dollars in gold and the promise of a captaincy in the British navy! This is about the worst thing that could happen to us when we're trying to bolster our defenses against the British invasion!"

"What has Tulci heard that is so disastrous?"

"The pirates are plotting with the British! He hasn't only heard it from Dominique, one of Lafitte's first lieutenants, but he's seen the brig-of-war with the British flag flapping in the wind anchored off Grand Terre. Not only did Jean Lafitte sail out to meet them in his small boat, but right now he's entertaining Captain Lockyer and several other officers from the British navy!" Antoine's face reddened and he jumped to his feet. "It's disgraceful that we didn't wipe out that nest of pirate traitors when we had the chance. But no. Too many people looked upon Lafitte as some sort of Robin Hood." He glanced at Danielle. "Now we're in for it!"

"Perhaps," Adelaide said smoothly, "Lafitte will inform the British that he intends to fight for the Americans."

"Ha! Not Lafitte! Not when thirty thousand dollars in gold are dangled before his greedy eyes! No doubt he's making a deal right now." Captain Verlaine pushed back his chair and hurried into his study.

"Mother," Danielle said, "I can't believe that Lafitte would attack New Orleans with —"

"Believe it!" Antoine stormed back into the room, carrying a rolled scroll, which he brandished under his daughter's nose. "Do you realize what their conference means?" He unrolled the map and placed it in front of Adelaide and Danielle. "Look!" He pointed to the island of Grand Terre about fifty miles below New Orleans. "You can see Grand Terre controls the swampland below the city and the Gulf. The British, with the help of these damned pirates, will find it easy to invade us. Our force is small and the British ships are already assembling, circling in the Gulf like sharks before a kill."

Danielle was stunned to hear that Lafitte

was meeting with the British. He had always professed his loyalty to America, and said the only thing he wanted was to earn his American citizenship. "What about Andrew Jackson?" she asked hopefully. "Isn't he on the way to New Orleans?"

"That's the message Monday's packet boat brought in, but who knows if the general will make it on time?"

"What else did Tulci say?" Adelaide asked, and although she appeared unruffled, Danielle noticed that her hands trembled as she poured more coffee.

"The British are being feted with Lafitte's finest wines and meats, and they have been invited to remain on Grand Terre." Antoine hit his fist on the oak table so hard that the cups rattled in their saucers. "This could be the end for New Orleans! The British blockade along the eastern coast has kept our navy bottled up, and there is no way they can spare manpower to the south. If we're captured, the British have threatened to cede Louisiana back to the Spaniards! Well, as God is my leader, it won't be an easy victory for them."

Danielle found her coffee difficult to swallow. Was it only yesterday that she was blithely riding to New Orleans and thinking how far removed Cypress Manor was from the war?

There was still a glint in her father's black eyes, but he had become deadly serious and was thinking logically. "I don't want either of you staying alone on the plantation. Be ready to move in with Madeline any day."

Aunt Madeline! Father's sister would not be easy to live with in her small house stuffed with Louis XV furniture. Nonetheless, she was a saucy, petite widow who still imagined she was quite the coquette. In fact, Aunt Madeline was being escorted about New Orleans by a colonel in the American army. It was gratifying to see Creoles and Americans getting together, because they usually didn't mix. The Creoles in New Orleans viewed the Americans as interlopers and rough-mannered newcomers . . . not at all up to the Old World standards of these Spanish and French settlers who had come here years ago. Danielle, as a Creole, really didn't know any Americans well, but those she had met, she had liked. It was strange; the Americans stayed on their side of town and the Creoles on theirs. She hadn't even met Aunt Madeline's American gentleman yet.

"I'll start packing," Adelaide said, laying her hand over Antoine's. He responded by rubbing it gently and looking into her eyes. The love between her parents was so touching that Danielle's heart filled with happiness at the sight of them. Would she ever find such a love?

Danielle glanced at the grandfather clock in a corner niche. It was one o'clock and almost time for her spinet lesson with Aunt Madeline.

"You'd better leave for your lesson," her

mother said, as if reading her thoughts. "Aunt Madeline will worry if you're late."

Her father nodded. "You're excused, chérie, and do not worry. It is that infuriating Lafitte! He makes my anger boil over! Our soldiers are rough frontiersmen, and our defenses will hold. I did not mean to alarm you."

But on the way to the stable, Danielle was alarmed. The British could attack any day, and her father would be on the front lines.

Saddling Ebony, she rode down the lane and turned her stallion onto the main road to the city. The sun had disappeared, and rain clouds were beginning to form.

She hadn't gone far when she saw a figure dart behind an oak. What if it were a British spy? She dare not let him escape back to the enemy ships. Without a thought of her own danger, she pulled on Ebony's reins, halting him.

"What's wrong, Ebony?" she crooned. "Did you lose a shoe? Let's have a look." Quickly, she jumped off and pretended to examine her mount's hind leg. After a pause, she straightened and reached into the saddle-bag, hauling out two horse pistols. Slowly and quietly, she cocked the guns and edged around Ebony's left flank.

"All right," she said loudly. "Come out." Although there wasn't a sound, she noticed a white sleeve protruding alongside the tree's bark. "I'll count to three," she said firmly. "One, two . . ." The flared sleeve fluttered a bit, but the culprit stubbornly remained hidden. ". . . three." At the final count, she waited for the space of three breaths then fired, blasting a piece of the bark off the trunk, very near the rustling white silk.

"Whoa! Don't shoot again." A well-proportioned young man stepped forth, hands in the air. His full-sleeved shirt was open at the neck, exposing a chained medallion that flashed in the sun. He wore a wide red sash, blue trousers, and boots. Brown ringlets covered his head like a halo around his tanned, handsome face. He grinned. "Hmm, what have we here?" He kept advancing.

"Don't come any closer," Danielle warned, her heart picking up a beat.

"Ah, I couldn't be captured by a more lovely enemy . . . if you are my enemy, which I doubt." Casually, he hooked his thumbs in his sash, and stood with feet wide apart, surveying Danielle. "You can ride and shoot like a man. What's your name?"

"Never mind who I am. You're coming with me!"

"And where is that, may I ask?"

"Into town where you'll be tossed into prison."

"*Bon!* Prison is exactly where I am headed!"

Danielle snickered. "Then you won't mind walking in front of my horse for the next five miles."

"I'd prefer to ride."

"I'm sure you would. Come." She motioned

with one of the pistols. "Let's get started!"

She slipped one gun into the leather saddle-bag, all the while watching her prisoner, but as she tried to mount, her foot slipped from the stirrup and the second pistol clattered to the ground.

With a movement as lithe as a cat pouncing on a grass snake, her captive had pinned her arms behind her back.

Kicking his shins, Danielle gained her freedom.

Dashing underneath Ebony, she began to run, but she could hear his pounding boots close behind. Within a minute, he had tackled her, sending her sprawling in the dust. She twisted and struggled, attempting to flee. She kicked and beat on his chest with a fury she didn't know she possessed, but her efforts proved no match for his strength. The more she fought, the tighter he gripped her wrists.

"You're hurting me," she gasped.

When he loosened his grasp, she lunged forward, biting his hand, again making a dash for it.

The dark boy reared back in pain. "You hellcat!" This time he caught her ankle and toppled her to the ground. "Stop it!" he ordered roughly, not relaxing his hold. "Enough is enough! Behave yourself!" His words were clipped and short, and she knew he no longer regarded this as an easy bout with a girl.

She became quiet. She tried to catch her breath, but to her chagrin, she felt a tear of frustration slip down her cheek. "Who are you? If you know what's good for you, you'll liberate me this instant or you'll have Captain Verlaine to answer to!" With a swipe of her hand, she brushed away a tear.

"Captain Verlaine!" He gave a low whistle. "Then you're Danielle Verlaine." The young man rose, brushing off his trousers and warning her with his eyes that no more escape attempts would be tolerated. "You are quite well-known, mademoiselle. And perhaps you've heard of Jean Lafitte?"

She nodded, not taking her eyes off him. "Of course. Who hasn't?"

"I'm Geoffrey Lafitte."

She tried hard not to display her amazement. Geoffrey Lafitte, Jean Lafitte's nephew . . . the son of Jean's sister, who had died in childbirth nineteen years before. "I thought the Lafittes were entertaining British officers and wouldn't dare show their faces in town." With a sniff of disdain, she turned to steady Ebony.

Geoffrey laughed. "Then you haven't heard? My uncle sent the British packing after letting them stew for several hours in the guardhouse."

Danielle glanced over her shoulder at Geoffrey and couldn't help smiling. She had been right all along about Jean Lafitte. He was an honorable man.

Geoffrey returned her smile. "Does that please you?"

"Naturally. If Jean Lafitte had allied himself with the British, it would have doomed New Orleans to almost certain defeat." Rubbing Ebony's nose, she added, "It will still be difficult to win—our troops are few and General Jackson hasn't arrived yet."

He walked over, turned her to face him, and his dark eyes danced. "You're well informed, my little wildcat." Untying his neck bandanna, he wiped a smudge from her nose.

There was a pleasant tingle when his fingers touched her. Flushed, she tucked back a curl that had fallen across her forehead. "I — I must look like a swamp woman."

"Ah, but no, Danielle Verlaine. You are a most lovely sight."

She backed up a step, bumping straight against Ebony. The horse neighed in surprise. She stroked his forelock reassuringly. "Oh!" She placed a hand to her forehead. "My lesson! Aunt Madeline will have the militia searching for me."

"And what kind of lesson? The latest dance step, the gavotte, perhaps?"

She shook her head. "Nothing that much fun. Lessons on the spinet."

"Someday you'll play for me." His tone was confident.

She was about to retort sharply, but suddenly his look of assurance made her believe it, too. A few minutes ago, she was struggling to flee from his grasp, but the magic name, Lafitte, and the fact that he was not pro-British, had changed her.

As if seizing his advantage, Geoffrey said,

"I don't suppose you'd give me a ride into town?"

"Oh, I couldn't possibly," she said. For once in her life she would act with proper decorum, just the way her mother wanted her to. Besides, she had only just met this charmer, and she had no intention of doing his bidding in a matter of twenty minutes. Still, there was something about this tanned, good-looking pirate . . . something about his appealing, dark eyes.

"I understand," he said smoothly. "It wouldn't do, would it, to befriend a pirate? They're tainted and you might become contaminated." He flashed a half-teasing grin, which took the sting out of his words.

He didn't know her. She'd never hold one's status against a person! "You have no horse?" she asked suddenly.

"It would be quite a trick to load a horse onto a pirogue."

Pirogues, small boats cut out of logs that could easily maneuver the swamps, were not exactly made for heavy loads. She laughed at the image of a horse and a pirate on a pirogue. "Where did you beach your boat?"

"On the shore of Alligator Swamp."

Danielle, preparing to mount Ebony, was conscious of Geoffrey's admiring gaze and lifted her skirt higher than necessary — to the top of her boots. "And why," she questioned, "are you so eager to go to town? Isn't it dangerous?"

Geoffrey sobered. "I must see my uncle. He's not well."

"Pierre Lafitte?"

"He's the one. He's been in prison far too long, and those cursed jailers won't remove his chains. You can be sure we plan to do something about the situation!" The darkening of his eyes changed their sparkle into an ominous cloud. But then his cheer returned. "I have a bad case of being a very evil pirate! But I'm dauntless, and if you won't give me a ride, I'll walk." His eyes watched her as if hoping she would relent.

"You didn't look so dauntless," she said, looking down at him, "when that bullet went whizzing by your nose."

"Ah, well, even pirates can be vulnerable, especially at the hands of a lovely lady like you, Danielle Verlaine. It was my good fortune to have met you. One of these days I hope I can do a favor for you."

She felt her cheeks flush. "I'd like to help you, but I can't this time." *Damn decorum,* she thought. Why couldn't a person meet someone, trust him, and aid him? But she only said, "Good-bye, Geoffrey. I hope your uncle doesn't have to remain in prison too long."

"He won't," the pirate responded confidently, and gave her a wave.

She dug her heels into Ebony's flanks and the horse broke into a gallop. Her thoughts raced along with the horse's flying hooves. Was Geoffrey Lafitte going to study the

Cabildo, the city hall, so he could plot Pierre's escape? She wondered how Geoffrey got along with his two uncles. There seemed to be a fierce loyalty between them. No doubt pirates pledged to defend one another if they should be captured. She hoped Geoffrey would never be captured and doubted if ten soldiers could hold him. He was a scrapper, and there was a toughness about him that could not so easily be overcome. A half-mile down the road, raindrops splattered against her face, and she thought of Geoffrey walking.

On impulse, she wheeled Ebony about and galloped back. "Climb on back," she said, leaning down and giving him a hand.

Once seated, he held onto her and they were off. She shouted above the clopping hooves, "If my father knew I was helping Geoffrey Lafitte, he'd be so furious that I wouldn't be surprised if he'd sell me to the Choctaws."

"You're much too spirited. You were meant to be a corsair's lady. Antoine Verlaine needs to meet Jean Lafitte, and then he'd find out we're not such a bad breed."

She believed him. Geoffrey was charming and handsome. Jean Lafitte had sent the British back to their ships and would most certainly now side with the Americans. The world that had seemed so insecure at lunch suddenly seemed a much safer place. With Geoffrey's arms about her waist, the light rain falling, her hair flying, and the smell of salt cane in the air, she felt wonderful. The

Lafittes weren't traitors after all. And with her was the most dashing pirate of them all!

That night she slowly undressed, not wanting to slip into bed and fall asleep. She wanted to remain awake so she could savor the day's excitement. She stood in her lace petticoat before the full-length mirror, tilting it for a better view. The smooth curves, narrow waist, and rounded hips showed she was finally becoming a woman! Her once plump face had given way to a pure oval with a finely chiseled nose, firm chin, and hollow cheeks. The blondness of her hair made her skin seem creamier and her eyes bluer. She smiled, thinking of Paul's description. Eyes as blue-green as a choppy sea. But she quickly dismissed Paul and allowed her mind to dwell on Geoffrey. She wondered what he liked best about her. Her mouth? She wet her lips, pouting provocatively. Her eyes? She narrowed them and noticed how they appeared to sparkle. Her hair? Her long mane felt soft and silky over the warm glow of her shoulders.

As she turned, she saw the bruise on her upper arm. Geoffrey had been rough, but she couldn't blame him for thwarting captivity. If her father had seen that mark and realized a Lafitte had manhandled his daughter, he'd set sail for Grand Terre and personally horsewhip Geoffrey. At least she had had the presence of mind this afternoon to ask Geoffrey to dismount on the edge of town so no one could report that "the Verlaine girl had helped a Lafitte, and wasn't that a good joke on Captain Verlaine!"

Beginning to brush her hair, she contemplated her father's words at dinner. He had scoffed at Jean Lafitte's dismissal of the British and said the pirate would never lift a finger to help the American cause. In fact, he implied that Lafitte's help wasn't wanted and promised that Lafitte and his cutthroats had a nasty little surprise in store for them in a week or so. Danielle, troubled, slipped into her nightgown, pulled back the star-designed quilt, and turned off the lantern lamp.

As she lay in bed, her worries were forgotten. Again pleasant fantasies eased into her dreams. How exciting it would be to see Grand Terre with Geoffrey at her side! Perhaps one day he'd come riding to Cypress Manor, sweep her off her feet, and carry her to Barataria Bay. She drifted into a half sleep. They would stroll in the moonlight by the sea. From Barataria Bay they would set sail for India, from which they'd bring back fine cottons and rich silks. They would become wealthy privateers and they'd sail around the world — to Spain, to Africa, to the East Indies, to South America — and her life would be filled with love and adventure. What a lovely future, what thrilling years lay ahead for her. . . .

---•---

Chapter Three

SEVERAL days after Danielle's encounter with Geoffrey, his uncle, Pierre Lafitte, escaped from jail. No one could figure out how it was done, but the chains had been cut and Pierre was gone. The talk was that Jean Lafitte had bribed the jailers. Governor Claiborne was in a rage and had posted a reward for Pierre's recapture.

As Danielle touched a bit of lip rouge to her lips, she again thought of Geoffrey and knew that he had had a hand in the breakout, but she was too happy to be concerned with the escape, which was inevitable. Everyone was surprised that Pierre had languished in prison this long. She ruffled up her high collar, slipped into her green outdoor pelisse with the short scalloped sleeves, and prepared to meet Paul.

Humming, she closed her bedroom door,

filled with an aura of anticipation. Every time she rode or walked the City Road, she half expected Geoffrey to spring out from behind the old oak. She wondered if he even remembered her.

As she went down the graceful, winding staircase, she lightly touched the wrought-iron banister with its delicate grillwork. The September breeze wafted through the shuttered windows, and the late sun threw shadows on the steps. She was aglow, for somehow she felt Geoffrey would be in St. Anthony's Square today.

In the meantime, she would enjoy Paul's company. He had a two-day pass from the *Carolina,* for the British ships no longer menaced the Gulf waters. They had moved farther out to sea, and there was no naval activity. They were probably rethinking their attack strategy on New Orleans since the pirates had refused to throw in their lot with them.

Paul, waiting at the foot of the stairs, held out a gloved hand. "Good afternoon, mademoiselle. You look lovely as always. I'm proud to be your escort for the Sunday promenade."

Danielle relished the compliment, for she had carefully chosen the white ruffled dress and the pelisse, a short-sleeved overgarment. If Geoffrey would dare to appear in the square, she wanted to be at her loveliest. For one fleeting moment, a heart-stopping thought crept into her mind. What if Geoffrey were with an attractive girl from Grand Terre?

However, as quickly as such an idea entered her mind, she just as quickly dismissed it.

Paul looked smart in his midshipman's uniform with the white trousers, short navy jacket trimmed in gold buttons, and a high white collar. He was tanned, and his blond hair was bleached by the sun. "Here, Danielle, let me help you with your shawl." Gently, he encased her shoulders in the fringed silk and held her against him for a moment longer than was proper.

"Thank you." She faced him. "I'm glad you have two whole days, Paul."

"Afraid not. All leaves have been canceled, and sailors will be piped aboard at midnight."

She gave him a sharp look. "Does that mean the British ships are closing in?"

"No, we've been recalled for another task."

She arched her brows, waiting for a further explanation.

"You'll hear about it soon enough," he added with a grin. "It's something you'll no doubt disagree with the U.S. Navy about."

"What is it?" She could usually inveigle secrets out of people — even Father — but not Paul.

"Our mission will be over in the next few days, then you'll find out. In fact, all New Orleans will hear of it!"

"Is it dangerous?"

Paul lifted his shoulders. "It could be."

"Are you raiding one of the islands or searching for British ships?"

"No more." Paul held up his hand. "You

know I can't give away military orders."

She sighed. "All right, Paul." There was no point in continuing. She would have to be patient. Tying her white silk bonnet under her chin, she took Paul's arm as he led her to the open carriage with the two white horses. They were bedecked with red plumes on their head harnesses and seemed to preen themselves with the desire to show off their prancing handsomeness as much as the promenaders.

As their carriage entered Dumaine Street, Paul jumped out, tethered the horses, and offered Danielle his hand.

Under the sycamore trees, they walked to St. Anthony's Plaza, and she thought how pleasant today's activity was compared with all the duels that were frequently fought on this site. In the background were the spires of St. Louis Cathedral with the gold cross atop, glinting in the late afternoon sun. Danielle, recognizing several couples also converging on the square, nodded.

A notice had been tacked up on one of the pillars of St. Louis Cathedral, and she walked over to investigate. She read the proclamation aloud:

$1,000 REWARD

Will be paid for the apprehension of Pierre Lafitte, who broke out and escaped last night from the prison of the parish. Said Pierre Lafitte is about five feet ten inches in height, stout-made, of light complexion, and somewhat cross-eyed; further description is unnecessary, as he is very well known in the city.

The above reward will be paid to any person delivering the said Lafitte to the subscriber.

J. H. Holland
Keeper of the Prison

Danielle said matter-of-factly, "He'll never be caught."

"You're very sure of that, aren't you?" Paul said. "Your pirate friends aren't invincible, you know." Paul took her hand, for the promenade was about to begin. "Lawbreakers deserve to be punished, and you look positively pleased that Pierre Lafitte escaped."

"Why, no, Paul. I'm as shocked as you are," she said mockingly. "Let's line up in formation. The walk is starting."

As she strolled about the square with other New Orleans girls, she tried to appear demure and keep her eyes downcast, but she couldn't help sneaking a glance at the onlookers. Walking slowly past the palm trees every few feet, she checked the faces, but Geoffrey Lafitte was not to be seen. She had been a fool to believe he would dare make an appearance just to catch a glimpse of her. He was where he belonged, back on Grand Terre. And she was where she belonged, in New Orleans with Paul.

The boys circling the plaza in the opposite direction from the girls wore smiles as wide as Rodriguez Canal when they came face-to-face with the maiden of their choice. When Danielle met Paul, she tried to smile, but as she passed him, she could only manage a small quirk at one corner of her mouth. She tried to imagine what Geoffrey was doing on this early Sunday evening with the sunset shimmering over the area bayous. Was he perhaps squatting before his uncle as Jean Lafitte counted out to each of his men gold doubloons that had been stolen from a Spanish galleon? Or was he strolling with a bayou girl? She shook her head, not wanting to think of it.

Suddenly, a contingent of eight horsemen rode pell-mell down the narrow street and into the square, sending the promenaders scurrying in all directions. Some sought sanctuary on the cathedral steps; others stayed with their backs to the wall of the buildings along the plaza. By the rifles they held high in the air, she could tell the horsemen were Kentucky frontiersmen, arriving in the city to join in the fight. Everyone knew of the famous long Kentucky rifles and the marksmen who owned them. They trotted first one way, then another, disrupting the regal Spanish promenade tradition. "Kaintucks" were uncouth and ill-bred. What did they know of custom? Last week, a few Tennesseeans had come into town; their appearance was as frightful as these bearded ruffians. Everything was in disorder: girls screaming, riders whooping and hollering and firing their pistols in the air. Some dared to speak to the younger girls, sending their chaperons into a verbal tirade against them, a fact that delighted the wild riders even more.

Paul, who had been on the other side of the square, came rushing to Danielle's side. "Are you all right?" He put his arm around her waist and stood defying the riders who circled them like a band of Indians.

Soon, however, the horsemen, dirty and tired from their arduous journey, left the promenaders in peace and galloped down the cobblestone street.

Danielle's bonnet was askew; as she straightened it, she reassured Paul. "I'm fine. Are *those* the kind of ragtag troops that are coming in to defend us?" There was fire in Danielle's eyes as she glared after the departing horsemen. "They're like the flatboatmen on Girod Street — riffraff! I don't understand how Father or anyone else can whip those ruffians into any kind of disciplined fighters — least of all, Andrew Jackson."

"You forget, Danielle, that Jackson himself is from Tennessee. Don't worry, he's not nicknamed 'Old Hickory' for nothing. He's as hard as hickory and twice as sturdy. We couldn't have a better leader."

Danielle didn't reply, but she doubted if Jackson could live up to his reputation or arrive in New Orleans in time to be effective. She lifted her skirt to avoid a mud puddle as they walked to their waiting horses. The evening was too glorious to be in a bad temper, and her good humor almost immediately resurfaced. "Mother and Father are waiting dinner for us. Mother has prepared a special dish for you, Paul. Wild duck."

Taking her elbow as she stepped up and into the carriage, he chuckled. "Adelaide spoils me."

"Doesn't everyone, Paul? You're so"— she searched for the right word and found two — "so personable and likable." Then she added in a dry voice, "You'll be the perfect naval officer, always making the right decisions, always pleasing the ladies."

Lightly snapping the whip over the horses' rumps, Paul shot her a strange look. "That bothers you, doesn't it? Sometimes, Danielle, I think you'd rather I were an outlaw. There's only one person I want to please . . . only one lady." He gave her a sidelong glance. "But she's hard to please."

"Oh?" she said playfully, "and who might that lady be? . . ." But when she saw his serious face, she didn't finish her silly retort. "I know who it is, Paul, and I'm not so hard to please."

Paul kept his eyes on the trotting horses. "I wish I could believe that. I always try to do the right thing where you're concerned, Danielle, but lately everything I do or say seems wrong."

She gave a light little laugh. "Oh, Paul, you're imagining things again. Let's not ruin our last evening together. From the sound of things, I may not see you for a while." She touched his arm. "You know how fond I am of you."

The smile she had tried to coax forth before now reappeared, and Paul said, "I think you'll see me sooner than you anticipate. If the British don't sail back into Gulf waters, I'll only be called for patrol duty, which means more passes."

"But I thought you had a mission to perform."

"We do, but it won't take long."

By the grim set of his mouth, she knew better than to try to wheedle his secret out of him. For the rest of the way to Cypress Manor she was quiet.

In a few days she discovered Paul's secret mission, and as she sat beneath the willow tree along the stream in back of the stable, she was sick at heart. Grand Terre had been destroyed. Everything that Jean Lafitte owned had been burned to the ground. Storehouses had been razed, and half a million dollars' worth of gold and merchandise seized by the Americans. Even Jean Lafitte's mansion had been gutted. How her father had enjoyed telling the story. Six American gunboats and the schooner the *Carolina* had taken part in the raid that had netted a pirate cruiser; seven schooners; and a felucca, a sleek, narrow Mediterranean-style ship. Commodore Patterson, the American in charge, reported that the buccaneers did not fire one shot in return and that most of the pirates had fled into the swamp. Lafitte's orders not to fight had been obeyed, but out of one thousand Baratarians, only eighty had been captured.

Danielle's thoughts were turbulent, her spirits as low as the ground-sweeping branches of the weeping willow. What had happened to Geoffrey? Was he safe? Had he been taken prisoner? She'd heard that two of Lafitte's right-hand men, Dominique and Cut-Nose, were in jail.

It was only yesterday that Lafitte had written to Governor Claiborne, offering his services and citing again the strategic position they held on Grand Terre and what a powerful striking force they could become for the Americans. She chewed a blade of grass as she once more reviewed the condition he asked in return for this alliance. Only that he and his men should receive pardons, and the one phrase that Jean Lafitte used stuck in her head: "I'm a stray sheep wishing to return to the fold."

In disgust, she flung away the blade of grass and wondered how Lafitte's proposal could be ignored. Instead, Father and Governor Claiborne and Paul had deliberately wrecked the stronghold of Lafitte. Who was on the right side now? She smiled grimly. For once Paul was wrong. Who were the men of honor? Certainly not her father or Claiborne or Paul! She jumped to her feet. If only she could do something. Maybe she should load a pirogue with food and bandages and sail alone to Grand Terre. She dismissed this idea quickly, for she would never be able to find it in the maze of bayous and swamps. After all, Grand Terre was fifty miles away. What would come of all this? In despair, she gazed over the sugarcane fields bathed by the setting sun. She wouldn't blame the pirates if they set New Orleans ablaze in retaliation for Claiborne's cowardly and stupid act. It would be ironic if Jean Lafitte fired on the city, instead of the British who had threatened to.

She feared Jean Lafitte's revenge would be terrible, but October and November passed and there were no incidents. In fact, he had written Claiborne and again offered his sword in the coming fight. Again Claiborne had ignored his request. Instead, the governor had forwarded Lafitte's petition to Andrew Jackson, and the general's reply was worse than no reply at all. In fact, it was an insult to Lafitte's generous offer. He had turned down any help from Jean Lafitte, referring to him and his men as "hellish banditti."

Danielle wondered when the men in charge of her city and her life would wake up and realize they needed every man and woman who could fire a musket. The British outnumbered them four to one, and now that the British had defeated Napoleon at the Battle of Leipzig, they would be able to devote their full attention to the pesky Americans. And since their numbers were so superior, the

British doubtless were confident of easily swatting and killing the Americans.

On the first day of December, sitting in the window seat of her bedroom, Danielle's thoughts were on the book *Candide,* which lay open on her lap. Voltaire had graphically described the horrors of war through the eyes of Candide. What would this war bring? Famine? Rape? Pillage? Burning? She shivered even though the sun, streaming through the small windowpane, was warm. Winter gave the landscape new colors. The green sugarcane fields had turned to a light buff color, and the chinaberry trees by the well were losing their yellow leaves. What would happen to the pirates, to Father and Mother, to Aunt Madeline, to Paul, and, finally, to her?

When she saw the rider swing up the lane, it didn't register at first who it was, and then she recognized Tulci. His face beneath the wide hat was so wizened and browned from the sun that she could scarcely make it out. But there was no mistaking the loose way he sat his saddle.

Father was at a meeting with Governor Claiborne, preparing for Andrew Jackson's arrival tomorrow. Mother was supervising the sugarcane quota.

Dashing downstairs, Danielle greeted the old man with respect, even though he reeked of swamp water and his clothes were in tatters. "Ho, Tulci," she called, running out onto the veranda. "Father's in town today.

Sorry you rode all this way. Is there a message I can give him?"

He removed his hat, scratching the few hairs left on top. "Well, I'll tell you true, it ain't your pa I want to see." His open smile revealed only four yellow teeth. " 'Tis you, Miss Danielle."

"What is it?" Despite the cool December morn, she was aware of small beads of perspiration forming on her upper lip. Tulci was in contact with the pirates. Could his message be from Geoffrey? Dare she hope for such a farfetched thing?

Tulci sat, hat in hand, grinning down at her.

"What is the message, Tulci?" Impatience edged her voice.

Chortling, he slid off his horse and held out a folded paper, but when she reached for it, he dangled it in front of her. "Old Tulci's got a secret, but he ain't gonna tell a soul. Nary a soul."

"Tulci," she pleaded, "stop teasing and give me the note." She moved a step closer.

This time, with an elaborate flourish, he handed the missive to her. "It's from that young devil, Geoffrey Lafitte. I think he's sweet on you." He remounted and watched her next move.

Calmly, she slipped the message into her pocket and said, "Tulci, this is personal. Geoffrey and I are only friends, that's all, but I'd rather you wouldn't speak of this to Father."

"Funny thing. Geoffrey told me the same thing. Old Tulci's no fool. I don't aim to have Jean Lafitte gunning for me. Don't fret, Miss Danielle, your secret's safe with me."

She wondered. Tulci was known to sell any bit of gossip for gold, but this was so trifling that it really wasn't worth his while. At least that's what she hoped.

He lifted a finger to his hat. "Good day, mam'selle. Enjoy your love note." Chuckling, he turned his mount and disappeared beyond the cypress trees.

She raced inside and up to her room, not wanting to risk a surprise visit from Mother or one of the servants, although, because of the war, Father had sent most of the workers away.

Geoffrey. Geoffrey Lafitte did remember her after all! Sweeping aside the mosquito netting, she threw herself across the bed and read the message:

Tomorrow at 10:00, during the parade for General Jackson, can you meet me in front of the Old Spanish Custom House? Dearest Danielle, I must see you again.

Your admirer,
G. L.

After rereading his scrawled note, she lay back on the bed, staring at the embroidered canopy overhead. He hadn't forgotten her. He *did* want to see her again. He was brave to venture into town with a price on his head, but he was intelligent, too. He would be safe, lost in the crowds that would jam the street to catch a glimpse of General Jackson, the man who was to save New Orleans. The parade and festivities all were pushed into the background when she thought of Geoffrey. She hoped she would know how to act and know what to say. Did he want her help in a scheme, or had he fallen in love with her? She whispered his last phrase once more: "Dearest Danielle, I must see you again."

Chapter Four

GENERAL Jackson was arriving today, but the most important thought on Danielle's mind was Geoffrey. She was about to see him again at last. She didn't even notice the chill, misty morning. As she rode down St. Charles Street, she heard the band playing the new anthem from Baltimore. It was written by an American who had watched the British bombard Ft. McHenry in September. The stirring song was in honor of a British defeat. The Americans would defeat the British again at New Orleans, she vowed, as she silently mouthed the words:

O say, can you see,
By the dawn's early light,
What so proudly we hailed
At the twilight's last gleaming?
Whose broad stripes and bright stars,

Through the perilous fight
O'er the ramparts we watched
Were so gallantly streaming.
And the rockets' red glare, the bombs
    bursting in air,
Gave proof through the night
That our flag was still there.
O say, does that star-spangled banner
    yet wave,
O'er the land of the free and the home
    of the brave?

The anthem filled her with pride. It was easy to understand why it had become the rage of New Orleans. She passed the general reviewing stand that had been erected in front of the Cabildo, where the officials of the city would sit, including her father.

Danielle was relieved to be on her own today, for her mother had decided to pack their most prized possessions before the British arrived.

Heading for St. Philip Street, she threaded Ebony through the swelling crowds. When she reached Lafitte's blacksmith shop on Bourbon Street, she noticed it was deserted and padlocked. Nevertheless, she slowed as she rode by. The small building, shaped like a French colonial cottage with a steep, over-hanging roof, was charming. It was hard to believe it was considered a front for Jean Lafitte's nefarious activities.

On she traveled to St. John and Moss streets, and there, in front of the Old Spanish

Custom House, beneath the sloping West-Indian-style roof, stood Geoffrey.

Her pulse raced at the sight of him. He was clothed in black, his lean, muscular body outlined beneath his silk shirt and trousers, which flared at the ankles. Over his shirt he wore an embroidered vest, and his thick hair curled just above his ears. His arms were folded over his chest as he leaned against the heavy wooden door. The Custom House was shuttered and closed for trade today. Usually it was bustling, handling goods that were shipped along the bayous where they were checked and stored. But few businesses remained open today, for almost everyone lined the streets ready to welcome the man known as "Old Hickory."

Danielle stopped before a hitching post. Before she could dismount, Geoffrey hurried over to help her off Ebony. He kissed her hand and smiled. "I'm glad you came." His warmth was contagious and her nervousness dissolved.

"What else could I do? I received your summons, m'lord," she said gaily, "and rushed to see what your bidding might be."

He laughed heartily. "Ah, my little wildcat. Always the one in charge, aren't you?" He crooked his finger. "Follow me."

Puzzled, she trailed after him until they reached Pirate's Alley. He grabbed her hand and they ran together until they reached the back door of a warehouse. Geoffrey unlocked the door and they entered. It was dark and musty-smelling, with merchandise stacked to the ceiling.

"Where are we?" she asked, staring about in open wonder at the heaps of goods on display.

"This is my uncle's storehouse and not too far from his shop on Royal Street." He pulled free a bolt of damask and unrolled it, spreading its heavy richness on a nearby cotton bale. "We're selling most of this merchandise at The Temple tomorrow."

"I've heard of Jean Lafitte's famous auctions. He has the wealthiest families in New Orleans buying from him."

"Not the Verlaines, however."

"Not the Verlaines," she echoed, laughing.

"Why don't you attend the sale tomorrow? I can meet you at the Crossing of the Five Muskrats and take you there."

She sucked in her breath. Should she risk it? She knew slaves had once been sold there; Father and Mother would be furious with her. "I'd like to . . ." She paused. "But —"

"Do come," he urged. When he saw she was wavering, he capped his argument with an "I dare you."

Without hesitating, she retorted, "I'll be there." And she would, too — if she had to swim.

"*Bon.* Three o'clock tomorrow at the Crossing."

A tiny thrill tingled along her spine. She had always wanted to attend a pirate auction, and now she had an invitation.

She gazed about in awe. "Do you own all of this?"

"My uncle does," he said simply. "Every privateer on Grand Terre has a share in it." He waved his hand about him.

"And is this plunder taken from Spanish ships?"

"Most of it. Jean Lafitte has been granted a letter of marque from Cartagena, Colombia. Since the Colombians are at war with Spain, they gave my uncle the right to loot any Spanish ships he encounters." He glanced around him. "And he's encountered quite a few! Being a Frenchman, my uncle considers any Spaniard fair game. Napolean Bonaparte never could conquer Spain. Maybe he will try again when he finishes recruiting a new army. I guess my uncle wants to do all he can to help Napoleon. Napoleon is not one to give up. They say he's been planning and scheming how to gather his troops together ever since he was exiled to the island of Elba."

"I'm sure the British will be ready for him." Danielle, not wanting to discuss Napoleon's exploits further, ambled down one of the aisles, viewing silks, cotton, spices, rum, snuffboxes, jewelry, and guns. She had never seen such an array.

When she came back, Geoffrey held a gold chain with a large black pearl in his hand. "I want you to have this necklace."

"It's beautiful, Geoffrey." But Danielle didn't touch it. "No, I can't accept any gifts from you, Geoffrey. I just can't." The thought flickered through her mind of who had owned this necklace. Surely it was stolen, and the memory of a wealthy Creole lady who had sailed from New Orleans and who subsequently disappeared came back to her. The woman's jewelry, however, had shown up in Lafitte's possession. Was this black pearl part of that woman's jewelry? She shivered slightly.

Geoffrey studied her face then said coolly, "I'm sorry, but I understand." He dropped the pearl in his pocket. "Perhaps one day you will wear this chain for me."

She stared at him. "I must get back," she said faintly, suddenly realizing she was with a very confident, very determined young man, alone in a deserted warehouse. "It isn't proper to remain here."

He grinned, and his dark eyes sparkled. "Since when is Danielle Verlaine bound by convention? She can't accept a gift, she can't stay with a freebooter more than ten minutes. Why? I only wanted to look at you to see if you are as lovely as my memory had painted you." He lifted her hand to his lips, all the while observing her. "And you are!"

"Why, thank you, Geoffrey Lafitte. And now, please, we'd better go. Will you be all right when we leave? What if you're apprehended?"

He sat down on a nearby chest, lounging with his arm encircling his bent knee. He begged, "Please, another five minutes." And then in answer to her question, he continued,

"The militia will only throw me in prison alongside Dominique and Cut-Nose. Besides, they might be released soon."

She relaxed and leaned against a large crate. "I don't think there's anything Jean Lafitte can say to convince Governor Claiborne to free his men."

Geoffrey frowned. "We're finished dealing with that stiff-necked Claiborne. My uncle intends to confront Andrew Jackson!" He rose and reached for her, pulling her close. "There's nothing like a face-to-face meeting to make your feelings known."

For a moment Danielle thought he might kiss her on the lips, and that would be an unforgivable liberty. As she was pressed against him, she held her breath; however, he only brushed her hair with his lips. "As soft and perfumed as a magnolia blossom," he said, and stepped back lightly. "I'm sorry if I offended you, my Danielle."

Her voice was shaky and she longed to embrace him, but she held herself in check. "I must leave." All she would have to do would be to step back into the warm circle of his arms. He was waiting for her. Instead, she turned. "Geoffrey, take care of yourself."

"Will you meet me tomorrow at the Crossing?" His voice was matter-of-fact; the magic moment was gone.

"I'll try. Everything is in such a turmoil. A week from Friday, Mother and I are moving in with Aunt Madeline. Perhaps I can skip my spinet lesson and attend the auction.

I've always wanted to see one. I'm surprised your uncle still holds them. I haven't seen any advertising handbills."

"No, lately the authorities watch us too closely — they're hoping to catch Uncle Jean in a trap." He opened the door, looking in both directions, then motioned for her to follow. "We've spread the word to our best and richest customers. There will be ladies there, too."

"I'll really try to meet you at the Crossing."

"Knowing you, my sweet, you'll be there."

As he shut and locked the door behind them, she reached out and touched his arm. "We'd better leave separately. I don't want anything to happen to you, Geoffrey." She lifted the hood of her cloak over her head, for it was raining.

He blew her a kiss. "I'm like a cat, with as many lives. . . . I'll be fine." And he sprinted around the corner and was gone.

She hurried to catch part of the parade. As she wended her way back to Royal Street, the drums rolled, and the bright blue-and-silver dragoons marched into view. In the middle of the bodyguard sat General Jackson, tall and unbending, on his magnificent charger. But the commanding officer of the Seventh United States Military District appeared far from magnificent himself. In fact, he cut a rather dismal figure.

Danielle, amazed at his gauntness, stopped and stood on tiptoe to observe the steely-eyed soldier's drawn, thin face over the heads of the parade-watchers. Was this the savior of New Orleans? He looked neither to the right nor the left. It had begun to rain, and around his shoulders was wrapped a short, blue Spanish cloak. His boots, encasing lanky legs, were worn and dirty. Where was the spit and polish of a real officer? Where were his medals and gold epaulets? Where was his dashing United States uniform?

Jackson rode directly to his quarters on Royal Street where Governor Claiborne and a few officers, including Captain Verlaine, were to meet privately and apprise him of the city's defenses.

Disappointed, Danielle returned to Ebony and rode back to Cypress Manor.

When she entered through the great double doors, she shook off her wet cloak over the black-and-white tiles.

"Is that you, Danielle?" her mother called from the parlor.

"Yes, Mother." She entered the living room, and her mother, looking like a young girl in a white blouse and dark skirt, was sitting in front of the purple-colored porphyry fireplace, carefully packing the cameo collection. Her mother and father had collected these medallions of stone with the classical profiles cut in raised relief for many years. They had over two hundred in their collection; the stones were worth almost as much as Cypress Manor.

"Here is the cameo given to you by your Aunt Madeline and Uncle Francis when you were born, Danielle." Between her thumb and forefinger she held up a tiny blue gem with a carved white head.

Danielle smiled. "I know. Someday I'd like to have a brooch made of it."

"It's yours, dear, to do with as you please." Adelaide carefully placed the baby cameo amidst the folds of velvet. "This box will travel with us to Aunt Madeline's and be treated most tenderly." She hefted the box, which was smaller than a loaf of bread. "Just think, this would finance a British brig-of-war. Wouldn't they love to confiscate such a treasure?" She handed the tin box to Danielle. "Slide this under your bed until next Friday." She smoothed back her golden hair. "I'd better bathe before we leave for dinner."

Danielle covered her eyes with her hand. How could she forget! Tonight was Andrew Jackson's evening. He would be formally greeted by the officials of New Orleans.

"You didn't remember? And just after you've seen the general, too. Tell me about him."

Danielle sank into one of the tapestried armchairs and rested her feet on the needle-point footstool. She described Jackson's poor entrance into the city and ended her description by saying, "I'm sorry I can't be more enthusiastic about the party."

"Danielle! At fifteen, you should love balls, no matter what the occasion, yet lately you've been preoccupied. Is something bothering you?"

"No, Mother. It's nothing." She must appear calm. She had no idea she was causing suspicion. Although her mother was sympathetic to many of her escapades, she certainly wouldn't be tolerant of a tryst with Jean Lafitte's nephew. Danielle managed a slight smile. "I'm just tired, I guess."

"Then take the strongbox to your room. I've laid out your prettiest frock. If you want to bathe, I left the yoked buckets by the tub, but you'll need to fetch the well water yourself, since Josephine and Etienne have fled for Baton Rouge."

So the last of the servants had gone. Soon she would leave Cypress Manor, too. She gazed about the living room with its comfortable chairs, the Gobelin tapestry of a hunting scene above the fireplace, the heavy brocade drapes that matched the insets in the wall panels. Each piece of furniture stood out in sharp outlines. When she entered her bedroom, she looked even more fondly at her own things. Blue-and-white chintz covered the chair, the curved settee, the bed, and even trimmed the dressing table. She had chosen the blue-and-white floral pattern and had never tired of its cheery appearance. She walked over to the white marble fireplace and touched the white porcelain clock on the mantel, guarded by a porcelain dog on one side and a porcelain cat on the other. She slowly walked to the window seat and sat for a moment. She gazed at the sugarcane fields. The Verlaines belonged here at Cypress Manor; she didn't want to leave. Sadly, she picked up her gown to dress for the reception.

However, the banquet and ball, held at Mr. Livingston's home, lifted her spirits considerably. Livingston was the most prominent lawyer in New Orleans. Jean Lafitte had retained him to remove the charge of piracy, but as yet, even Livingston and his staff couldn't clear his name.

Danielle's father, splendid in his captain's uniform with the dress saber at his side, hurried to meet them. "Ah, you both make me so proud." Taking the arm of his wife and daughter, he led them into the ballroom. "General Jackson will be surprised at how civilized the inhabitants of New Orleans are."

Myriads of tiny candles in the crystal chandelier leaped and glittered over the shine of oak floors, the gold-rimmed crystal goblets, and the satin chairs at one end of the ballroom.

"Captain Verlaine!" a deep voice boomed. "I must meet these beautiful ladies you are escorting."

"General Jackson, good evening," Antoine Verlaine greeted his superior.

Danielle turned and almost gasped audibly. Was this the same bedraggled man she had seen this morning? General Jackson, a white-gloved hand resting on his sword hilt, waited for an introduction. His dress uniform with dark trousers and short green jacket was impeccably tailored to his lean frame.

"I'm honored, sir, to present my wife, Adelaide Verlaine, and my daughter, Danielle."

Jackson bowed low, showing thick gray hair. Brushing his lips over their extended hands, he said, "I'm pleased to meet both of you. I've heard rumors to the effect that the ladies of New Orleans outshine the rest of the country and now I can report that the rumors are, indeed, true." He held out his hand to Danielle. "Could I persuade you, my dear, to be my partner for the cotillion?"

"I would be pleased," she replied shyly, and stepped gracefully forward to accept his arm. She had heard of his charm with the ladies, and now she believed it.

They swept onto the dance floor, and as soon as the band struck up, he twirled her about the floor in the lively French dance. She knew she looked her best in her light muslin lavender dress that reached just to her ankles. The beaded bodice and hem caught the sparkle of the bright candlelight. If she were to represent the women of New Orleans for just one dance, then she would do them proud. Not once did she falter in the intricate steps. She had to admit that her partner was faultless in his execution of the dance pattern.

She yearned to forget she was supposed to be a simple beauty and to ask him what he proposed to do for their city's protection. She sighed, and when she noticed he was watching her, she smiled prettily. This was not the time and place to talk of military matters. She would learn soon enough what this strong, resolute soldier had in mind for her safety!

Chapter Five

GEOFFREY, waiting for Danielle in his pirogue, picked her up at the Crossing of the Five Muskrats and quickly rowed over to the *chênière,* one of the many swamp islands covered with white shells.

As Danielle stepped ashore, she was amazed at the number of men and women congregated in a clearing surrounded by live oak trees, awaiting the auctioneer's opening call.

Suddenly, she held back. "Geoffrey, there's Mr. Grymes. He's an attorney who knows my father."

"He knows my uncles, too." Geoffrey grinned. "He's the second attorney, along with Mr. Livingston, that Uncle Jean retained to remove the indictments against the Lafittes and to free Pierre. Even though they weren't able to deliver, Uncle Jean still paid their fee, which was twenty thousand dollars each." He laughed. "Poor Grymes. He stayed on Grand Terre to gamble and lost every penny."

Danielle had heard Mr. Grymes was the playboy of New Orleans, but right now she was only interested in avoiding him! If he recognized her, he'd report back to her father, gloating all the while. She remembered that her father had criticized Mr. Grymes for accepting Lafitte's money, and now here she was also associating with the pirates. It would place her father in a very bad light, indeed.

They reached a small hill where she could survey the proceedings without being seen. "Let me stay here on this knoll among the trees. I'll be able to see and hear everything and yet I won't be conspicuous."

"Whatever you say, sweet Danielle." He pointed to a large wooden platform that had been built in the clearing. "That's where the sale will take place."

For a fleeting moment, she wondered why he had brought her to this illegal auction, but she was sure he sensed her love of the daring and intended to show her a slice of his adventuresome life. Then, too, she had gladly gone along with his invitation.

"I'll be back soon. I need to organize the sale of the Persian carpets that will be going on the block." His dark eyes studied her, amused. "I trust you will be all right while I'm gone?"

"Of course, Geoffrey. I'm comfortable, and I'll sit on this stump and watch the proceedings." She shooed him away with her hand. "You go ahead."

"I'll be back before you can make one bid!" With light, easy strides, he was down the hillock and soon disappeared behind the large platform.

Idly she watched the well-dressed men and women conversing in animated voices as they milled about. Jean Lafitte mingled with these buyers, speaking Spanish to a fat merchant, French to a cloaked lady, and English to a trader in a tall beaver hat.

The auctioneer, a beefy, ruddy-faced pirate, leaped up on the platform and displayed sacks of cinnamon, curry, and pepper. Buyers immediately started the bidding. Most stores in New Orleans stocked their shelves from these auction sales; the authorities seldom bothered The Temple, not with the townsmen thirsting for these wares and supporting Jean Lafitte's privateering.

"Well, if it isn't Miss Nose-in-the-Air Verlaine!" Gambi towered above her, leering down.

Danielle's heart turned over at the sight of this stocky bully who hated her so much. She shrank back a bit, for he was reeking of rum, and his eyes were red-rimmed.

"Afraid to show your face at the auction yonder?" He jerked a thumb backward and prodded her foot with his heavy boot. He cackled, but there was no joy in his laugh, only contempt. "I'd like to show your father where his precious daughter is right this minute!"

Scrambling to her feet, she said between clenched teeth, "Gambi, leave me alone." Her words were braver than she felt, for her knees were like water, yet she didn't dare call for help.

"Oh, I know your protectors are down there — the Lafittes." He gave that awful snicker again. "Especially Geoffrey." He rubbed his snub-nose, contemplating her. "One of these days you won't have a champion near. Then watch out! Jean Lafitte is soft in the head when it comes to dealing with the Americans. They can burn his house, his settlement, and all his possessions, and still he gives orders not to fire on them. If I were running Grand Terre, we'd have scuttled the likes of you a long time ago!"

She shivered. The memory of Gambi's attempted takeover from Jean Lafitte several years ago flickered through her mind. Gambi had refused one of Jean Lafitte's orders. Later, one of Gambi's men had shouted for Jean Lafitte to come out on the porch, and when he did, Gambi's defiant lieutenant told him that "he would only take orders from Gambi." Jean Lafitte hadn't hesitated. He pulled out his pistol and shot him dead.

It was a lesson the pirates hadn't forgotten, although it was plain to see that Gambi wanted to take over Lafitte's leadership. One mistake or one weak decision on

Jean Lafitte's part and Gambi would be right there to instigate discontent and rebellion.

"I'm sure you'd like to challenge Jean Lafitte," she said angrily, her eyes as hot as his. "But he's too popular. Why would his men substitute *you* for a chief who has a reputation for fairness and has made most of his Baratarians wealthy?"

"Someday," he muttered, and moved closer, shoving her against a sapling, almost causing her to fall. "Someday," he repeated, "you'll find yourself alone, and old Gambi will catch you!" Then he half stumbled, half slid down the hill.

She had a sharp jibe on her tongue but thought better of it. She didn't want this cutthroat returning.

Her pulse still hadn't settled down as she observed Geoffrey stacking and tagging beautifully designed rugs on the platform. Once he turned in her direction and smiled. She wished she could respond to his happy mood, but Gambi had clouded her adventure.

Please hurry, Geoffrey, she pleaded silently. The day that had begun so brightly had changed. She wanted to leave this place called The Temple, where slaves once had been sold. The oak branches overhead seemed to mesh together, closing out the daylight and filling the knoll with shadows. Why had she come to this eerie place?

Once back in the pirogue with Geoffrey, her foolish fears evaporated, and his sunny disposition made her laugh. Happiness flooded through her once again. But, looking back at the narrow waters and the black trees, she knew she'd never return.

The following week, on Thursday, Danielle's father had come home to help with the final packing arrangements before the family left Cypress Manor in the morning. She was glad her father was spending the night, for the plantation had taken on a deserted and lonely air. The servants were gone, and white muslin covered the furniture.

Captain Verlaine leaned back comfortably in the armchair and unfastened his stiff military collar.

Danielle sat on a footstool, hugging her knees, watching her father sip a brandy. He appeared quite debonair in his U.S. uniform with the smart short jacket and black trousers with the scarlet stripe along the side. She was eager to hear about the latest news of troop movements.

"What are our chances against the British?" she asked coolly.

"There's every reason to believe we can whip them!" He gave her a radiant smile, and even his long mustache seemed to twitch with good humor. Danielle's hopes soared again. Jackson was an inspiration!

"Jackson's Tennessee regulars and the Mississippi dragoons have arrived and, believe me, those soldiers are rugged veterans!" He continued with Jackson's accomplishments. "He's ordered the reconditioning of all the forts. The bayous between New Orleans and the Gulf of Mexico are being jammed with fallen trees." He reached over and gave Danielle's hair a stroke. "Gunboats and over seventeen hundred men have been added to our ranks, but still we need more uniforms and weapons."

"I know," Adelaide commented. "General Sir Edward Pakenham and his British troops are already at the mouth of the Mississippi." She observed her husband. "I worry about you, Antoine. General Sir Edward Pakenham has over twelve thousand men, which completely outnumbers our force."

Danielle suppressed a smile. Only her mother would use Pakenham's full title.

Adelaide added with a hint of concern in her voice, "Our militia companies are completely thinned out. What can Jackson do about those?"

Antoine crossed his ankles and lit a cheroot. "My dear Adelaide, the general has given us such strength of defense and such organization that it's unbelievable. The militia companies of the Hulans, the Chasseurs, the Foot Dragoons, and the Louisiana Blues have formed a single fighting battalion under Major Jean B. Plauché." He leaned back, puffing on the small cigar.

"Ah, it's good to relax with both of you." Lines appeared across his forehead. "Our lives will be upside down after tomorrow." He looked fondly at Danielle. "After the war, when things are normal again, we can plan your betrothal party, darling. After all, you'll be sixteen in March."

Yes, sixteen, she thought hotly, *and I'm being treated as if I were ten!* She tried to be poised but couldn't keep her voice from rising. "I do not intend to marry Paul Milerand!"

Her father, taken aback, looked at her sharply. Irritated, his fingers tapped on the arms of the chair. "What do you mean, Danielle? It's all arranged!"

"Yes. That's the problem. It's all arranged! Why haven't I been consulted? Why do you just assume that I want to marry Paul? I'm not sure . . ." She faltered at her father's reddening face and glanced helplessly in her mother's direction. There was no arguing with her father when his mouth was set that way and when his eyes took on that steely glint.

"Antoine, dear," Adelaide interceded. "Now is not the time to talk of wedding plans. Danielle needs some quiet time to plan her own future." Her eyebrows lifted, and there was a small quirk around the corners of her generous mouth. "Antoine, remember when you courted me? When you gave me a diamond ring, you also announced that you had set the date for our wedding."

Antoine's face crinkled into a smile, and he visibly lost his anger. "Yes, you let me cut sugarcane for another six months, and I had to tell my friends that I wasn't sure if there would be a wedding or not." He cleared his throat. "A trifle embarrassing, but I loved you too much to give up!"

"Yes, I finally relented after half a year, didn't I?" Her lovely face softened. "Did you know I loved you as much as you loved me? It was very hard not to answer your messages, but you had to learn that I wasn't a subject and you weren't my lord."

Antoine chuckled. "You taught me a lesson, all right, and even though I still have no patience, I have more than I used to when I was young . . . and all because of you, Adelaide."

Danielle listened to this exchange, fascinated. This was the first time she'd heard of her mother's holding back. Perhaps now her father would understand her need and listen. She ventured her viewpoint. "You see, Father, I'm not the only one that doesn't want to rush into marriage."

Her father's smile was tender, but there was still a firm look in his eyes. He had not given up on his plans for her. "We'll talk about it later. I shouldn't have brought it up with all that's happening."

She said uneasily, "Yes, we'll talk about what I'd like to do after the war."

Right now it was more prudent to change the subject. "I — I heard Jean Lafitte was going to meet with Jackson and offer to fight for us," Danielle ventured, not wanting to look at her father.

Antoine Verlaine cocked his head to one side. "And where did you hear that?"

"I — I don't remember," she lied, feeling her cheeks redden.

"Well, you're right. Lafitte met Jackson at the Old Absinthe House last night, and it was morning before their conference was over. Jackson needed flints for his guns, and Lafitte promised him seventy-five hundred flints plus more muskets he had hidden away in the swamp. He also asked that the Baratarians be able to serve in the army. Jackson accepted."

"Wonderful!" Danielle clapped her hands before she could stop herself.

Her father gave her a quizzical look. "Yes, I suppose it is wonderful. The pirates' information will be invaluable, for they know the inner passages in each and every bayou and fen as well as I know every acre of Cypress Manor."

He rubbed his chin with his thumb. "Of course, Jean Lafitte never does anything without a price. He has demanded that any pirate in jail must be released, and after the war, each one of them must be given his citizenship."

"We need the Baratarians," she said earnestly. "They can help with supplies, they are good fighters, they have ships, they can . . ." Her voice trailed off. Why was she explaining to her father, a military man, the advantages the buccaneers could bring to their side? He knew full well what they could do for them. Now, if he would only accept the Lafittes, like Andrew Jackson had done, her future might even change. Perhaps, someday, she would be able to introduce him to Geoffrey Lafitte.

"Damn pirates," Antoine muttered. "Maybe you're right, Danielle, about needing every man in our army, but never forget that Jean Lafitte's wealth and his little kingdom on Grand Terre were built on the sale of slaves." He clenched his fist. "I'll never accept Jean Lafitte as an equal!" he said with a stubborn set to his jaw.

It was as if a cold waterfall had spilled down her spine. She had forgotten this aspect of Jean Lafitte. She had *wanted* to forget. After all, he didn't sell slaves now, and certainly Geoffrey had taken no part in this loathsome trade. Geoffrey would never sanction such a despicable practice. She bit her lip. She was positive of that.

"Ah, my dears, it's time for bed." Antoine rose and stretched. "I need to report to the Exchange Coffee House for a seven A.M. meeting with Andrew Jackson and Claiborne, so I'll be leaving early." He lifted Adelaide's chin and kissed her nose. "Are you sure you can travel into town alone tomorrow?"

Adelaide laughed, and her green eyes crinkled at the corners. "You forget, darling, that Danielle and I are two very independent women. We'll be leaving Cypress Manor around noon, and we'll go directly to Madeline's. Don't worry, we'll be perfectly free from harm!" She took his hand. "You look tired, Antoine."

"We've been drilling for days and I'm bone-tired." He reached for Danielle. "Kiss your old father good night since I won't see you in the morning."

She kissed his forehead and he hugged her close. For some reason, this made the war seem so immediate.

When she went to bed, her eyes moistened, and fear clung to her like the mist in the bayous. Despite her misgivings, she eventually dozed. Early in the morning, she vaguely heard a horse's hooves. Her father was leaving.

When she fully awoke, the sun's rays beamed through the shutters, and while she dressed in her riding garb, she thought of their trip to Madeline's. She would ride Ebony alongside the carriage. They would only pack a few valises and take the cameos.

Then there would be no life left on Cypress Manor. Even the stable would be empty, for the sugar mules had left last month to haul timber for building fortifications around the city. The thirteen they owned would be good draft animals. All of them weighed between thirteen and fifteen hundred pounds, twice as much as the little Creole mules used in the cotton fields. Sugar mules had been brought in from Missouri; they had to be extra large for plowing the river's soil so deep. Then, too, the hauling at harvesttime was laborious.

Well, it might be a long time before Cypress Manor harvested another sugarcane crop.

Folding her nightgown, she placed it in her valise and tucked in her bedroom slippers.

She made the bed and straightened the room so everything would be neat and ready for her return. On impulse, she took down the porcelain cat, wrapped it in a cape, and packed it also. She would have one thing of her own amidst Aunt Madeline's many knick-knacks.

Dropping to her knees, she peered under the bed and pulled forth the metal box that contained a fortune in cameos and placed it by the door along with her valise. With only the shutters left to lock, her hair to braid, and the furniture to cover, she would be ready on time.

"Come and have coffee and bread before we leave," her mother called from downstairs.

"Yes, Mother. I have a few things to do and I'll be right down."

"Fine, dear. I'm securing and locking the shutters in every room downstairs. The coffee will be brewed in ten minutes."

"All right, Mother." She quickly shook out the muslin and covered the settee, but as she was tying it, she heard her mother talking to someone. Who would be calling now? She hurried to the window and peeked out between the slats. Perhaps Tulci had ridden over with a last bit of news.

What she saw caused her to grasp the bedpost and hold on with every fiber of strength. Dear God in heaven! They hadn't left Cypress Manor in time! There, stretched out along the dusty lane, was a column of British troops, standing at stiff attention.

She rushed to her half-closed bedroom door and saw a roomful of British soldiers, her mother facing them. Danielle's heart raced as she tried to think what to do. She had to hold herself back from doing anything foolhardy, like challenging them with a pistol. That wouldn't do either her mother or herself any good. The one thought that dominated all else was that she must get away and warn General Jackson.

The tall officer who confronted her mother said in a loud voice, as if he were reciting a memorized passage, "I am Colonel William Thornton of the British army. You, Madame Verlaine, are under house arrest."

How did he know their name? Then Danielle saw the short, olive-skinned man at the colonel's side. She recognized the blue shirt and tarpaulin of the Spanish fishermen from Moccasin Springs, a small fishing village on the Mississippi. They were British sympathizers and evidently had acted as their guides through the treacherous subtropical marshes. The troops never could have made it on their own. She half crouched, standing absolutely still, trying to catch every word.

The colonel spoke again as he removed one

of his gauntlets and glanced about. "It looks as if you intended to abandon your plantation. Are you alone here, madame?"

Adelaide put aside the veiled hat that matched her gray traveling suit and took her time in answering. Then she lifted her head and said serenely, "Yes, I am. I was to join my husband in town." She glanced at the fisherman. "I'm sure you know who that is from your informant."

A brief smile flitted across the colonel's stony features. "Indeed. Captain Antoine Verlaine." He wiped his brow. "We had a hard march through the swamp, and even with the help of Miguel" — he indicated the fisherman with a flip of his glove — "trying to find a solid pathway took some doing. Fortunately, we found one bayou, Bayou Bienvenue, that wasn't choked with tree logs. We're glad to have found your lovely plantation, madame, and I can assure you, we will respect you and your possessions. We do, however, expect your cooperation."

At these words, Danielle picked up the tin box and grasped it tightly.

Colonel Thornton stared at Adelaide for a long moment. "You appear to be an Englishwoman, well-bred and genteel. Your countrymen need your help, Madame Verlaine."

Adelaide, slender and straight, returned his long look unflinchingly. "I assure you, sir, I am an American, and I'll defend Cypress Manor and New Orleans with every breath in my body."

"How very noble of you," he sneered. With a quick half turn, he motioned to a nearby soldier. "Lieutenant, tie her in a chair!"

Shaking, Danielle watched as two soldiers roughly shoved her mother in a chair and bound her hands behind her.

"We won't bother to gag you," Colonel Thornton said disdainfully. "You can scream all you please. No one will hear you. Now"— he stood in front of her, slapping his glove against his boot — "I know you have a daughter, and I'm sure she's hidden somewhere in this house. Rest assured, madame," he said in an icy, calm voice, "that we'll find her."

"I am alone," Adelaide reiterated, observing her protagonist with equal disdain. "You'll find nothing here."

"Alone? I doubt it. If you were truly English, I might take your word, but being so proud of being an American, I'm sure you've adopted their lying ways. They are cowards, every last one of them. Barbarians who shoot from behind trees and ambush my men in the swamp. No, I'd never trust an American."

"You are the invaders! Americans are only defending their homes," Adelaide said with a defiant toss of her head, her eyes flashing.

Swiftly, the colonel strode forward and slapped Adelaide across the cheek with his glove.

Danielle gasped, bringing her knuckles to her trembling lips.

The colonel lashed out, "Enough of your insolence, madame! You are my prisoner of war." He seemed infuriated that she didn't cower before him.

"Lieutenants Roth and Emerson. Search the premises. The Verlaines have a daughter, and I mean to find her."

Saluting, the two men began their hunt, one going into the dining room and the other into the pantry.

Panic seized Danielle. She didn't have a moment to lose, for they would soon be coming upstairs. She gave one last look at her brave mother and crept down the hall to the back stairs, trying to remain out of sight, scarcely breathing. What would Jackson say when he heard the British were only five miles from New Orleans?

Suddenly, a soldier passed the opening, and she flattened herself against the wall. Her throat clamped shut, and her mouth became as dry as tinder.

She remembered her mother's words when she had told the colonel that she was all alone. She was giving her daughter time to escape. She knew, too, how vital this information would be for the Americans. For a fleeting moment, the young girl wondered how she could leave her mother, but there was no other way. A tear slid down her cheek. *Poor Mother, in the hands of these fiends!*

Quietly, Danielle unbolted the back door and raced down the stairs out into the courtyard. She dreaded crossing the open space to the stable, but it had to be done before troops swarmed all over the plantation.

Taking a deep breath, she dashed across to the stable, ducking inside. There stood Ebony, patiently waiting, not realizing his swiftness could determine the fate of New Orleans. If the British were this close and could surprise Jackson's forces, the city would be lost without a fight.

Throwing the saddle over Ebony's back, she hurried to fasten the girth, but her fingers were awkward and trembling. Her heart pounded. The strongbox, too large to fit into the saddle pouch, was securely tied behind the saddle.

Mounting efficiently and silently she whispered, "Easy, Ebony, easy. Soon I'll let you go faster than you've ever gone." With her riding crop, she gently urged the black stallion out into the yard. In a flash, the bridle was seized, startling Ebony into jerking his head backward, almost unseating Danielle.

"Well, my lass!" came a shout. "Where do you think you're off to on such a fine December morning?" A British soldier held the reins fast!

*Chapter
Six*

EBONY reared, forelegs pawing the air. The British soldier, in dodging the hooves, loosened his hold on the reins.

Without a moment's pause, Danielle slashed her riding whip across the man's cheek, and instantly a red welt sprang to the surface. The soldier fell back, bellowing with pain and yelling for reinforcements.

Danielle was off at a mad gallop toward the seldom-used Swamp Road. She didn't care much for this back road, but it was safer than trying to skirt past the regiment in the front.

She didn't expect the soldiers to follow her because rumors were that the British were afraid to step on the spongy soil of the "Trembling Prairies" in Louisiana.

However, she was wrong, for two horsemen rode after her.

"This way, Charlie! She can't get far," yelled one British soldier. "After her!"

The blood rushed to her face and her pulse throbbed. She had to escape the British at all costs. It would be difficult to outdistance seasoned cavalrymen, but she was an accomplished horsewoman, too, and she had a tremendous advantage, for she knew every twist and bend in the Swamp Road. She clung low on the saddle and headed toward the city. A moss-covered overhanging branch brushed against her face, but she didn't stop. Her brain was working feverishly. There must be some way to escape the soldiers.

All at once she knew what she could do. Although the plan was risky, anything would be better than to be captured.

When she reached the turnoff at Alligator Swamp, she pulled Ebony up short, jumped off, and led him into a thick grove of cypress trees, heavily laden with Spanish moss. The ground was liquid mud, and she had to slog her way into the cove, thick with cattails.

She patted Ebony's quivering nostrils. "Quiet . . . quiet. Not a sound," she whispered reassuringly.

She pulled a handkerchief from her belt and entwined the white lace square in the branch of a nearby cypress tree. It fluttered in the chill morning like a Greek siren beckoning Ulysses' sailors onto the rocks; only in this case, the bit of lace would lure British soldiers into a morass.

She waited motionlessly among the ferns

and high reeds, willing the soldiers to return and fall into her trap.

She gasped with relief when she heard the two horsemen talking on the nearby Swamp Road. Soon they were bound to discover the hoof impressions leading into the cypress grove, but she was so well concealed that they'd never suspect she was near. She only prayed Ebony wouldn't neigh or paw the ground. She would bait them into the tangled grove, and when they saw her handkerchief, hopefully they would be enticed farther into the swamp and ride well past her sheltered niche. If her plot succeeded, they would ride ever deeper and become mired in the never-ending grasses where it looked secure, but beneath all was ooze and water. Once they had gone beyond her, she would return to the main road and ride full tilt for General Jackson's headquarters.

She must have waited fifteen minutes at the longest, but it seemed like hours before they retraced their way. All was still except for the cawing of the sea gulls and the movement in the brush where a black turtle crawled.

Their voices broke the silence as one soldier hacked ruthlessly with his sword at the low-hanging moss. "What a filthy country. Cold and clammy. I don't think I'll ever be warm again."

"I don't mind the cold," the second soldier responded. "It's this swamp with the mud and birds and snakes."

"Look!" the first soldier whooped, stopping a swath in midair. "Her handkerchief! We're on the right track!"

Their voices faded as they delved deeper into the swamp.

She waited a few moments, then without a sound, she led Ebony back onto the solid path.

Once in the clear, she remounted and started at a gallop for New Orleans.

The Swamp Road, with its curves and mud, took longer than the City Road, but eventually she came upon the trappers' houses on the city's outskirts. The houses were deserted, for the trappers were off in the swamp, setting muskrat traps.

She had made it! Only a few more miles to Royal Street. Ebony was covered with lather, and once, when she remembered the cameos, she twisted about in a panic, but the box was still securely bound.

Her hair was tangled. There had been no time to braid it, and her boots were covered with mud. For a second, she wondered if General Jackson would remember her, and if he did, would he believe her incredible story?

Down the narrow street she galloped, until Ebony came to a shuddering stop before Jackson's headquarters. She jumped off the horse.

A sentry guarded the door, and when she tried to brush past, he lowered his musket across his chest. "The general is busy," he snapped.

"I must speak with him at once. Get out of

my way . . . my news won't wait!" She would not be thwarted now when she was so close.

The sentry, a young boy in a leather jerkin, shook his head stubbornly. "The general is busy." His tone was more uncertain, however.

"I don't have time to argue!" she shouted. "Let me in at once. The war could depend on my information!"

Her disheveled, desperate appearance unsettled him, for he faltered and lowered his gun. He persisted in blocking the doorway, however.

With a shove, she pushed him against the building and raced inside.

"Come back here!" He followed, grabbing her arm.

General Jackson, poring over a map with an aide, glanced up, amazed. When he saw Danielle, he straightened to his full height. "What the . . ." Then he looked sharply at the sentry. "What's the meaning of this, sergeant?"

"General Jackson!" she burst out. "You must listen to me. Don't you recognize me?"

His wide gray eyes narrowed. "Danielle Verlaine," he murmured. He waved the sergeant aside. "It's all right." Then he gazed at her, hands on hips. "My dear, what's this all about?"

Without wasting time, she told him the story in two sentences. "General, the British have taken over our plantation. My mother is their prisoner!" She stopped for breath.

"The Verlaine plantation!" he echoed,

dumbfounded, glancing at his aide. "That's only five miles from here. How did you escape?"

She knew he was groping for confirming evidence of such a wild story, hoping it wasn't true. "I ran out the back door, taking the Swamp Road. Two of the British soldiers followed, but I sent them on a false trail."

"Great heavens!" Jackson almost smiled at her, but the hollows of his cheeks seemed deeper, and his skin had a sallow tone. "Do you realize what this means?"

"I think I do, sir." She sank into a nearby chair. "The British won't be able to take you by surprise."

"That's right!" He rubbed his chin. "In fact, I might surprise them!" Over his shoulder, never taking his eyes from Danielle, he ordered, "Sergeant, bring our valued courier a cup of tea."

The general strode to the window and after a moment's thought spun about, smashing his fist into his hand. "They won't sleep on our soil! I'm going to fight them tonight!" He then turned to the young Creole at his side. "Rousseau, fetch Major General Carroll immediately and fire the signal gun to alert the 44th and 7th infantry at the city barracks."

"Yes, sir!" The young Frenchman was out the door on Jackson's last word.

Danielle gratefully drank the tea and waited for her heartbeat to slow, all the while watching Jackson and hoping he was well. She knew he suffered from malaria, and the way he looked, he probably should have been resting.

"Sergeant," he ordered, "get me four couriers. You send a courier directly to Brigadier-General Coffee and his Tennesseeans who are only four miles north of here at the Avart plantation, and tell him to double-march to the de la Ronde plantation. I'll handle the other three messengers. Oh, and sergeant, as soon as those orders are carried out, return to your unit."

Jackson donned and buttoned his jacket and buckled on his saber. He checked his pistols and snorted. "So the British call the Americans 'dirty shirts,' do they? We'll see who comes out the cleanest in this fight!" He hurried back to the map. "How many troops do you think the British had, Danielle?"

"There was a long column, led by a Colonel Thornton."

"Colonel Thornton, eh? According to my scouts," he mused, "he was leading an advance assault troop that would be about eighteen hundred men." Then he gave her his full attention. "Danielle, what can I do for you? The United States Army owes you a great debt."

"Let me help in the war in some way," she pleaded.

"You've helped me more today than an entire battalion."

"Sir!" The three couriers entered the room, saluted, and awaited their orders.

Jackson scribbled out a directive, folded it,

and handed it to the first messenger. "For Major Plauché on Bayou St. John. If his troops can't be in this position within two hours, he's to contact me." The general then turned to the second courier. "This is for Colonel de la Ronde. He's to act as my guide. If he can't be here in thirty minutes, he's to let me know. There's a second message for General Carroll. His troops are to break camp and go directly to Bayou Bienvenue."

Danielle drank more tea. Colonel Denis de la Ronde was their neighbor. She knew him well and wondered where Françoise and Mignon, his two young daughters, were hidden.

To the third messenger he gave another sealed missive. "For Commodore Patterson. I need him to drop down the river and keep his guns in a ready position."

The couriers withdrew immediately.

A bugle sounded, and Danielle felt so helpless. *She* could be a courier, too. She could shoot. She could assist in some way.

Outdoors, the drums and fifes played and there were cries of men and the sound of caissons careening down the streets. Jackson hurriedly put on his two-pointed black hat, muttering, "My whole army is coming down the Mississippi on flatboats. If I only had another day." He opened the door, giving her a last look. "Thank you, Danielle Verlaine. Your courage will not go unrewarded."

"Sir, could I help by? . . ." She stood up, clutching the cup of tea.

"Do you have a place to stay?" the general asked.

"My aunt's, Madeline Verlaine."

"Please. Go to your aunt's. Stay inside. There will be a battle tonight — that's the way you can serve me best." He was out the door before Danielle could protest.

Stay inside, indeed, she thought. She had no intention of languishing behind shuttered windows while Americans would be fighting and dying for their country. She would go to her aunt's, but later she would find some way to aid the cause.

Dispirited, she gave one last look around Jackson's austere office and left for Aunt Madeline's. All she wanted was to help the war effort. Was that too much to ask? Well, Jackson would see that she had courage for more than just a ride along the Swamp Road.

As she rode into the Vieux Carré, the Old Square District, she halted several times to allow running militia men to pass, a U.S. marine unit to march by, and the volunteer lads of Beale's Rifles, all expert marksmen and wearing blue hunting shirts and wide-brimmed black felt hats, to dash by. Once, she had to make way for mules loaded with cotton bales for breastworks along the front.

At last, reaching Rampart Street, she tied Ebony to the hitching post in front of Aunt Madeline's pretty pink-brick town house with its supporting columns on the first level and the cast-iron balcony on the second. Many of the town houses had the same type of architecture, but her aunt's was so well maintained and had the added features of a profusion of roses and irises in season and a bubbling fountain in the back courtyard.

Untying the tin box and tucking it beneath her arm, Danielle hurried up the wooden walk, opened the gate in the scrolled grill-work fence, and pulled the rope on the bell. While she waited, a group of yelling Baratarians ran past with sabers drawn, some with knives between their teeth.

The door was flung open by Aunt Madeline. The small, lively woman cried, "I've been so worried. Troops are marching through the streets. Bugles. Drums. Horsemen going this way and that. Come in. Come in, my dear." The tiny brunette hugged Danielle but almost immediately released her. "Where's Adelaide?"

Danielle encircled her aunt's tiny waist with her arm. "It's quite a tale, Aunt Madeline. I'll tell you all about it over a cup of coffee." She remembered ruefully that she never did taste the morning coffee that her mother had said would be brewed in ten minutes. Was that only this morning? A few hours ago? She could hardly bear to think of her mother. Where was she? How was she being treated?

"Sit down, Danielle, and I'll bring in a tray." Aunt Madeline looked with distaste at her niece's bedraggled appearance. "Oh, and take off your muddy boots before entering the parlor."

Danielle, tugging off her high boots, shook her head. She should have remembered her aunt's fetish for cleanliness. Usually she was amused by Aunt Madeline's concern for eliminating every dust particle in sight, but today it was only irritating. Men were dying, her mother was a prisoner, everything was in chaos, and Madeline was fretting over mud on her carpet.

The coffee tasted bitter, but it was bracing. As Danielle sipped, she told Madeline the whole wretched story of Adelaide's capture while her aunt, at certain intervals, clicked her tongue in disbelief.

Danielle held out her cup. "Is there some more?"

Madeline shook her head. "Sorry, Danielle, but coffee is scarce. Only the smuggling Baratarians have an ample supply. Even William can't find any for me."

"Colonel Ellinger?" Danielle asked, sweeping a sidelong glance at her aunt beneath her long lashes and smiling while she gently moved to and fro in the rocker.

"Yes, what other William do I know?" She held out her small hand. "You haven't seen my latest gift." There, on her third finger, was a sparkling diamond surrounded by four bright rubies, winking in the afternoon sun.

Her aunt edged forward on her chair. "After the war, we plan to be married . . . hopefully in June, if there's a peace treaty by then." She smiled, and her whole face lit up. Her pert nose and upswept black curls gave her a saucy air. "William is with General Morgan, who is one of Jackson's right-hand men. They'll soon be coming south, not too far from Cypress Manor."

She stood up and walked to the Christmas tree by the spinet and tilted one of the candles into an upright position. "We had hoped to spend Christmas together, but it seems there's a battle to fight."

Danielle thought of the holidays with a pang. Christmas was only two days away, with her mother a prisoner and her father in the army, heaven knew where.

Aunt Madeline paced back and forth, her cinnamon-colored dress swirling about her slender ankles. "I've been going to the Ursuline Convent every day, rolling bandages and preparing blankets for our soldiers. The legislature finally allotted blankets, and they're coming in by the wagonload. It's been so cold and damp this December. At any rate" — she sat again, still leaning intently toward Danielle, her enormous hazel eyes serious — "a contingent of women are following the army to the front with bandages and medicines. We're assembling at the Cabildo." She reached for Danielle's hand. "You'll be safe here. I may need to be away for several days — do you mind?"

Danielle touched her aunt's hand, admiring her strength and dedication. She looked so tiny and helpless but she was not at all. Danielle said gently but firmly, "Aunt Madeline, of course I mind. I intend to go with you.

The last thing I asked General Jackson was to be able to help. He rushed out, telling me to come here."

Aunt Madeline's hand closed on hers. "Good, I knew you'd want to go with us." She jumped again to her feet. "Now, there are things to do. I'll change into a more practical gown."

Danielle indicated the metal box. "I've brought the Verlaine cameos. Where's a good hiding place?"

Madeline looked about the cluttered but cozy parlor with its pictures, pillowed chairs, heavy drapes, and directed, "Slip it under the draped table. I have no vault, and it will be as safe there as anyplace."

Danielle fetched the box and shoved it under the covered round table.

"Shutter the windows, dear. Are you sure you don't want to lie down for a few minutes? You look so tired."

Danielle was tired to exhaustion, but she said, "I'm fine, Aunt Madeline. You go ahead. The sooner we get to the front, the sooner we'll be able to tend the wounded."

Latching the windows, she felt elation along with her weariness. She could be of some service after all. Her pulse quickened, sensing the hardship and danger that faced her.

Chapter Seven

IT was dark by the time the hospital wagon was organized to leave the Cabildo. Torches illuminated figures running, women and children on balconies cheering troops pouring into the city, carriages rattling toward the front, mules hauling cannon, messengers dashing across the plaza. Danielle's heart was pumping hard, and her throat was parched. What would it be like at the front? She hoped her courage would remain steady. The lively strains of "Yankee Doodle" were being sung as their wagon creaked by a coffee house. It was odd to see such activity because for weeks Jackson had had martial law imposed on the city. The curfew meant no one could be out after nine o'clock, and sentries, posted everywhere, saw that the law was enforced.

The wagon, filled with ten women and three orderlies, was followed by two more wagons loaded with tent equipment, medical supplies, and blankets.

Despite the chill, moonless night, Danielle was warmed by excitement and patriotic fervor. She clenched her fists, vowing to be resolute and as brave as a soldier.

Out of the darkness, a rider galloped, scattering handbills right and left. "Citizens of New Orleans," he bellowed. "I come from General Keane, the British commander. Read these words. They could affect your future!"

Danielle snatched one of the handbills fluttering down and read the message aloud:

> Louisianians:
> Remain quietly in your homes.
> Your property will be protected.
> We make war only on Americans.

Aunt Madeline scanned the contents, then tore the paper in two. "What nonsense!"

Danielle said angrily, "The British must think we're still loyal to France. Just because we haven't been in America as long as some Easterners, they consider that we won't fight as Americans."

A woman, an American, sitting directly across from her, answered, "You must admit that most citizens of New Orleans were not very friendly when the Americans first entered the city."

"The Louisiana Purchase was eleven years ago. Since then we've *become* Americans." Madeline bristled.

"Personally," the American woman said, "I like the French and Spanish settlers here. They're friendly and" — she patted her stomach — "I love the food."

Half the city's population was of French and Spanish ancestry. Even Mayor Girod needed a translator when he first met General Jackson, for Girod spoke only French. Danielle had been born in Louisiana, however, and felt a fierce loyalty to the American flag. "I'm loyal to the United States," she said quietly.

"Most Creoles are, but what about those merchants that went to see General Jackson last week?" someone else asked.

Danielle bit her lower lip. She couldn't find any excuses for those businessmen who had asked Jackson to surrender the city without firing a shot because they were concerned about their bulging warehouses stuffed with merchandise. They knew that if the British invaded, their goods would either be destroyed or confiscated. Fortunately, Jackson had thrown them out of his office. Jackson was wonderful. He had unified the population and rallied everyone to save their city as no one else could have done.

Madeline broke in, her hazel eyes snapping. "Those privateers were despicable and by no means represent the majority. They were just greedy men . . . like anyplace else."

"I agree with you," said the American. "My name is Betsy Summers." Her smile spread across her broad face. Danielle held out her hand. "I'm Danielle Verlaine, and this is my aunt, Madeline Verlaine."

Unexpectedly, cannons boomed, sending tremors along the ground. Was the fight commencing? Danielle was thrilled yet frightened at the same time.

They passed a group of pirates along the river levees, manning cannon aimed at the British on the other side. Dominque and Cut-Nose, the two Baratarians recently released from prison, were expert artillerists, and as they went by them, Danielle wondered if those two pirates were overseeing the firing.

As they neared the de la Ronde plantation, she could see the flickering bonfires of the British on the other side of the river. It was a cold night, and vapor rose from the river. The British must be frightened to be camped in a swamp in a strange country.

When the wagons halted about five hundred yards from the bank, several soldiers met them to set up the large hospital tent. Danielle and the other women helped unload the medical supplies, and it wasn't long before there was a line of frontiersmen asking for blankets. Danielle was kept busy, parceling out the wool blankets. She just wished there were more because it wouldn't be long before their meager supply would be depleted.

The mist settled over the river and mingled with the cannon smoke. It was almost impossible to see into the gloom. She could, however, make out the outline of the *Caro-*

lina, whose guns were firing at the British camp fires. Paul must be directing the sailors. He was such a short distance away, yet he might as well have been in New York. How she would love to see him and be reassured he was safe. They had grown up together, and she had a strong affection for him. Darling Paul, who had always been so protective of her. Who, now, was protecting him?

Sporadic rifle fire cracked nearby.

"Major La Costa! Move your men to the orange grove!" came a deep voice out of the darkness. The all-black battalion of two hundred eighty men marched smartly forward. Many of these men were Dominicans who had fought for Haitian freedom.

For a short while, the rifle fire stopped, but the two cannon kept exploding at the British outpost. British soldiers emerged from the mist to attempt to capture the fieldpieces.

Suddenly, there was Jackson on his white charger, shouting, "Save the guns, boys, at any sacrifice!" He wheeled his horse about, and Danielle glimpsed his vibrant eyes. He no longer seemed ill.

The Tennesseans moved forward, and she could make out men fighting in hand-to-hand combat. *Dear God,* she thought. Without moonlight, men couldn't tell who they were stabbing . . . British or Americans. As if to confirm her thoughts, a voice yelled, "John, what are you doing with that bayonet? It's me, Steve!"

In a few hours, both sides had to withdraw, for the heavy fog enshrouded them like a black veil. A few casualties were brought in on a stretcher, and Danielle helped to dress the wounds of three soldiers.

One boy, a Beale's rifleman, sat on the edge of a cot while she bandaged his arm. When she finished, he grabbed his long rifle and energetically began to clean the red-soaked bayonet. He had fiery hair and a freckled face.

He looked at her approvingly. "What's your name, miss?"

"Danielle," she replied, wishing he wouldn't use his wounded right arm with such vigor.

"Pretty name to go with a pretty face."

"What's yours?"

"Christopher Rollins from Nashville, Tennessee, and chomping to return. Christmas ain't no time to be away from the old homestead."

"Was the fighting bad?"

He laughed victoriously. "We kept those Lobster Tails on the other side of the river where they belong, but to tell you the truth, it ain't much fun mucking about in the swamp . . . in the pitch dark."

"I'll bet you won, though?" She smiled, too, for his laugh was infectious.

"Hardly." He sobered, and Danielle thought he was probably only fifteen, her age. "Tell you what, though," he went on, "those Britishers learned one thing tonight."

"And what was that?" Aunt Madeline questioned, joining them, her sleeves rolled to the elbows. Lines of fatigue creased her brow.

"They learned that taking New Orleans ain't going to be the pushover fight they thought it'd be, ma'am." Finishing cleaning his bayonet, he slipped it into his boot and rose. "Well, ladies, thanks for the bandage. Got to go now." He winced, putting on his backpack. "Jackson's ordered every man to report to his commander to help fill in and fortify that trench they call the Rodriguez Canal."

He tipped his wide-brimmed hat to Danielle. "Hope to see you again, little lady, but it ain't likely. Soon's we lick the British, I aim to head back to Nashville." He pulled back the tent flap and was gone into the cold night.

"Good luck, Christopher," she called after him.

As Danielle folded a blanket, she turned to see her father. She moved toward him, filled with surprise.

"Father! Father!" She flew into his waiting arms. "Were you hurt?" She stepped back to examine him.

"I'm fine. Only tired and dirty. General Carroll told me you were here." Even though his uniform was soiled with mud splatters, every button was in place, and his hat sat squarely on his head.

"Antoine!" Madeline stepped forward. "What about a hug and kiss for your sister?"

"Ah, Madeline. I'm so tired. I only have eyes for one thing at a time."

He turned back to Danielle. "Are you all right, darling?" He held her at arm's length, gazing at her with concern. "General Carroll told me you had a wild ride along the Swamp Road this morning."

"Yes. Then you know about Mother. Was the plantation retaken tonight?"

"No." He lowered his head. "The British are solidly entrenched at Cypress Manor. You must try not to worry about her, Danielle. Remember, Adelaide is resourceful and calm. She'll be safe until our return."

Danielle's eyes misted. "I hated to leave her."

Captain Verlaine tilted her chin upward. "You did a brave thing, and the only thing you could do. Your escape was well thought out, and you had to leave your mother. We can only hope that the British won't harm a defenseless woman. The fight went very well tonight. If General Keane had attacked this afternoon, before Jackson had had a chance to organize his men, it might have been a different story. After we lost five gunboats to the British, the *Carolina* did herself proud, pinning down the British along the levee so they couldn't advance."

"And the Baratarians?"

He shrugged his shoulders. "The pirates' artillery shielded Jackson's left flank.

"Look, my dears" — he rubbed a dirty glove across his forehead — "I don't have much time. I need to return to my troops at the canal. We'll be working all night trying to fill that dry gulch." He smiled wryly. "I did come here for a purpose. Your field hospi-

99

tal will be moved behind the canal, and you are to return home. Jackson expects that no fighting will resume until after Christmas. Even the British will believe in a truce over the holidays. There may not be open battle, but there won't be any holiday for us." He touched Danielle's cheek and held Madeline's hand. "The two of you will have a quiet Christmas alone this year. God willing, we'll all be together next year, and," he added with a twinkle, "under an American flag."

"Have you heard anything about William?" Madeline enquired eagerly.

"Nothing, sorry." He edged to the opening as if hating to leave the two women. "Go back home, Madeline, and be as comfortable as possible. You'll be summoned when the fighting commences," he said, and added under his breath, "or when the cannon open up again. Take heart." And he was gone.

Danielle turned to Madeline, and the two held each other for a long moment. Returning home to wait for the war to start again would be difficult.

Christmas Day was dismal, even though the candles on the tree were lit and Aunt Madeline, as a special treat, made pralines. For a while they played cards, but even this soon bored them.

"I'm going for a walk, Aunt Madeline. Won't you come with me?" Danielle was concerned, for her aunt was not her usual vivacious self. Madeline had asked everyone she came in contact with if they knew the whereabouts of William, but there was no news.

"I don't think you should go out, Danielle," Madeline cautioned.

"Aunt Madeline, it's as quiet as a tomb out there. I have to breathe fresh air after being cooped up for three days. I'm numb from sitting. From reading. From playing cards."

Her aunt didn't argue. "Don't go past the square," was her only warning. The dark circles under her eyes meant she hadn't been sleeping well. "I have a headache. I think I'll lie down for a bit."

"I'm sure William is all right," Danielle said, trying to comfort her aunt.

"I hope you're right, Danielle, but I can't help worrying. My mind keeps seeing William as I last saw him. Dressed in his uniform and on his brown horse, he waved to me and blew a kiss. He's in my thoughts constantly. He's such a dear man. I hope you have a chance to meet him someday." There was a catch in her voice.

Danielle flung her cloak around her shoulders. She knew what Madeline was thinking. Perhaps she'd never meet this American army officer, but she pretended otherwise. "I'll not only meet him, I'll be part of the wedding party." She smiled, but Aunt Madeline turned her back, walking to the sofa and stretching out. "Don't be long, Danielle."

"I won't." Getting out had been very easy. Danielle could tell Aunt Madeline wasn't herself or she wouldn't have consented quite this readily.

Danielle wandered into the back courtyard, bleak and flowerless in the crisp morning light, and slowly walked around the fountain filled with dead leaves. She breathed in the river breeze. Stepping lightly over to the wooden gate, she leaned her elbows on top, looking up and down the street for some sign of activity.

Unlatching the gate, she walked along Rampart Street. It was deserted, and the boarded-up residences were depressing. She shivered a little in her velvet wrap and pulled it closer around her chin.

When she came upon the square, two pirates were cleaning a large cannon. By the ropes and pulleys entwined over the barrel, she knew they were preparing to haul it to the front lines.

Her heart beat hard. Dare she ask about Geoffrey? She was eager to know how he was . . . where he was. If she was clever, perhaps she could find out without her intense interest being obvious. Her walk slowed. She mustn't begin the conversation, for it wouldn't be proper. She stamped her foot a little and gave them a side glance, but they were vigorously polishing a twenty-four-pounder and paid no attention to her.

From her quick look, she knew Cut-Nose must be one of the men directing the overhaul of the cannon. He'd been given the nickname because half of his nose had been lost in a saber duel.

Danielle deliberately stumbled on a loose plank and went down on all fours. Cut-Nose rushed to her side and lifted her to her feet.

"Mon Dieu!" he exclaimed. "Mademoiselle, these walkways are treacherous. Did you hurt yourself?"

"I — I think I'm all right," she said, pretending to be dizzy. She shakily placed her fingers to her temple.

Cut-Nose was a big man with a swarthy complexion and heavy lines around his large mouth, but it was his nose that gave him such a forbidding appearance. Besides being half gone, there was a scar running from his nose to his jutting chin.

"Come over here and sit down, mademoiselle," he said sympathetically.

"Are you Cut-Nose?" she asked, allowing him to hold her elbow and direct her to a stone bench.

He roared with laughter. "How did you know? Ho! Dominique. This little lady knows about us Baratarians."

She was glad her trick had worked and that he didn't ask who she was. "The citizens of New Orleans appreciate the Baratarians and what they're doing to protect the city. I've met Jean Lafitte and his nephew, Geoffrey. Are they helping you, too?" she asked casually.

Dominique, with a wide grin on his broad

face, swaggered over to the bench, thrusting a big boot up on it and leaning his arm on his knee as he peered down at her. "Ha, Jean Lafitte knows nothing of artillery. I learned all there is to know in the French Revolution. I am an expert!" He expanded his chest.

Cut-Nose answered her question more directly. "Right this minute, Jean Lafitte is meeting with General Jackson at the McCarté House."

Danielle knew that the McCarté House was an official residence near the Chalmette plantation, just behind the Rodriguez Canal.

She was a little jittery. Should she be bold and ask about Geoffrey? She almost asked when Cut-Nose volunteered her sought-after information.

"Geoffrey is on Grand Terre, but he, along with about five hundred other Baratarians, will be coming in by pirogues tomorrow. They will help complete the canal's fortifications. There's where the big battle will take place."

So Geoffrey was safe. She wanted to dance about the square but restrained herself. She rose and said in a calm voice, "I feel fine now. I had better return home or my aunt will be worried." She shook hands, first with Dominique and then with Cut-Nose. "I'm pleased to have met both of you."

"Our pleasure," Dominique said, nodding and grinning like a little boy.

That afternoon, she and Aunt Madeline went to the convent and rolled bandages, then in the evening played more cards.

When she went to bed, sleep eluded her. She thought of Geoffrey, rowing his small pirogue and skimming over bayou water. She must see him again . . . somehow . . . some way.

At seven o'clock the next morning, she was awakened by a heavy bombardment. Hurriedly, she dressed in her dark riding gown, ready to go to the front, if need be.

Aunt Madeline waited for her at the bottom of the stairs.

"Are we leaving for the front?" asked Danielle.

Her aunt slowly shook her head, and tears glistened in her eyes, then spilled over, coursing down her cheeks.

Danielle grasped her hand. "What is it, Aunt Madeline? Is it William?"

"No, it's . . . Danielle, try to be brave." The words strangled in her throat.

"What is it? Tell me." Danielle's voice rose to match her rising panic.

"It's the *Carolina*. It's been sunk."

Chapter Eight

SHE stared at her weeping aunt in amazement. When she finally found her voice, the words came out in a rush. "Are you certain? How do you know?"

Wiping her eyes, Madeline swallowed hard and composed herself. "A messenger came in and reported that the ship sank fifteen minutes after the British trained their guns on her."

"What happened to the crew?" Fear made her voice shake.

"No one knows if there are any survivors. If there are, they'll be taken directly to the field hospital." Her aunt hesitated. "There's no point in going to the hospital until we're sent for. Couriers will keep us informed."

"Aunt Madeline, you know I can't sit and wait to find out about Paul. I need to know

now. I have to know if he's alive or . . ." Her voice faded.

"Dearest Danielle. If Paul drowned, we'll know soon enough. General Jackson doesn't want anyone going to the front unless authorized."

"I have a pass, remember? I work at the hospital."

"You must be patient, Danielle." Tears sprang to her aunt's eyes once more.

Danielle surmised Madeline was thinking about William, but she couldn't stay and comfort her. She grabbed her cloak. "I'll be back as soon as I can."

She ran to the City Horse Barn, but Ebony was gone — probably being used as a draft horse.

Frantically, she ran back to the street and was able to hail a cart piled high with logs. The cart was slow as it lurched and bounced over the cobblestones. As they neared the front, she jumped out and ran the rest of the way. When she approached the canal, hundreds of men were filling it in with tree branches and spiked iron balls. On the edge of the dangerous pit, cotton bales were stacked breast-high and close together. They had also piled up wicker baskets, open at both ends and stuffed with mud. These, too, would be used to stop British bullets.

Racing past McCarté House, she wondered briefly if Jackson were inside. She was stopped several times by sentries, but her hospital pass allowed her to go on her way.

The tent loomed ahead of her. Silently, she uttered a little prayer. "Please, God, let Paul be alive."

A number of sailors, bedraggled and wet from their recent brush with drowning, stood in front of the tent entrance, talking in worried little groups. Paul wasn't among them.

She rushed inside where Betsy Summers was treating a cut on a bleeding midshipman. "Are all the men from the *Carolina* here?" she asked, looking about frantically.

"Danielle!" The plump woman noticed her face, which must have been as pale as the white bandage. She continued to swathe the sailor's head in bandages. "All the navy men that made it to safety are here. We don't have a dead or missing list yet."

"I have a friend on the ship. He's tall and blond. A midshipman," she explained. "His name is Paul Milerand."

"I don't know," Betsy said in a consoling tone.

The young sailor glanced up and shook his head. "I saw Paul and then he disappeared."

Betsy said, "Check the beds in the ward over to the right. They are filled with sailors who for the most part suffered only cuts and bruises . . . nothing serious. Go ahead and look."

Murmuring her thanks, Danielle hurried to each bed, asking several seamen if they knew the whereabouts of Paul. None of them had any idea. Distraught, she tried to hold back the tears. Did Paul drown? Was he killed in the explosion?

She stopped alongside a sailor who was sitting in a chair, wringing out his shirt in a bucket. "Did you see Paul Milerand?" She almost sobbed out the name.

"I don't know," he mumbled, not bothering to look at her. "I was lucky enough to jump before the ship exploded. What was the name again?"

"Paul Milerand." She almost screamed the name, but instead enunciated as clearly as she could.

His head moved from side to side and his expression was dazed.

A voice behind her said, "Are you searching for me?"

She spun about and there was Paul, appearing cool and possessed; such a calm attitude would serve him in good stead when he became an officer. He had a jagged cut down his cheek as long as a crawfish.

"Paul! You're safe!" She dashed into his arms, hugging him tightly. "I was so frightened when I heard the *Carolina* went down."

"I'm not hurt," he assured her, holding her close. "I'm only shocked at losing the ship."

"It must have been horrible."

"Let me take you back to your aunt's. I'm to report to Commodore Patterson in the morning." His crooked smile was a bit rueful. "He gave all able-bodied seamen twenty-four hours' rest after the 'ordeal,' as he called it.

To me, it was more of a disaster. Now the British will be able to attack Jackson's line without being concerned about the *Carolina*'s guns."

His gaze shifted to the sailors around him. "She was a sweet schooner. The largest ship the Americans had. Commodore Patterson has already gone up the river to scout for another ship. The *Louisiana* alone can't protect the entire river."

She hadn't realized how deeply she cared for Paul until now. Seeing him secure and so vulnerable made her want to cradle him in her arms. They began to walk away from the front.

Halfway down Rampart Street, Paul drew her into a terraced garden, surrounded by a deep hedge. In the center of the dry and cold garden was a large statue of Louis XIV, looking very regal and haughty. No wonder he was called the Sun King. She didn't have long to contemplate the French monarch, however, for Paul put his arms around her and tenderly kissed her. His lips were warm, and she responded with gratitude that he was alive. Then she closed her eyes, and for a split second Geoffrey's face was before her.

"My last thoughts, when the ship listed and began sinking, were of you, Danielle. When the muddy waters closed over my head, I didn't know if I'd ever see you again." He looked at her tenderly. "When the wind ruffles your hair . . ." He held her close again. "Oh, it's sweet to hold you in my arms. If only you

110

knew how much I love you." He kissed her again.

"I do know, Paul." She couldn't believe he had actually kissed her. Paul, who was always proper, who always behaved correctly. He must really have thought he was about to die. "Paul," she cautioned, "when the war is over, we'll talk about us."

"I love you," Paul said simply, looking into her eyes. "I thought I'd never hold you like this."

Stepping back, he untied a small leather pouch dangling from his belt and drew forth the emerald ring. "I know you won't wear this on your third finger, but will you at least keep it for me until after the war and we can decide our future? Perhaps you'll wear it on a neck chain."

The shimmering memory of the gold chain with the black pearl that Geoffrey had offered her replaced the emerald ring in her mind's eye. Why hadn't she accepted the necklace? A memento of Geoffrey would be so precious to her now.

"Will you keep the emerald for me?" Paul repeated.

"I can't, Paul. I'm fond of you and depend on you, but . . ." Again she thought of Geoffrey.

"But I'm more like a brother, is that what you're trying to tell me?"

She sighed, staring into the blank eyes of Louis XIV. "You're more than a brother, Paul, and you know it. I've said before that I need some time. Don't push me. I want our relationship to be built on a love that's beyond any doubts. Can't you understand that?"

Paul half turned, kicking at a dead branch on the walkway. "I'm trying to understand, Danielle. When I have my own ship, there's no reason you couldn't come with me. Do you think I'll keep you confined like some exotic bird in a cage? I want you as free and proud as you are right now. I wouldn't dream of quenching your spirit." He added wryly, "I doubt if anyone could tame you into being a docile wife who dogs her husband's footsteps.

Perhaps Paul meant what he said, but she resented being pushed into a marriage. "Paul, I said I needed time." Her words were deliberate and spaced far apart.

"Time to know if you love me or not?" he asked bitterly. "Obviously you don't. Tell me, is there someone else?"

For a breath, her pulse stopped.

Paul gave her a second look. "Well, is there?"

She couldn't look at him. "Let's discuss this when life is back to normal."

"All right, and I'm sure when the war is over, your excuse will be the same: You need more time!" He lowered his voice. "I'll love you forever, Danielle, but don't expect that I'll take your vacillation forever."

"When I'm ready," Danielle said carefully, "I'll ask for the ring."

"Good." There were little fires in his dark eyes. "Because I won't offer it again."

A stab of remorse shot through her. Paul was alive, but in the morning he'd be gone, perhaps on another ship, perhaps again to be shot out of the water. This time Paul might not emerge unscathed. Why couldn't she return his love? Why did her thoughts constantly dwell on Geoffrey? Geoffrey Lafitte, whom her father would hate. If she married Paul, her parents would be happy, but a wedding with Geoffrey would be utterly inconceivable.

"Paul," she said, taking his hand and giving him her most dazzling smile. "Aunt Madeline will be frantic. You are to come with me for a pleasant dinner and to stay overnight and sleep in a soft featherbed tonight."

His fingers finally encircled her hand, but he was no longer the ardent lover.

She rose early the next morning and prepared coffee and croissants for Paul. When she kissed him good-bye, she studied his rugged handsomeness and was puzzled why he couldn't excite her like Geoffrey.

Later that day, she and Aunt Madeline once again left for the front. As the cart rumbled toward the Rodriguez Canal, her thoughts were as bleak and heavy as the fog. The new British general had arrived on Christmas Day, and since that time, cannons constantly shelled Jackson's line. They said General Pakenham, a dashing thirty-eight-year-old commander, was determined to break through the American position by blasting the cotton bales in order to open up a hole for his advancing troops.

The new British general, had a strong incentive for winning New Orleans, for he had been promised an earldom and the governorship of Louisiana, if victorious. His victory seemed more and more likely as British reinforcements poured in daily, coming up the bayou in long boats.

Major-General Sir Edward Pakenham. The British leader's name reminded Danielle of her mother's use of his entire title.

With a pang, she disconsolately reflected on Adelaide's imprisonment. How was she faring with British troops all around her? Was she forced to cook for them? Mend their uniforms? Bind their wounds? Did they treat her as a traitor because she was English yet remained loyal to the Americans? The thought of her mother being abused sickened her; yet, Danielle was confident of her mother's courage and knew she wouldn't be intimidated by the soldiers, no matter how many invaded Cypress Manor. Her mother was made of sturdy stuff.

A sigh escaped Danielle's lips. Aunt Madeline gave her a keen look.

They neared the field hospital, and in the distance, along the Rodriguez Canal as far as she could see, were soldiers lined up behind cotton bales and wicker baskets of mud. What day was it? she asked herself. Wednesday. She should be taking her spinet lesson and riding Ebony. How far away she was from the everyday routine of the plantation. She thought with foreboding of her new life: mud, shells, soldiers, and bloody bandages.

Chapter Nine

NEW Year's Day had come and gone with very little notice, 1814 slipping into the dawn of 1815.

For a week, Danielle and Aunt Madeline had been living in a small tent behind the hospital tent at the front while the British cannon constantly shelled the American lines, trying to no avail to tear a gap in the breastworks.

With this daily bombardment, it was amazing that only seven wounded had been brought into the hospital. The American troops' entrenched position was almost impossible to penetrate. Jackson's men were exacting a much heavier toll.

The weather continued to be miserable, cold and rainy. One thing that helped the bivouacked soldiers was the much-needed five thousand more blankets that had arrived.

General Jackson could be seen riding up and down the line daily, encouraging his men, stopping to drink smuggled coffee with the Baratarians and chatting with his favorites, the Tennessee frontiersmen.

Danielle filled her days by walking behind the lines, mending uniforms, and talking to soldiers who came by for a dose of sulphur and molasses for colds or dysentery.

On January fifth, Jackson's army was reinforced by twenty-three hundred Kentuckians under Major Adair. Although these additional troops were desperately needed, the general was bitterly disappointed, for only seven hundred of the men came with guns. Whoever heard of Kentuckians without their long rifles? Again a plea went out to the citizens of New Orleans for firearms of any kind, and again a few more rusty muskets were rounded up and distributed. For the most part, however, the Kentuckians would have to depend on their hunting knives. Danielle had turned in her two horse pistols on the first call for weapons in early December.

The next day, when she was walking in the orange grove of the Chalmette plantation, a knife went whizzing by her shoulder and struck a tree to her left.

Alarmed, she ducked behind a bush, afraid it might be a British soldier who had infiltrated their lines. As she peeked out, she glimpsed a shock of red hair jutting out from a cap. Christopher Rollins! He threw another knife, which hit the trunk of the small tree.

"Christopher!" She stepped gingerly forward, glancing warily at the two knives stuck in the tree.

His eyes widened and he grinned. "Well, I'll be hanged, if it ain't Dan-ee-yell!"

She smiled. "Yes, it's Danielle, and if it isn't Christopher from Tennessee. What are you doing in the orange grove?" His freckled face and pleasant smile lightened the whole day, despite the leaden sky overcast with gray clouds.

"What's it look like? Target practice. I aim to stalk me a British soldier in a short while, and I don't want to miss!"

"With a knife?" She shuddered.

"Yup. Five of us are going on a little hunting party to see how many we can nab."

"I've heard General Pakenham has sent a letter of protest to Jackson complaining about the Americans' fighting habits. He says our soldiers don't know the etiquette of warfare." She kicked a few dead leaves aside and sat down on a fallen log, observing Christopher in his leather-fringed jerkin, leather pants, and knee-high boots.

He guffawed. "Don't blame 'em for not liking the way we fight. We've already bagged fifty sentries just by creeping up behind 'em and slitting their gullets." He demonstrated the technique by stepping lightly through the leaves and not causing a rustle. "Then," he continued, "we come back to camp and give Jackson a little rundown on where their troops are located and if they've changed cannon position." He chuckled, taking off his raccoon cap and running his fingers through his long, straight hair, as fiery red as a maple leaf. "Them Choctaws are great scouts. They know this area better than I know the hills around Nashville." He sat down beside her.

"You've killed fifty Englishmen on sentry duty that way? That's more than the Americans have lost in this whole campaign."

"Yup, sentry duty is something the British dread. Can't say I blame 'em any."

A raindrop fell on her cheek. She rose, wrinkling her nose. "It's going to rain."

"This is the dangdest, rainiest land I ever did see." He winked at her. "It'll make for better hunting, though."

A fine rain fell in earnest now. "I'd better run back to camp, Christopher. Good-bye." She waved to this appealing mountain lad. He was sweet and naive, even if he did talk about killing British as nonchalantly as he would about squashing spiders.

"I'll come by and see you, Dan-ee-yell, afore I head back to Tennessee," he shouted after her.

The rain pelted against her face, and she looked back once as he pulled the knives from the orange tree.

She was glad to reach the tent where Aunt Madeline was eating a hard biscuit. Their meager rations were the same as a soldier's.

"Danielle!" Madeline ran to her and grabbed her hands, whirling her around. "William is safe! One of General Morgan's soldiers told me. The soldier had been bitten by a rat and swam across the river, underwater mostly, for treatment."

Danielle nodded her head abruptly. Typical patient. For a week, they had been treating bites, colds, and dysentery. "And?" she prodded eagerly. "What was the soldier's news?"

"This!" She triumphantly held out a torn piece of paper. "Read it! You can't imagine how relieved I am."

Danielle scanned the hasty scrawl:

I am fine. We are located on the west bank with General Morgan's force. Have been on a scouting mission. I'll see you soon, my darling Madeline.
                              Your future husband,
                              William

Madeline, eyes sparkling, danced a few spinning steps about the tent, unhampered by her heavy wool dress and apron. "Isn't it wonderful?" she beamed.

"Oh, yes," Danielle said, smiling, delighted at her aunt's transformation. It was as if a mask of gloom had been lifted and replaced with one of joy. "I'm happy for you, Aunt Madeline." She went over to a pile of clothes. "However, we have work to do. This heap of jackets, pantaloons, and trousers was sent in by the women of New Orleans. We need to take the wagon and dole them out to the boys who are out there freezing."

"Yes, yes." Madeline's quick, energetic movements were back. "How I wish we could give some of this warm clothing to Morgan's men."

"We can hardly row across the river with British guns trained on us."

Betsy Summers bustled by with a pot of boiling water. "Now, before you girls do anything, I want you to sit with me for a minute and drink a cup of hot water. I wish it were coffee, but we've run out, and there's not a bean to be found. This is the next best substitute." When she glanced at their unbelieving faces, she added, "At least it will warm your insides."

"That would be good," Danielle said gratefully as she watched Betsy pour the steaming water into a tin mug. With a stab of hunger, she remembered the crab gumbo and rice her mother made. What was she eating? Were they giving her enough to eat? How marvelous it would be to have a bowl of her mother's gumbo now. Her mouth watered, but she accepted the cup thankfully. She shouldn't complain, for they had lived on hardtack for only a week. The soldiers were the ones who suffered. They weren't dressed warmly enough and had to subsist on a few biscuits and water.

Madeline drank her hot water and set it down, sighing. "It wasn't long ago, Danielle, that we were having a cup of coffee in my parlor."

"I know," Danielle replied. "Don't remind me."

Betsy laughed, her small eyes twinkling in her plump face. "I'm a tea drinker myself."

"Where are you from?" Danielle questioned, curious about this jovial woman's background.

"My husband and I are from Baltimore," she said wistfully, but in a clear voice. "Jeremiah." She stopped. "Jeremiah Philip Summers, my husband, was a fisherman in Chesapeake Bay, but we had a chance to come to New Orleans after the government purchased it from Napoleon in 1803 and the area had settled down. Such fishing! We own two shrimp boats, but I don't go out in the Gulf as much as I used to. But take it from me, when this war is over, I intend to go out with Jeremiah every day. I haven't seen him for three months," she sighed heavily.

Danielle looked down at her empty cup. "Do you know if he's safe?"

Betsy's smiled returned. I know he's safe with General Morgan and those Tennessee boys. Jeremiah is a good man. You couldn't ask for a better fighter. He's strapping big with enormous shoulders." She paused, rolling her eyes. "How I'd love to have those huge arms around me now." She laughed heartily. "Jeremiah is just a plain, hardworking fisherman. But it's the likes of him that will do in the British, you'll see."

Danielle believed her. The soldiers she had observed were tough and could live under the worst conditions imaginable — scanty rations, rain, mud, and facing an army four times larger than theirs.

"You're one of the first American women I've ever really sat down and talked to," Danielle said. "Some Creoles hate Americans and are constantly comparing them to the 'Kaintucks.' I wish they could know more Americans like you, Betsy. They'd soon change their minds."

"The war has brought us all together," Madeline said. "They say even General Jackson, who at first didn't trust the Creoles, is now pleased with their fighting spirit."

"You're right, Madeline. We're all soldiers in this together. Creoles, Americans, and Choctaws," Betsy said with a huge grin.

"Speaking of soldiers," Danielle exclaimed, jumping to her feet and reaching for her cloak, "we have clothes to distribute."

"Oh, yes," Madeline said, throwing a muffler around her neck. "And soup to make!"

"Soup? Out of what?" Betsy asked.

"Ah, you haven't seen what two Mississippi flatboatmen brought in. There're twenty black turtles out back just waiting for the stew pot. Do you know," Madeline continued, "that those river flatboatmen were quite well behaved? I always heard they were such rowdies."

Danielle hefted a load of jackets into her

arms. "I guess when you're in a situation like this, everyone has to pull together. I've changed my ideas about people, too."

As they loaded the wagon, she was still thinking about her last statement when she saw three pirates pulling a cannon behind the cotton bales and then removing a bale so the barrel could poke through, aiming at the British line.

The bombardment abated, but the acrid smell of smoke hung in the air as Madeline and Danielle trudged in ankle-deep mud, leading a horse-drawn cart laden with clothes. Once Danielle turned and fished out a biscuit and fed the horse. It looked so worn and overworked. With an aching heart, she thought of Ebony. Who had her horse now? Would he be returned to the horse barn after the battle?

When they arrived at the river's edge, Colonel Ross's troops were frantically pulling out flaming cotton bales that had just been hit. They tipped them into the slime of the Rodriguez Canal where the cotton smouldered and hissed, sending up more black smoke.

While Danielle and Madeline tossed out jackets to eager hands, Colonel Ross appeared on his magnificent chestnut and ordered the still intact cotton bales hauled to the rear.

After the cart was emptied, Danielle glanced over at several soldiers and shivered, not so much from the cold as at what they were doing. They were slashing open the bales and stuffing the cotton beneath their shirts for warmth. The sad sight unnerved her. She had led such a luxurious life at Cypress Manor. She remembered last winter when she had sat before their fireplace, gazing into the flames while her mother did needlepoint and her father read aloud from *Robinson Crusoe*. Ah, what she wouldn't give for an evening like that now.

Madeline saw the shivering men, too. "Poor soldiers, but it will soon be over. One of the frontiersmen told me they've spotted the British making scaling ladders."

"That means they're preparing to go over the wall," Danielle said.

Colonel Ross rode over to them. "Ladies, go back to the hospital tent. Don't venture near the river again."

Her pulse raced when she realized they were expecting the attack at any time.

Chapter Ten

THE next morning, when Danielle sleepily peeked out of the tent, the American line was crammed with soldiers with their guns ready. Up and down the line, soldiers and more soldiers. Danielle had a good view of the Chalmette plain because Jackson had ordered the farmhouses blown up. In this way, when the British advanced, there would be clear visibility.

As she watched through the spyglass, several British soldiers scooped up the black sugar that had spilled from the cases they used for fortification and began to eat. Their rations, rum and a few biscuits, were even more sparse than the Americans'. But to eat unrefined sugar! Didn't they know it was filled with cane splinters and grit?

"There will be lots of British soldiers that won't be able to fight today."

"Oh? And why is that?" Madeline asked, tugging her wool blouse over her disarrayed curls.

"They'll be too sick. Remember when I was five and got into a barrel of unrefined sticky sugar? I kept Mother and Father up all night. Mother held my hand while I threw up. I thought I was going to die."

"You were into everything as a child, Danielle," said Madeline, looking fondly at her niece. "I can't believe you're almost a grown woman now, ready to marry Paul."

Danielle bristled at Paul's name. Even Aunt Madeline took it for granted that she and Paul were to be married. Wasn't there anyone who would accept the fact that she was perfectly capable of making her own decisions?

She was ready with a sharp retort when cannon boomed, and all thoughts of the future flew out of her head.

Madeline instinctively ducked her head. "How much longer do you think the British are going to bombard us?" She folded a blanket. "Ugh, even the wool is damp and smells!"

"The British are going to send in the infantry," Danielle said knowingly. "Take the spyglass. You'll see them scurrying about with ladders and scaling hooks."

Madeline waved the long glass away. "I'm not interested. I have more practical things to do than to worry about what the British are doing. You could watch them all day long and fret and stew over every activity." Danielle marveled at how practical Aunt Madeline was under stress.

Her aunt added, "There's still some soup left. I'll heat it for the wounded soldiers."

"You have the right idea," Danielle agreed. "We can't change anything." She laughed. "I'll run to the pump so we can have our 'savory' cup of hot water."

"You had better not venture out, Danielle. Remember what Colonel Ross said," her aunt called to her.

"He meant that we shouldn't go near the front lines. Don't worry. I'll be back in five minutes."

She hurried outside with a bucket before her aunt could protest again and headed for the large mangrove tree that sheltered the wooden pump. This might be the only respite they would have for a long time.

She had scarcely given Paul a thought, but now, in the early morning hours when she was alone, she pondered her future. If she accepted Paul's ring, she would make everyone happy, and who knew, perhaps she'd even make herself happy.

The memory of Paul two years after his mother's death, when he was only twelve and Danielle was nine, came back to her. He and his father, Captain Henry Milerand, had been invited to Cypress Manor for dinner. She remembered staring at this serious, strange boy who sat across from her at the dinner table. He looked very neat and well scrubbed in his cabin-boy uniform with his white cotton trousers and high collar.

After dinner, the two fathers had gone into the parlor for their brandy and cigars. Was it that night that they discussed their children and what a good match it would be to blend the Verlaine family line with the Milerand name? The one family in sugar and the other in ships. What could be a more perfect merger? She knew Paul's father had carefully plotted out his son's future, very early providing a special tutor for him, but seeing to it that, at age seven, he received practical experience by serving aboard his father's schooner. Fortunately, Paul had loved ships, the sea, and the study of navigation, and never once strayed from the goal his father had chosen for him.

When she and Paul had gone outside to play, she had been filled with energy and wanted to play tag or hide-and-seek, but he had his own ideas. From his back pocket, he pulled out a piece of rope and began to tie various knots. As they sat in the swing, she watched, fascinated, as his adept fingers transformed the rope into various loops and knots. She soon forgot about the games she had begged to play and, instead, coaxed him into teaching her how to tie knots. It wasn't long before she could tie a square knot, a bowline, a figure eight, and a cat's-paw. She learned all about the different types of ships and their riggings. As they grew up, he had always been near, but he had never directed her or given her orders. He admired her accomplishments and wanted her to continue with whatever new thing she tackled. She liked that about Paul. What she didn't like was being told whom to marry and at what age. She had a good mind and meant to use it.

Reaching the pump, she wielded the heavy handle, which was difficult to move. A thin stream of brackish water trickled out. She pumped harder. Everything in this camp was a struggle.

Suddenly, the handle was grabbed and pumped vigorously, sending the water gushing forth. She spun about, almost expecting to see the boy she had been thinking about. But it wasn't Paul. It was Geoffrey! He was flashing that famous smile that made her dizzy with happiness.

"If it isn't my little wildcat. This is no work for an aristocratic lady," he teased, filling the bucket with water.

A tingle of pleasure flowed through her, and she laughed with sheer gladness, yearning once again to feel his arms around her. "This aristocratic lady has done more distasteful tasks than pumping water," she responded in the same light vein, but she wouldn't tell him about the cleansing of infected wounds or the emptying of waste buckets.

Geoffrey held her shoulders, looking into her eyes. "I talked to the Kentucky rifleman who described this pretty blond girl with the bluest eyes he'd ever seen. I knew immediately he was talking about you and I tracked you down."

He smoothed back a wisp of her hair. "I only have a few moments, but I had to see you. The Baratarians are in the middle of the line where I'm helping Gambi and Dominique with the artillery. When this is over, I want you to come to Grand Terre as my guest. My uncle would be pleased to have you." He laughed. "Besides, I think he'd like to see his nephew upgrade himself with a charming belle from an old New Orleans family. Wouldn't you like that?"

She didn't want to be coy and play the coquette, yet she couldn't tell him yes. All at once, she hung back. Was it her Creole aristocratic background that attracted Geoffrey to her? What was wrong with her? This was what she had dreamed about. She didn't want Paul, but she wasn't sure she wanted Geoffrey, either. She was just a headstrong girl who might find herself so independent that for the rest of her life she'd be going her own way, alone.

"We'll have time later to settle our affairs," Geoffrey said, leaning close to her face and brushing his lips across her cheek. "I might even see you this evening. The battle is shaping up to be short and final." He tipped her face up to his and kissed her lips.

Her legs weakened. Geoffrey loved her. There was no doubt in that kiss.

"Who's there?" a burly pirate yelled, moving menacingly forward.

Danielle stepped back from Geoffrey as if she'd been shot.

The stocky pirate frowned at the two of them, tapping his fingers on his cutlass, a short, broad sword that most pirates wore. He faced Geoffrey. "We need you to help move the twenty-four-pounder. The barrel needs to be swabbed out and prepared for firing."

"All right, Dominique." Geoffrey turned back to Danielle and gave the growling pirate an airy wave. "One more minute."

His nonchalant attitude infuriated Dominique and he roared, "Now!" His long beard fairly quivered with rage. "Your uncle put me in charge of the artillery, and I've just given you an order."

For a minute Geoffrey glowered at the seething buccaneer; then he emitted a short chuckle. "I'm coming, Dominique — *sir*." He smiled at Danielle and said in a low voice, "Later."

He stalked off, shooting Dominique an insolent look.

"Please take care, Geoffrey," she said beneath her breath after his retreating back.

Dominique stayed behind and glared at her. "You had better watch who you choose to dally with, miss. You're playing with a lit fuse in Geoffrey Lafitte. You don't know how many crying girls he's left behind!" Dominique strode away, leaving her to carry the bucket.

Retracing her steps, she tried to remember what Geoffrey had said . . . that Jean Lafitte would like her, and perhaps he would. Their first meeting had certainly been congenial, but of course, that was before she had fallen in love with his nephew. Her father was the big worry. If only she could choose her own mate without any interference. People didn't always marry whom they were expected to marry. Look at Andrew Jackson and his wife, Rachel. *They* had lived as man and wife before Rachel's divorce decree was final. Jackson had taken more than one nasty sneer over that, but since he was an excellent duelist, the talk soon died down.

The bucket became heavier, and she switched hands. What difference did background make if you truly loved the person? And what if Geoffrey had left a few trampled hearts in his tracks? You couldn't expect a good-looking man like Geoffrey not to have a past. He didn't know about Paul, either. However, Geoffrey and she had a unique love. She was special to him. She just knew it. Besides, she could hold her own with any woman. She stepped proudly ahead but stumbled, sloshing water over her skirt.

When Danielle entered the tent, Madeline was wiping the forehead of a Choctaw warrior. She motioned to a soldier on a cot near the entrance. "Danielle, see what you can do for that young man over there. They found him in the swamp." Silently, she pressed her lips together and moved her head back and forth.

Danielle's heart hammered when she noticed the flaming red hair. "Christopher," she gasped. She sank to her knees beside the cot and gently turned the groaning lad toward her. "Christopher, what have they done to you?"

Although he recognized her, he didn't speak. However, he made a supreme effort to raise up on one elbow.

"Please, lie down," she ordered crisply as her deft fingers unbuttoned his blood-soaked leather shirt. She almost wept when she saw the gaping chest wound. "Christopher, close your eyes while I clean away the blood and bandage you." She bit her lip, trying not to sob aloud. Her throat was so dry, she couldn't swallow. Her pulse throbbed as she worked furiously to rinse out the wound and stop the blood flow with a heavy cotton bandage.

She called to the runner by the tent flap. "Find the doctor. He's at Jackson's quarters."

"The McCarté House has been blown up," the young courier said, his eyes wide with fear at the sight of Christopher's wound.

"Well, I don't know where he is, then," she snapped, frantic with the urgency of her request. "He's doubtless on the front lines. Find the general and you'll find the doctor."

"Yes, ma'am!" He bolted out the door.

Christopher opened his eyes. "Dan-ee-yell.

I thought I'd be in Tennessee afore I'd ever see you again." His breath was short. "Our huntin' party warn't very successful. I was in the swamp when several British soldiers came out of nowhere. I winged one with my knife, but another, moving fast as a mountain cat, jumped out from behind a tree and shot me 'fore I could duck."

Weakly, he held up his hand and pointed at his heart. "Shot me and left me for dead." He gave her a lopsided grin. "But it ain't so easy to kill a Tennesseean!"

Soaking a cloth, she wiped away the perspiration on his pale face.

He shut his eyes, and his raspy breathing frightened her. The fresh bandage was already bright with blood. She glanced at the entrance, but the doctor still hadn't arrived.

"Christopher," she whispered. "Hang on. The doctor will be here any minute." Shakily, she poured a glass of water, but with a feeble wave, he pushed it aside. Dipping a cloth into the water, she moistened his parched lips instead.

"Hold my hand," he said in a faint voice.

Tenderly, she took his hand in hers.

"Listen to me. If I don't make it, will you write to my ma and pa at Toad Hop Ferry, outside of Nashville? Tell 'em I was a good soldier."

"Shh," she cautioned. "The doctor will soon be here. You're going to be all right."

"You wouldn't be funnin' me, would you, Dan-ee-yell?" His smile became a grimace.

"Don't forget the letter," he murmured. I need . . ." He turned away and was still.

"Christopher." She made no move to touch him. She knew he was dead. Poor Christopher. He'd never return to Nashville. She put her head in her hands and wept.

Chapter Eleven

DANIELLE remained kneeling until her tears finally subsided.

Aunt Madeline stroked her shoulder. "I'm sorry, chérie, so sorry. Did you know the lad?"

"Y-yes. Christopher Rollins from Tennessee." She rose, and again the tears streamed down her cheeks as she leaned against her aunt. "Oh, Aunt Madeline, he was so young. Just my age."

"What a shame," Madeline said softly. "Come. One of the pirates left a small packet of coffee. Let's have a cup." She frowned briefly. "I imagine it's smuggled, but it does taste like heaven."

With thanks, Danielle sipped the hot brew and wiped her eyes. Suddenly, the band struck up "Yankee Doodle." The two women stared at one another in astonishment. The strange little band, the Orleans Battalion, had marched in last Sunday for a New Year's Day celebration but had been interrupted by a heavy bombardment and had been silent until today.

Danielle went outside and drew in her breath at the sight before her. The fog had lifted and the sun glistened over row after row of British soldiers. The drum rolled, and with three great hurrahs, they advanced in perfect unison. She heard the guns from the west bank and wondered if Paul were manning the cannon. It was strange the British hadn't tried to knock out Patterson's battery before they proceeded.

With her spyglass, Danielle observed the splendid British columns filling the field with red and white. Their flag fluttered in the breeze, and company banners were high in the air over each battalion. She could make out a regiment carrying ladders lagging in the distance.

The Americans, behind the breastworks, tensely waited for the signal to fire. They stood three deep, front row carefully sighting along their gun barrels. She prayed their marksmanship was as true as their reputation and would save them from the troops moving inexorably toward them like a river.

Suddenly, General Jackson, on his war horse, thundered up and down the line. "Fire, boys, fire! Make every bullet count!"

There was a deafening roar as cannon, rifle, and musket burst into life.

However, Danielle couldn't believe her eyes, for despite the volley, the troops kept moving forward.

In a split second, the results of the deadly bullets became apparent. British soldiers began to topple, and the whole line wavered. It was as if a giant playing with toy soldiers had tired of the game and swept them from the board.

The first American line stepped back to reload, and she could see the British general, Sir Pakenham, astride his horse, waving his sword and urging his men forward. The depleted ranks had regrouped, the gaps filled in, and they kept coming.

The second American line aimed, delivering its deadly musket fire.

The band once more struck up "Yankee Doodle."

One soldier yelled, "Do you see those crazy men, Robert? Don't they know we can hit a squirrel at forty yards?"

The second soldier hollered down the line, "The Lobster Tails are marching right into our guns, and those white-cross belts across their chests make mighty fine targets."

"If they want to commit suicide, I'll help 'em out," came the answering bellow.

Jackson, riding by again, shouted, "Give it to 'em, boys!"

And the American soldiers did. The second column of British soldiers fell in swaths, like sugarcane beneath the knife. The British line was shattered, and the soldiers remaining on the field were confused. Most of the officers on horses had been killed, and without leadership, the soldiers broke and began to run to the rear. General Pakenham was still alive, however, and was riding back and forth, trying furiously to stem the tide of their race to the entrenchments behind the levee.

He pointed with his sword at the American line and did manage to gather a new formation to follow him into the deadly fire.

All at once the general went down, but he was soon seen on another horse. He was brave, but a second bullet caught him and he dropped his sword, his arm dangling limply at his side. Yet, he rode on, shouting wildly for a regrouping. A third bullet caused him to tumble from his horse. Several soldiers immediately gathered him up and carried him toward the large oak in the center of the field.

A wave of pity washed over Danielle, making it difficult to speak. Finally she cried, "Aunt Madeline, Aunt Madeline, General Pakenham has been shot." She moaned softly. "Oh, it's so horrible. Terrible. We're winning, but the poor British . . . The plain is a sea of blood." She offered the spyglass to her aunt.

"No, please." Madeline shook her head. "Even with my poor vision, I can see as well as I want to." Shielding her eyes against the bright morning sun, she gazed up and down the American line. A tear ran down her cheek, and she reached for Danielle. Clinging to each other, stunned, they watched the carnage.

It seemed impossible that the British would have any soldiers left. Danielle wondered if the battle could be over in less than half an hour.

She broke away from her aunt. There, marching across the flat ground, were the Scottish Highlanders in their dark green tartan kilts and leather bonnets. They were magnificent, tall warriors who advanced boldly as the bagpipes skirled. They must have been a thousand strong.

Once more the Kentucky and Tennessee riflemen concentrated their guns on the Highlanders and their ranks soon thinned as entire squadrons fell.

When they were approximately five hundred feet from the ramparts, the Scots stopped, only a few upright. They stood as if blindfolded, awaiting the bullets of a firing squad. At last, the few Highlanders remaining recoiled from the barrage and retreated.

The Americans didn't cheer. They could only watch in mute horror at the results of such a brave, foolhardy death march.

In the quiet of the smoke and the fallen men, the band swung into "Hail Columbia." The victorious Americans came to life, throwing their hats in the air and beating each other's backs. Several soldiers dashed over to the hospital tent, coaxing and pulling the women forth to dance with them.

Danielle ached at the bloody battle scene, but at the same time, she was relieved. The war was over. They had won! She could return to Cypress Manor and be reunited with her mother and father. She longed to see her mother. It had been two full weeks since her capture. She prayed the British wouldn't be vengeful and shoot prisoners of war.

The question flickered through her mind as to why the enemy wasn't being pursued. Jackson had evidently ordered his men to remain behind their barricades.

Danielle picked up her skirts and began running to the center of the line, but the crush of the dancing, singing soldiers prevented her from struggling through to see Geoffrey.

Finally she gave up, for, even if she did manage to elbow her way through, there was no guarantee she'd find him.

She returned to the hospital tent where six covered bodies had been placed outside, ready for burial. She hastily averted her eyes, trying not to think of Christopher.

Entering the tent, she noticed a few wounded had been brought in, so she helped Betsy bind a soldier's leg. Madeline was tying an arm sling for another.

Betsy grinned at her. "We're to go to our homes. These men will be moved to St. Ann's Hospital. Jackson has given orders that no one is to go south of the Rodriguez Canal. The British camp is still bristling with a strong reserve unit. Although, right now, I imagine all they're doing is licking their wounds." She indicated a Mississippi dragoon. "He told me the British have sent a flag of truce over for a burial detail."

"A couple of British soldiers made it over the palisade." Betsy jerked her head in the direction of two soldiers being guarded by a sentry. "They're prisoners of war. I did what I could for them, but the corporal is pretty well shot up."

Danielle went over to them with a canteen of water. One was unconscious, but the other looked at her with such fear in his eyes that she stroked his hand, trying to quell his hideous nightmare.

"It was awful. My best friends died on either side of me . . . my major was shot. I . . ." His lips trembled, and for a moment Danielle was afraid he was about to cry; but instead he drew in a ragged breath and meekly accepted the canteen. After drinking deeply, he handed the metal canister back to Danielle. "Do you notice how clean-shaven I am?" he inquired, rubbing his hand over each cheek.

Puzzled, she nodded.

"All the troops were commanded to shave this morning, in order to make a neat appearance for our triumphant entry into New Orleans." His voice was unnatural and he snickered. "Now the boys will be clean and neat for their own funerals."

"Where are you from?" Danielle asked,

trying to take his mind off the terrible battle he had just experienced.

"London."

"Do you have a family?" she asked gently.

"My wife Caroline and my two-year-old son Danny." His racing pulse was becoming steadier. He attempted a smile. "My son is a wild one, he is." He shuddered, seeming to relive the battle. "I'll be glad to get back home and forget this whole bloody mess."

A soldier stuck his head into the tent. "The wagon is leaving in a few minutes for the city, miss."

"We'll be right there," Madeline answered for Danielle.

Danielle turned to the enemy soldier and patted his hand. "You'll be fine after a few days' rest. You're just dazed at your defeat. Try not to think about your friends. Don't worry. General Jackson is a fair man, and I'm certain they will soon arrange for an exchange of prisoners." As she said the words, she pictured her mother. Perhaps she would be swapped for this young man. She hoped the trade would be soon. "Good-bye. You'll be as good as new in no time." She smiled at him, but his gaze went beyond her and he didn't seem to hear.

Madeline, cloaked and holding a wrapped bundle, waited for Danielle.

Already soldiers were entering, placing the wounded on litters and carrying them out to the wagons.

While she and her aunt helped load supplies into the cart, she noticed three officers and a general talking to Andrew Jackson.

Jackson thrust his face at the officer with all the fancy braid and medals, and shouted, "Morgan, you retreated! By heaven, I'll have your stars."

General Morgan! Danielle glanced more closely at the three officers, wondering if one of them was William Ellinger. She cast about for her aunt, but she had gone back into the tent.

She couldn't hear General Morgan's reply, but when Madeline emerged, she pointed at the three officers. "Do you recognize any of those men?" she asked eagerly.

Madeline squinted in their direction and turned back to Danielle with a blank look.

She sighed, forgetting how nearsighted Madeline was.

"I'll fetch the spyglass," Madeline said abruptly, and immediately ducked back into the tent.

"I'll have you court-martialed!" Jackson stormed. "Morgan! Come with me."

General Morgan, walking beside Jackson, was gesturing with his hands in a graphic explanation as they disappeared into a staff tent. General Morgan's three officers turned to go back to their duties. One lieutenant headed to the canteen wagon. The other two strode away.

Madeline leaped up on a cotton bale and peered through the lens.

"Danielle!" she said excitedly. "It's him.

It's William." Then lifting her voice even louder, she called, "William, William Ellinger!"

The tall man turned and when he spotted Madeline, broke into a run.

Upon reaching her, he embraced her tightly while Danielle watched, smiling. They murmured endearments to one another, giving her a chance to appraise this distinguished soldier that Aunt Madeline had chosen for her second husband. His dark hair, streaked with silver, was wavy. He was clean-shaven, except for a mustache above his full mouth.

The cart driver, perched atop the wooden seat and holding the horses' reins, gave them an impatient look. "Ladies, I have to make another run."

"We'll be right there," Madeline promised, her voice ringing with happiness. She pulled Danielle forward. "William, meet my niece, Danielle Verlaine. Danielle, this is Colonel William Ellinger of the U.S. Army." Her body was straight and filled with pride as William's arm encircled her shoulder.

"I'm honored, Danielle." His handshake was firm, his look unswerving, and his smile charming. His tone was deep and resonant. "I've been trying to locate Madeline for the last two weeks. I've been on maneuvers in the swamp and then we bivouacked across the river."

"Do you know what happened to Patterson?" Danielle blurted out. "He's the commander of Paul Milerand, a friend of mine."

William chuckled. "They're safely aboard the *Louisiana*. They had to be towed down the river."

"I'm glad you're here, William." Madeline gave his hand an affectionate squeeze.

"Ladies!" The driver was clearly irritated.

"Darling, I'll see you soon," William said. "Jackson is planning a victory celebration, and we'll all be given free time." He assisted Danielle into the cart.

"Why are the British still camped on the Chalmette plain? I thought we'd won," she questioned.

"We have," William answered, "but both sides need time for negotiating. The British still hold the Verlaine plantation and grounds. They don't appear to be in any hurry to pack up and leave, either. Of course, they have a lot of burying to do. Jackson is keeping a sizable force along the canal to keep an eye on them."

Holding Madeline, he gave her one more kiss before lifting her up into the cart.

As the cart trundled back to town, William's depressing news caused her heart to sink. As long as the British held prisoners, her mother would remain captive. There would be no early reunion. The image of her mother tied and threatened by Major Thornton returned, and she longed to do something. What good was winning the Battle of New Orleans if her mother was still in danger?

Chapter
Twelve

THE cart clattered down a gravel road, which was lined with gigantic moss-draped cypress trees. The city was beginning to awaken to the victory news. It was unharmed and, most important to the merchants, undamaged. There were scattered cheers as a few soldiers straggled back toward the military hospital. Then the cart turned down Burgundy Street between rows of shuttered town houses, and farther along the tree-lined avenue were small cottages where, beneath the flat tile roofs, women were flinging open attic windows. Everything looked sharp and clear to Danielle. She couldn't absorb enough of the city scene stretching before her. The cottages, daubed with mud and Spanish moss, were more charming than the town houses. Standing on their stilts to protect them from floods, they appeared ready to take a bow. On the second floor of one of the cottages where the living area was, a kerchiefed woman shouted, "Vive Général Jackson."

Danielle waved to her, and also to a dancing family on the porch next door.

In the square the band played "La Marseillaise." A group lustily sang the French anthem.

Some Kentucky sharpshooters were leaning on their guns and singing. They grinned and cheered when they saw the cart, and sang the words of their ditty loud and clear:

> Behind it stood our little force.
> None wished it to be greater,
> For ev'ry man was half a horse
> And half an alligator.

One of the Kentuckians yelled, "Eight o'clock on Canal Street! Come to the torchlight victory parade!"

As they went along, Danielle's heart swelled with pride. The cheer and happiness in the city was boundless.

"Mademoiselle," a young boy called down to her from a balcony. "Catch." He threw a small, wrapped American flag, which she caught deftly. She unfurled the Stars and Stripes and waved happily back at him. Both the tricolor and the American flag flew from rooftops, fluttering in the wind together. It was gratifying to see the French and U.S.

flags side by side, both of them red, white, and blue.

When they arrived on Rampart Street, Madeline's town house was a comforting sight. Opening the gate and walking up the wooden sidewalk, Danielle relished the tupelo tree, the wrought-iron oak leaves and acorns in the grillwork of the balcony, and the red-tile roof. The afternoon sun was astonishingly warm on her face. Impulsively, she grasped Madeline's hand and fairly skipped through the door into the dark sanctuary. They set to work opening shutters and allowing the light to fill the room. More shouts of joy were heard as American troops marched informally down the streets.

"Madeline, won't it be wonderful to have our first family reunion after what we've been through . . . especially with Mother."

"Ah, so wonderful, chérie!" Madeline, sitting in an armchair, echoed the words. "I want to look around and see if everything is in its proper place." She laughed. "*Bon.* The armoire has not moved and neither has the settee. Ah, back to our reunion." She clapped her hands excitedly. "We must have a sumptuous dinner at Cypress Manor, so William can see what a prestigious family he's marrying into, *non?*"

"Of course," Danielle replied with a smile.

Madeline put a finger to her cheekbone. "Let's see. Who will be included in our family gathering?"

"Well, there will be Father and Mother, of

course." Danielle began ticking off the list on her fingers. "Paul and Captain Milerand, you, and . . ." She paused mischievously.

"And William!" Madeline exclaimed indignantly.

"Oh, yes, and William. He will soon be part of the family, won't he?" She thought of Geoffrey and how marvelous it would be if he could be added to the party, but then Paul and his father would need to be excluded. She could see Geoffrey sitting across from her at their dining table. He would make such a handsome guest. She would wear her beaded dress, and Geoffrey would be oh, so gracious that he would immediately win over her father and mother. She sighed. Her dreams were more like fantasies.

Madeline was speaking. ". . . and he said to me back at the hospital tent."

"Who?"

"William Ellinger. Who do you think I've been talking about? He wants to marry me in two weeks. He says it's nonsense to wait until June."

"He's right. Why should you?" Danielle pulled out the cameos from beneath the table and opened the box to check the contents. "It will be fun to plan a wedding."

Checking over the cameos, she saw that they were all safely nestled in their velvet cocoon. She burrowed to the bottom and, in her hand, cradled a green cameo. "Father gave this to Mother last Christmas. Doesn't the white profile remind you of her?"

Her aunt said, "Ah, yes, especially that regal nose."

Danielle put the stones back. "If Cypress Manor has been damaged, these gems will help rebuild the plantation." She fitted the lid on the box and pushed it back under the table. "Aunt Madeline, I feel so torn. Although I'm happy the war is over, I'm frustrated because nothing is being done to rescue Mother. The British are allowed to occupy our plantation and won't budge until it suits their fancy."

"General Jackson knows what he's doing, Danielle. Trust him. I'm sure he would like to lead an attack, but why should he risk the lives of his meager force when he's accomplished his purpose? He's saved New Orleans. There's no point in pursuing a larger army when they'll retreat after they've moved their wounded and buried their dead. Besides," she added, "an injured wasp is more apt to sting than one left alone."

"You're right, Aunt Madeline. I realize that, too, but I can't think clearly when my mother is suffering. If she were here, the pleasure of this day would be complete. I keep remembering how she was shoved into a chair with her hands bound. Through it all she held her head high, and she wouldn't give Colonel Thornton one ounce of information."

"It must have been terrible. You can be certain right now that Adelaide is coping with Colonel Thornton. If I know her, she's helping with their wounded." She patted Danielle's hands. "Don't worry. Adelaide will remain cool and clear-thinking throughout this ordeal."

Danielle smiled briefly. "That's probably true, Aunt Madeline, but I can't help myself. I'll never forget that day. Mother is the big worry, but I even think about Ebony. Poor horse. Later, can we walk down to the City Horse Barn and see if he's been returned? The more soldiers that enter the city, the better chance someone will turn him in and I'll be able to recover him."

"Naturally, we'll do that."

Without Ebony, she would never have escaped from the British that day. He was so sleek and gallant. The memory of the swamp chase came back to her. She wondered if the two British soldiers trailing her ended up floundering in the quagmire.

Her aunt reached for her cloak. "I'm going to run over to Rolf's Bakery and see if he has started the ovens. I need bread."

"Perhaps some of the warehouses have been opened and are selling food."

"What's been stored isn't too edible. Molasses, rum, sugarcane, and cotton. However, if I can purchase molasses, I have flour in the pantry, and I'll bake." She put on her bonnet, eyes sparkling. "Then tonight we'll join the singing and celebrating with everyone else. Where did the soldier say the parade would be?"

"Down Canal Street," Danielle answered,

pulling off her worn boots. "What a relief to take these heavy things off." She dropped them by her chair.

"Dear me, yes. Let me take them out in the back hall." She wrinkled her nose and held them at arm's length. "They're ripped on the side, too."

Danielle looked down at her black dress, soiled and crumpled. She thought, *How nice it will be to wash and change out of this drab gown and heavy black stockings.*

Madeline came back. "Here are your black slippers. When the shops reopen, we'll go to Madame Louvain's and buy two of the most elegant gowns in the city for my wedding day."

Danielle slipped into the black shoes. "Hurry back. I don't want to miss the torch-light parade."

"We won't miss a moment," her aunt promised. She tied the ribbons of her yellow bonnet under her chin and, with a quick wave, went out the door.

With a sigh of contentment, Danielle gazed about. Before cleaning up, she'd sit for a moment and close her eyes. She saw images of her loved ones parade before her. Who would be the first to return to her? Probably Father. She was certain Paul wouldn't be allowed to leave the *Louisiana* for some time. How she'd love to celebrate tonight with Geoffrey. Dimly, the sound of singing and shouting gave her a preview of the happy revelry that would take place later as more soldiers streamed back into the city. She smiled, thinking of the soldiers who would be reunited with their families . . . of the ones who would be going back to Kentucky and Tennessee. There would be one soldier who wouldn't, however, and her smile vanished. She had vowed to write to Christopher's parents — and she would before leaving tonight. He must have been such a joy to his father and mother. She wondered if he had any sisters or brothers.

All at once, the doorbell clapper rang, followed by a wild pounding on the door.

Instantly alert, she rushed to the window and peeked out, thinking it might be American soldiers who were a trifle too exuberant from rum, and had started their own party early.

She wouldn't allow anyone in. She dashed for a chair to fit under the doorknob. However, she was startled when the door glass was shattered and a hairy arm reached in, twisting the doorknob from inside. She picked up the chair and, using it as a club against the intruder, began to slam it against his arm.

"Ow! Ow!" The arm jerked back out of sight. "That witch! Look at this gash." With a grunt, the man heaved himself viciously against the door.

Frantically, Danielle tried to keep them from breaking in, but it was no use. The door frame splintered, and two stocky pirates burst into the room. One was Dominique, the artilleryman, and the second was Gambi. For an instant her heart stopped.

"Get out! This is a private home. Get out this instant, or I'll call to the soldiers in the street." The singing was louder, and she knew they wouldn't be able to hear her.

"You'll call to no one," Gambi snarled, and pushed her so hard she sprawled on the floor.

She looked to Dominique for sympathy. Didn't he remember talking to her? But Dominique scarcely gave her a glance, for he was scrutinizing each and every knickknack, and stuffing his pockets full.

"Watch your step," she ordered as firmly as she could from her prone position. "My father is Captain Verlaine, a close friend of Andrew Jackson's!"

"We know who your worthless father is," Gambi snarled. "Why do you think we're here? Captain Verlaine, that scurvy, vile no-good. It so happens your father had a meeting with Jean Lafitte this morning, and he still won't support our bid for citizenship. God help him, he'll be sorry for his stand. You and every Verlaine should be fed to the alligators."

On all fours, she began to rise to her feet, but Gambi kicked her viciously in the side. "Stay down. I'll let you know when you can get up."

Holding her breath as Gambi advanced toward the little round table, tipping upside down everything in his path, she warily watched him. For a fleeting moment, she wanted to laugh through her pain when she noticed his mud-caked boots. Aunt Madeline would take him by the ear. She lowered her eyes, glad that her aunt wasn't here. Oh, God, if they were going to kidnap her, let them take her now before Aunt Madeline returned. They might kill Madeline. She prayed Gambi wouldn't find the cameos, but even as the thought crossed her mind, he picked up the table and tossed it aside with powerful arms.

"Aha! What is this?" He swung his big head in her direction, leering. The fear in her eyes must have been transparent. "Something of value?"

She said nothing, staring past him.

With a swift movement, he bent down and flung off the cover. He held up the velvet, spilling out the cameos, one by one. "Dominique," he yelled. "Get over here. We don't need nothin' more than this box and the girl. Let's get out of here."

"Wait," she pleaded. "Let me stay behind. I can reason with my father and persuade him to support your demands. You've helped defend the city, and I'm sure I can change his mind."

"He'll never change his mind," Dominique growled. "He's a stubborn man who treats Jean Lafitte as if he's worthless. Well, we won't take his insults. He supported the sacking and burning of Grande Terre, too. Don't worry, we intend to deal with him in language he understands. If he calls us murderers and pirates, then that's what we'll be!"

"The likes of you Creoles won't prevent us from getting the money and position we deserve." Gambi spat on the carpet, and Danielle cringed. "Before we're through, Captain Verlaine will beg us to become citizens so that he doesn't get his daughter back in little pieces."

She almost sobbed aloud. How could she let Aunt Madeline know that she was being kidnapped? Who would know where she had gone?

"Keep your mouth shut and follow me," Gambi commanded, tucking the box of cameos under his arm.

"One moment." She was thinking frantically. "There's a bottle of brandy in the kitchen. Could I have a swallow before we leave?"

"Quit stalling."

"Why not?" Dominique countered. "If little Miss Aristocrat wants her brandy, let her have a swig. Might even take one myself. Besides," Dominique urged, "it might keep her quiet on the boat."

"Make it fast," Gambi snapped.

She went into the kitchen with Dominque dogging her footsteps. The kitchen was a mess, and fortunately, flour had been spilled all over the table. She reached for the brandy bottle, eyeing Dominique. After taking a short swallow of the burning liquid, she coughed and sputtered, her eyes watering.

Dominique roared with laughter, grabbing the bottle. "I'll show you how to drink."

As he tipped up the bottle, he gulped the rest of the contents. Watching him every second, she half turned and traced the initials G. T., for Grand Terre, in the brown flour. She hoped to heaven Aunt Madeline wouldn't compulsively wipe it clean before she noticed the clue.

Finished, Dominique smashed the bottle against the wall and wiped his mouth with the back of his hand. "Get going," he ordered, pushing her forward.

When they walked out the door, Danielle measured every step she took. Was it less than an hour ago that she had walked along this banquette, so glad to be back at her aunt's? She sniffled, fighting back tears. She dare not cry. She needed to keep her wits. The celebrating soldiers in the street were her salvation. As she neared a group of whooping and yelling soldiers, one tootling on a fife, she watched for an opportunity.

Gambi loosened his grip as he shouldered his way past the men. In a split second, Danielle yelled with every ounce of strength she possessed. "Help! Help me! I'm being kidnapped!"

Dominique immediately hollered over her voice, "Three hurrahs for Jackson!"

The soldiers responded with three lusty cheers.

Gambi's hold on her arm tightened so severely, she whimpered. Twisting his mouth to one side, he snarled, "If you yell again, I'll break your arm."

The soldiers laughed and waved. It was useless. No one could hear above this din.

Dominique and Gambi forcibly jostled her through and away from the cheering crowd.

Chapter Thirteen

THE two pirates tightly grasped Danielle's arms all the way to the bayou where their skiff was partially hidden under a willow tree.

Pushing aside the foliage, Gambi stepped into the boat, roughly pulling her after him. The small craft swayed and rocked.

"Lie down," he ordered brusquely, under his breath. No doubt he was still worried that a wandering soldier, enjoying his new freedom, might overhear him.

Next, Dominique jumped aboard, making the tiny boat sway even more. The stocky man steadied himself and straightened the red bandanna on his head. His long beard and gold earrings gave him the look of a swaggering freebooter, but Danielle remembered him as the fine artillerist who had ordered Geoffrey back to work that day by the well.

She stretched out as Gambi ordered but lifted her head to look around, recognizing St. John's Bayou.

"Stay down!" Gambi hissed, "or I'll give you another kick."

She flattened herself in the bottom of the boat and watched as each pirate took an oar. Dominique pushed away from shore. The city was so close, yet so far. She shivered and, with a shaking heart, lay still. The air that had warmed her cheek such a short while ago now felt cold and damp. The ribs of the boat were uncomfortable, and the smell of decaying fish permeated the bottom.

Gambi threw a tarpaulin over Danielle. "Sleep," he snickered, "if you can breathe, that is."

Danielle remained as still and silent as she could, not wanting to antagonize Gambi further. He was likely to bind and gag her, and then she would die of suffocation. Sweat trickled down her back, and her throat constricted, making it difficult to swallow.

The heavy canvas made her gasp for breath. She tried to twist her head to form an air pocket and hoped they wouldn't force her to lie, covered, the entire voyage to Grand Terre, a distance of over fifty miles. She dug her nails into her wrist to keep back her tears of fright.

The skiff moved smoothly over the placid

water while the oars dipped and lifted noise-lessly in a steady rhythm.

"Careful of the swamp grass ahead," Dominique warned.

"I see it," Gambi muttered.

"What do you think Jean Lafitte will say when he sees the hostage we've brought him?" Dominique said gleefully.

"He'll give us a reward. You'll see. Danielle Verlaine is worth a fortune. Not only that, but he'll have Antoine Verlaine just where he wants him."

She squeezed her eyes shut. To think she would be the cause of her father's humilia-tion. He would do anything to save her. Well, he would find out very soon where they had taken her, when he was presented with the ransom demand. If only Aunt Madeline would figure out her sketchy message and a search party could be organized in time to ambush the kidnappers on the bayou, before they reached the island of Grand Terre.

It seemed like hours before Dominique threw back the tarpaulin, uncovering her head. She breathed deeply of the fresh air.

Cramped, she sat up and was amazed to see the sun setting. She was certain it had been close to midnight.

Her long hair tumbled about her face, and she noticed her sleeve was ripped, exposing a black bruise. Her side ached from Gambi's kick. She thought of her aunt's home and what they had planned for tonight. Right now, she would be dressing for the torchlight parade, and later, there would be dancing in the street. She felt so miserable when she thought of the horror Aunt Madeline would experience when she found her gone and saw her beautiful things strewn about and broken.

She sat in the middle seat, facing Gambi, with her back to Dominique. She observed the narrow bayou with the cypress trees dripping long strings of moss, the smooth, slow-moving water, and an occasional tern flying overhead. It was all such a tranquil scene, not at all in keeping with the stormy emotions raging inside her.

As unobtrusively as possible, she studied Gambi's weather-lined face, black from the sun. There was no compassion in his small eyes, only a hard glint of cruel greed. He was boorish and contemptible. She could expect no mercy from him. Her eyes moved to the box of cameos at his feet, and again she thought of her father, what she had cost him. Well, somehow she would escape. Soon. Some way. She could swim, row a boat, run, ride a horse, shoot and, glimpsing the knife in Gambi's sash, she thought she could even use a dagger if she were given the chance.

Gambi watched her. His narrow, glittering eyes seemed to uncover her secret thoughts. A slow grin spread across his bearded face. "What are you dreaming of, mam'selle? Do you like the looks of the knife in my belt? Wouldn't you like to stick it in my gizzard?" He threw back his head and roared. Then his menacing glower returned as he coldly assessed her. "I wish you'd try it!"

Pointing to an alligator that glided through the murky water, he shouted, "Look! It would be so easy to tip you over the side."

She shuddered. The broad snout of the alligator and the two teeth jutting out from his powerful jaws was a terrifying sight — especially when she was threatened with becoming his next meal.

"Alligators are always hungry," Gambi continued in a more cunning tone.

She rigidly grasped the edge of the wooden board she was seated upon, trying not to betray her fear and revulsion of Gambi. He was a loathsome plunderer. He fit the picture of what most people thought about pirates. Gambi was a true pirate. She remembered what Jean Lafitte had said many months ago: "My men are not pirates. Call them priva-teers or corsairs but never pirates." Well, Gambi was a pirate. He continued to leer at her while she attempted to keep her face impassive, but her thoughts were centered on a picture of Gambi. He was standing on a platform with a hangman's noose being fitted around his thick neck.

"Yes, sir. Alligators would find Danielle Verlaine a tasty tidbit . . . blue bloods are a delicacy!"

"Stop that talk," Dominique grumbled.

Danielle turned and gave him a grateful smile.

His grin, showing a missing front tooth, was reassuring. There was even a hint of sympathy in his brown-bearded face.

Gambi was silent.

She leaned back on the seat and prayed for rescue. She must have dozed, for when she sat up, it was dark, except for the shimmering moon making silver ripples across the water.

The pirates knew the intricate passages well, and guided their small boat through the tropical greenery, going out of one narrow inlet into another. Every muscle in Danielle's body was sore, and she was hungry and thirsty. The brandy had created a craving for water.

As they rowed by a large island, she saw fishermen's huts in the distance and wished there were some way she could signal her plight.

Finally, a large body of land loomed ahead.

"Grand Terre," Dominique crowed.

Yes, Grand Terre. She must resign herself. There was no search party. There would be no rescue. So she would have to advance to the next step and not panic. Jean Lafitte was a fair man. He would send her back home and punish Gambi and Dominique for their action. At least she hoped he would.

"My arm is tired, and I'm ready for a sleep," Dominique said.

"First things first," Gambi snapped. "We'll take Miss Aristocrat to Jean Lafitte."

"Do ye think he'll be back from the front?" asked Dominique.

"You can count on it. He left in a fury after his conference with Captain Verlaine."

Her blood ran cold at these words. She depended on Jean Lafitte. But he might not be her protector, after all. Would Geoffrey be there? If so, *he'd* be her champion, and his word would go a long way with his uncle.

But the next conversation dashed any hope of Geoffrey's being her rescuer.

"Where's Geoffrey?" growled Gambi, as if he knew of their liaison and was afraid of his intervention.

"He and Beluche are dismantling the cannon. They'll return tomorrow or the day after."

"Miss Aristocrat. Ha!" Gambi spat into the water. "Look at her. She's as ragged as a beggar maid." He thrust his face into hers and snarled, "Not much of a blue blood, are you?"

"I may not look like much, but I will soon prove my good breeding." She tried to keep her voice calm, but she couldn't hide the tremor.

She examined her torn dress and tried to brush away the wrinkles. She lifted her high collar, and when she smoothed back her thick hair, it simply fell forward again. If only she had a brush and could wash. She remembered her first meeting with Jean Lafitte, when her hair was in shiny coils and she wore a smart riding gown with highly polished boots. Would he even recognize her?

After the pirates beached the boat, the dawn light filtered through the mist, displaying small thatched cottages along the sandy shore; but as yet, no one was about. She watched as Gambi hid the box of cameos beneath a gnarled tree root.

"This treasure will be our little secret, eh, Dominique? No need to tell Jean Lafitte." Gambi's malevolent glare sought her out. "If you value your life, you'll say nothing."

She clamped her lips together. This could be a trump card at a later time. She knew where the cameos were, and she could bargain with her captors, she thought, as they walked past the tiny settlement to a gleaming white mansion dominating the center of an oak grove.

Lafitte's home had two outside curved staircases, reaching like a horseshoe to the balcony door. The new house appeared unfinished. Evidently the Baratarians had rebuilt his mansion after the Americans had raided Grand Terre last fall and destroyed their buildings.

She walked with renewed energy when she thought of the charming Jean Lafitte. She was confident he would never sanction Dominique and Gambi's kidnapping. In fact, he would punish them. She was sure of it. Good. They deserved it. She'd like to give them a horsewhipping — at least Gambi!

Going up the steps, Gambi reached the door

and flung it open. In a mock bow, he swept one arm wide, motioning for Danielle to enter.

Gingerly, she stepped into the gleaming hall with its elegant oak floors and crystal chandeliers. Boxes were piled about. The newly arrived merchandise was waiting to be unpacked. One box from France was labeled "porcelain," another from India, "silk," and yet another from Jamaica, "rum."

"Lafitte!" Gambi called. "It's me, Gambi. We have a hostage you'll want to meet."

Danielle, breathing hard, rehearsed what she wanted to say. Should she appeal to Lafitte as a gentleman and show him the bruises these men had inflicted on her? Or should she ask to be returned to New Orleans at once, before the Americans sped back with more gunboats? She abandoned the last idea, for Jean Lafitte was not the type to be afraid of threats.

Before she could plan another strategy, Lafitte entered. His black quill pen tapped impatiently against his white shirt. "What is it, Gambi?" He appeared annoyed at the interruption.

"We've brought you a guest." Chortling, he gave Danielle a little push forward.

Lafitte looked coolly at Danielle. "Mademoiselle Verlaine! Welcome to Grand Terre." Although his words were cordial, his tone was not.

She hesitated, not knowing exactly how to reply.

"This is a surprise, Gambi." He propped a black-trousered leg up on a chair, leaned over, and waited for an explanation.

"We heard about your interview with Captain Verlaine and learned he's still dead set against our citizenship." Gambi's beard fairly bristled as he glowered at her. "With his daughter in our hands, we can persuade him that Baratarians would make excellent citizens."

"You're right, Gambi. It doesn't happen very often, but this time I think you've had a good idea."

Gambi shot his leader a dark look, and it was evident he was wickedly jealous of Lafitte.

"Verlaine has brought me nothing but trouble," said Lafitte. "Almost ruined me!"

But not quite, Danielle thought, glancing about the rich hall.

Lafitte rubbed his chin, his black eyes contemplating her. "All right, Gambi. Perhaps in this little lady we'll have a new lever against Verlaine. Right, gentlemen?"

"Sir," Danielle spoke up, "these men are not gentlemen. They've kicked and abused me. I appeal to you to return me to my father."

"My men are not gentlemen?" Lafitte's eyebrows shot up. "Possibly, Danielle, you have led too sheltered a life. Or perhaps we have a different definition of the word *gentleman.* Certainly, I do not view your father as a gentleman just because he wears a fine uniform. He needs to be taught some manners."

Danielle drew herself up tall. "My father has principles and believes in fair play, even if he doesn't agree with your politics."

"Father and daughter are alike," Gambi said churlishly. "This brat is no lady. Look what she did to my arm." He held up his elbow, showing a long, jagged gash.

Lafitte laughed. "Maybe you've met your match, Gambi."

"Shall we throw her in the guardhouse?" asked Dominique, weary of all the talk.

"Sir," Danielle said, licking her dry lips and trying another tack. "If you allow me to return, I will plead your cause."

"If our gunners in yesterday morning's battle couldn't plead our cause, nothing could. I doubt if your interference would be welcome," Lafitte said coldly.

Interference! The word fell across her face like a lash.

"Throw her in the guardhouse!" Lafitte directed. "I think perhaps we can bring Captain Verlaine around to our viewpoint, after all."

She winced as Gambi grabbed her arm.

With a terrified, hopeless feeling, she meekly allowed herself to be led away.

Chapter Fourteen

As they approached the small log house, Danielle's docility changed to savagery. Lunging, she kicked Gambi's shin hard. She tried to wrest free of his grip, but even though he yowled with pain, his fingers became tighter talons on her wrist. She balked and refused to move another step. Uttering an obscenity, he dragged her the last few yards to the iron door and threw her inside. The momentum of his shove sent her flying against the opposite wall.

"Stay there and rot for all I care!" Her last sight of Gambi before he clanged shut the door and slammed home the bolt was his glowering face.

She beat on the thick door with her fists, but Gambi was departing, singing lustily.

Temporarily abandoning any hope of rescue, she tried to stifle her fear of small spaces and turned to scrutinize her surroundings. Examining every inch of the room for possible avenues of escape, she checked the thick wall, the heavy door, and the one barred window. They were all impenetrable. With distaste, she viewed the room's sparse furnishings. There was one chair, one table with a pitcher of water and a washbasin, and in the corner a pallet with the Spanish moss stuffing spilling onto the dirt floor. Dragging the chair to the window, she stood on the seat to observe the outdoors. She had a good view of Jean Lafitte's house and through the trees, the distant shore. No one was around.

She looked at her tiny room and again tried to quench the feeling of terror that rose in her throat. Confined spaces had always alarmed her, ever since the day when she had been a tiny girl and had crawled into one of the huge, open iron kettles used for boiling sugarcane juice. She remembered that the plantation bell had rung, sounding the end of the workday for the field hands, when she decided to examine the cavernous container. Climbing into the vat, she slid joyously down the sides, and using like clay the molasses residue at the bottom, she molded all kinds of strange shapes and even daubed pictures on the sides. In her artistic endeavors, she managed to smear the sticky goo all over herself as well. She plodded back and forth, finding walking difficult, for the thickened brown liquid clung to her shoes, holding her back as if she were wading in knee-high water. Eventually, she had fallen asleep in a dry corner. When she awakened, darkness had descended, and the molasses had hardened on her dress, in her hair, and on her face. Mosquitoes swarmed around her head. She tried to climb the slippery sides but kept slipping back. No one heard her shouts for help because the vats were set near the sugarcane fields. The thick syrup that had been so much fun to play with now trapped her in a quagmire, hampering her movements and tiring her, causing her to move like a snail from one side to the other. The goo that earlier had been wonderful to smear on everything now had become stiff, and smelled sickeningly sweet.

She didn't know how long she stayed in her deep cavern, but when her father found her, she must have been a pathetic sight with her tearstained, molasses-streaked face and clothes. Her mosquito-bitten body was sore and swollen. Her mother had hugged her and immediately filled the bathtub at home. How marvelous it was to soak in the warm sudsy water and have her mother shampoo her hair.

The memory of the contented, safe feeling with her parents almost overwhelmed her. How she longed for a happy reunion at Cypress Manor with them. Would it ever happen?

She shuddered, glancing at the prison walls, then reached for the pitcher and poured water in the basin, washing her hands and face. She felt refreshed, which brought back a bit of optimism.

Nonetheless, as the day passed, she sat dejectedly in the chair until Dominique brought her supper of bread and water. She immediately leaped to her feet, lifting her chin proudly. She'd show these pirates that she could bear any punishment they cared to mete out.

"Are you all right?" Dominique asked, peering at her from beneath bushy brows.

"I'm fine and glad to have some food." She took the chunk of bread and devoured every crumb.

"I'll bring you a blanket and a candle."

"Thank you, Dominique." Even Dominique must consider her surroundings bleak.

"Tomorrow I'll bring you more substantial food, too," he promised.

Tomorrow, she thought glumly. Did she have to spend another day in this dismal room?

That evening, she lay on her pallet, expecting Jean Lafitte to relent and release her. He had done that with the British officers, permitting them to return to their ships after only a few hours in the guardhouse. She understood that with the British he had only wanted to show them his power and authority, but in her case, he wanted to teach a Verlaine manners. Manners, indeed. She was losing respect for the mighty Jean Lafitte and his treatment of prisoners. Perhaps her father was right. New Orleans didn't need citizens like Lafitte and his men. Especially Gambi. He was a criminal of the most evil kind.

The evening shadows fell across the bars, forming a pattern of lines on the floor, and Lafitte still hadn't come to liberate her. Once more, she stood on the chair and looked out the window at his house, hoping to catch a glimpse of him. Evidently Geoffrey hadn't come back, either.

She went back to her pallet, flinging herself down, and tried to sleep. Suddenly her eyes flew open. A scurrying noise in the opposite corner sent a chill along her back. She had a nightmare image of a rat gnawing its way into her small quarters. In the waning light, however, she could see nothing frightening. Perhaps a mole. Next, she watched a centipede crawl across the wall. A cold sweat bathed her body. She wished with every fiber of her body that she could get away from this dreadful place.

Sleep finally came to her, even though she awakened several times in the night.

With the January sun streaming through the bars and awakening her, she jumped up. The first thing she did was to stand on the chair and survey Jean Lafitte's house. Gambi was climbing the steps to the balcony. What new skulduggery was he planning? He had done his worst as far as she was concerned. What further damage could he do? At least she knew where he had concealed the cameos, and had no intention of letting him get away with their theft. When the time was right, she would use them to her advantage. She wouldn't tell Jean Lafitte about the gems just yet. If she escaped, she would take them with her. If not, they would be her weapon against Gambi. She thought of her father. How worried he must be. He had her mother on his mind, and now Danielle was adding to his concerns.

She sighed deeply. To forget her imprisonment, she removed her black sash and began to tie the knots that Paul had once taught her. That day was so long ago. *Paul,* she wondered, *where are you at this moment? You might be even closer than Geoffrey if you're still on the* Louisiana, *plying the Mississippi River.* Her slender fingers tied the intricate bowline and then the cat's-paw, which helped her forget her predicament for a few moments.

After an hour, she retied the sash around the dress that she had been wearing for four days. Now, though, because of the chill in the air, she was glad she had it on and that she was wearing thick black stockings.

Once more she stood on the chair, peering out at the white house. There was no movement. There were a few pirates drying a large fishing net on shore. The sun, straight overhead, meant it was noon. Wouldn't Geoffrey ever get back? He would be her knight in shining armor, come to rescue his princess. She smiled at the fantasy. Well, she certainly didn't resemble a princess in her drab dress and disheveled hair.

The door clanked open.

Eagerly she dashed over, thinking it was Geoffrey. Her smile vanished, however, when Dominique swaggered in, placing on the table a bowl of shrimp gumbo and a cup of water. The steaming food looked good, but when she tasted the hot liquid, it was vile.

She pushed it away. "I can't eat this," she complained.

"You'd better eat it or go hungry."

She glared at him. Slowly, she pulled the bowl back. Dominique was right. She must keep her strength up, so she lifted a spoonful to her lips. Her stomach heaved, but she was able to keep it down. Another spoonful, and with each one she kept telling herself it would give her strength to flee this pirates' island.

"Dominique, what does Jean Lafitte plan to do with me?"

He shrugged his massive shoulders. "I think he has forgotten you. He has more important things on his mind."

In astonishment, Danielle stared at him. "More important things?" She wondered what could be more important than taking a Verlaine hostage. If he riled the American authorities too much, they might force him out of Louisiana, and he and his men would become exiles.

"Don't worry," Dominique said. "He'll send a message to your father in the next few days."

"Why the delay?"

Dominique grinned. The gap in his teeth seemed more ominous than it had previously. "To let your stubborn father stew awhile."

In frustration, she hit her fist on the table. Her fate was so nebulous, and hinged on Jean Lafitte's whim. He could let her live or die. Die. Her high spirits wouldn't even let her think about death. But what if by some quirk her father didn't get the message or was unable to pay the ransom? She dismissed this line of reasoning. It was ridiculous. Of course, Jean Lafitte would wait for his money or his citizenship papers, whichever came first. It was just galling to think that she was so unimportant. Why, he hadn't given her any more thought than he might the centipede she'd seen creeping along the wall.

"Is Geoffrey Lafitte back?" she blurted out. She hadn't meant to betray their relationship, but she had to know.

Dominique's keen look unsettled her, but she took another mouthful and said casually, "I thought you said he'd be back soon."

He lifted one shoulder. "One boat of cannoneers has landed, and no doubt his boat is close behind."

The news buoyed her spirits. At last. She could stand anything for a few more hours.

Dominique turned to leave.

"When Geoffrey Lafitte lands, will you tell him I'm in the guardhouse?"

He narrowed his eyes. "What's going on between you two? You were at the pump to-

gether, and now you want to see him again."
He suspiciously studied her face.

"We're friends, only friends," she fibbed.

"You'll need more than Geoffrey Lafitte
to get you out of here, but I'll tell him."

She reached out but didn't touch Dominique's hand. "Thank you," she said simply.
Now all she had to do was settle down and
wait for Geoffrey to hurry to her side. It
wouldn't be long. She was sure of it.

But the afternoon slipped away into dusk,
and still her love hadn't arrived.

For the second time that day, Dominique
came back and brought a meager supper of
soup and coffee. She asked eagerly, "Has
Geoffrey come in?"

The pirate gave her a long look. "He and
Beluche will be in sometime." He shrugged.
"Who knows where they are?" And he
winked broadly. "Maybe they've found some
young women to keep them company. Why
should they hurry back?"

Her cheeks flamed, but she wouldn't give
Dominique the satisfaction of showing
jealousy.

"Maybe he won't be back for a week,"
Dominique said with a laugh. "New Orleans
has more amusements than Grand Terre."

"If he doesn't get back, he doesn't," she
remarked coolly.

After Dominique left, she threw herself on
the pallet. The first boat of cannoneers had
landed. Why hadn't Geoffrey? Had he
actually found a girl he wanted to be with?

His good looks would attract any lady he chose. In her mind, she saw his bold smile and black eyes. On the other hand, he had no way of knowing she needed him. He might be staying in the city to look for her.

She stared at the log beams overhead. Geoffrey loved her. She was sure of it. But the memory of Dominique's statement preyed on her mind. What was it he said? Geoffrey might not be back for a week. Her father and aunt had no idea where she was. Would she ever get out of this pesthole?

That night she cried herself to sleep.

Chapter Fifteen

THE next morning Danielle rose, stretched, and scratched herself around the waist. She hoped the itching sensation was caused by the wool dress and not by anything that crawled.

When the bolt slid free, she was ready for her breakfast, skimpy as it was. She ran to welcome Dominique but stopped and stared. "Geoffrey!" she exclaimed. "Oh, Geoffrey! You're here at last!"

"My poor Danielle," he murmured with an astonished look at her appearance. "What have they done to you?"

Uttering a soft little moan, she rushed into his welcoming arms. How she had yearned for this moment.

He stroked her hair, making reassuring sounds. "My dearest love. I searched for you in New Orleans. What happened?"

"Geoffrey, I was kidnapped." She stepped back, knowing she looked bedraggled and woebegone. "Gambi was terrible. He and Dominique burst into Aunt Madeline's house and forced me to accompany them to Grand Terre. Gambi kicked me." Tears surfaced and threatened to spill over when she relived the ordeal. "He was going to throw me to the alligators. He was awful and —" She stopped abruptly. She was babbling on like a child.

He pulled her back into his arms. "Sweet Danielle, if only I'd been there. Gambi can be greedy and vicious." His eyes hardened. "I don't know why my uncle tolerates him. If it were up to Gambi, he'd make every Spanish prisoner we've ever taken walk the plank."

"Please," she implored. "I want to get out of this place. I've spent two nights in this wretched prison." She shuddered. "It's horrible!"

"I know. I know," he said soothingly as he held her head close into his shoulder. "You'll soon be liberated. My uncle sent a message to Captain Verlaine."

She pulled free, hands on hips. "And how much ransom did he ask for me?"

"There will be no ransom."

"No ransom?" Her eyes became as wide as saucers. "What do you mean no ransom? Am I worthless?"

"My uncle wants to see you. He'll explain things in detail."

"Did you persuade Jean Lafitte to set me free?"

"You don't persuade my uncle, Danielle. You can reason with him, but he'll make up his own mind."

She was confused. "B-but you're here . . . didn't you tell him to let me go?"

He laughed. "I'm here to take you to my uncle, but first I want to hold you." He embraced her. "And kiss you." His lips brushed hers.

For a long time, he hugged her close. It was so good to nestle against him and to feel his protective arms around her and to be tenderly treated.

As he led her to the great white house, she felt a sense of relief and fervently hoped she would never have to return to her awful cell.

Geoffrey left her standing in the hall with the words, "I'll be back in a minute."

Uneasily, she gazed around the quiet room. Where was everyone? Why had Geoffrey left her?

Geoffrey returned from the back of the house with a Santo Domingan woman who wore a black patch over her left eye. With her good eye, she looked Danielle up one side and down the other with disapproval. *"Mon Dieu, what can I do with this beggar girl?"*

Danielle shrank back a bit at this swaggering woman's fierceness.

"So, 'tis a Creole miss I'm to clean up and make presentable for Jean Lafitte, is it?" She walked around Danielle, muttering, "I have quite a job ahead of me. Come with Lupé. I fix you up. You're not a fit sight for Jean Lafitte."

Danielle followed the tall, barefoot servant, who wore a full skirt and a ruffled blouse, to a back room where a metal tub was filled with inviting soapy water.

"Here. I help you." The leather-skinned woman unbuttoned Danielle's dress and took her clothes between two fingers while holding her nose with her other hand. "Whew. These things I throw out in the hall." When she returned, she nodded approvingly at Danielle's blossoming figure. "I was young once. I, too, had a nice slender figure and curves in just the right places."

I wonder, Danielle thought, viewing Lupé's angular frame and skin, cracked from the sun. Could she ever have been young and pretty?

As Danielle soaked in the tub, luxuriating in the attar of roses scent, she lathered her entire body.

Lupé went out singing a strange little melody and soon brought back an armful of clothes — fresh pantaloons, a full skirt and red blouse. "Put these on when you're bathed. First I wash your backbone good." Lupé soaped a piece of wool and began to scrub.

Danielle winced at her rough handling but felt clean and pink when Lupé finished.

"Now," Lupé ordered, "wrap this blanket around yourself. Your hair is next. There's clean water." She indicated a white porcelain basin. "While you wash your hair, I take your dirty dress and other clothes to the laundress. They'll be scrubbed and pounded clean again." She left, closing the door after her.

As Danielle brushed out her abundant wet hair, donned her fresh peasant clothes, and thrust her feet in sandals, she felt like a new person, ready to confront Lafitte or even Gambi.

Lupé returned, one hand on a hip, and surveyed Danielle, again walking in a circle around her. "Much better, my Creole girl. Lafitte waits for you."

"Where's Geoffrey?" asked Danielle.

"He go down to shore and repair sails." She winked her good eye. "He'll be back for morning coffee and croissants. Hurry! I said Lafitte waits for you, and no one keeps him waiting. Not even rich Creoles like you." She sniffed disdainfully.

Danielle followed the woman, curious to see what Jean Lafitte had to say.

Entering a room lined with books and small model ships, Danielle stood waiting while Lafitte finished writing what appeared to be a long list . . . probably inventory or supplies, she thought.

At last he dropped his quill and leaned back, observing Danielle. "I hope your two days in the guardhouse didn't prove too distasteful."

Danielle gazed at him calmly, not replying.

Rising, Jean chuckled. "At any rate, I have a plan for you. I would like you to stay in this house as my guest for three days. I want you to be an ambassador, if you will. Then you can see for yourself what Baratarians are like and give a report to your father."

"My father will be frantic with worry."

"A message has been sent, assuring him of your safety and telling him you will be returned by Friday. We have shown we're men of honor on the battlefield, so he knows he can trust us."

For a moment, Danielle studied the wall map of the Louisiana Territory. This was a dream come true. She knew Jean Lafitte was a man of his word, even after her stint as a prisoner. She had always wanted to see Grand Terre . . . not the way she'd seen it recently, however. Here was her chance to see Grand Terre and to be an — an ambassador! She liked that. Maybe she'd be a peace emissary between Jean Lafitte and her father.

"Well, Danielle Verlaine. What is your answer? If you want to return to New Orleans today, I'll send an escort with you to your aunt's."

"I'll remain on Grand Terre," she said, buoyed with confidence at her diplomatic role. There could be good that would come out of her visit.

"Good. I thought you couldn't turn down such a tempting offer. There are not many people who have seen Grand Terre as you will get to see it." His usually serious face broke into a smile as he held out his arm for her to take. "Let's have our breakfast."

They went into the dining room where

they spotted Geoffrey Lafitte, who was already drinking his coffee.

Danielle sat down and watched as Lupé poured the steaming liquid into her cup. What a contrast from the breakfast she'd had yesterday of bread and water . . . and her surroundings! She looked about at the paneled walls, the white lace curtains, and the tablecloth of finest linen. The silver coffee server was highly polished, the porcelain was delicate, and the napkins of the finest damask.

Danielle quietly watched Jean Lafitte. He was so charming this morning, not at all like the cold individual who had sent her to the guardhouse. He was someone to be wary of and would be dangerous if crossed, doing always what suited his own best interests. She knew, too, that he was an expert duelist and had killed a man in a duel in Charleston.

"I will be busy with Jacques Lemoyne." He turned to Danielle and explained. "Jacques is one of my sea captains. We'll be checking in cargo. Geoffrey will show you around the island. If you need anything, Danielle, Lupé will fetch it for you." He rose, and his velvet vest and trousers showed off his lean physique. His face was tanned and youthful. He did not have the look of a tough pirate chief.

When Jean had left, she and Geoffrey were alone to finish their coffee.

Geoffrey grinned at her and fingered the sleeve of her red blouse. "You look like a little girl in that peasant garb." His eyes met hers as she reveled in the warmth of his gaze and tingled with pleasure at how happy the day with him would be.

"We'll have a wonderful day, chérie. We'll walk to the shore, and I'll show you the *Pride*, my uncle's ship. Then we'll walk along the beach and search for shells. I'll show you the privateers unloading their goods, and the new warehouse they'll be stored in. Since the Americans burned Grand Terre's buildings and sank our ships, everything is new or has been rebuilt."

He held out his hand, and lightheartedly, they walked to the sandy beaches. From the six ships anchored offshore, Geoffrey pointed out Lafitte's schooner.

"Isn't she a beauty?" asked Geoffrey. "The *Pride* is one hundred eighty feet long and carries eighteen cannon."

Danielle, hand to forehead, squinted against the brightness. "It looks as if there's a thunderbolt in the figurehead's hand. Who does the figure represent?"

"Neptune."

"How appropriate," she said, "to have the god of the sea on her sharp bow."

The ship rocked to and fro, her sails furled until sailing time.

Geoffrey said admiringly, "Because of her long, narrow lines, she cleaves the water like an ax."

"She is lovely," Danielle responded, wondering how many Spanish ships had been sent to a watery grave because of the *Pride*.

Next to the *Pride*, Danielle noticed that

one of Lafitte's ships was being unloaded by deckhands. Box after box was placed in large rowboats. Once fully laden, the oarsmen took them to shore. There, the pirates, in a line, passed the cargo from one man to the next, singing a pirate song as they worked. Danielle could only catch the words *blood* and *gold* over and over.

She noticed Jean Lafitte conferring with his captain beneath three gigantic oaks. The sun dazzled the white sand as Geoffrey led her away. It was fun to walk hand in hand along the shore, kicking the sand, until they reached an isolated cove.

When the sun was high overhead, they found a smooth stump to serve as a table. From a pouch Geoffrey pulled forth a wine flagon, some cheese, and a small loaf of bread. His dark face was intent as he brushed off the stump with his wide sleeve and spread out their simple lunch.

Ah, my handsome pirate, she thought as she watched his graceful movements. His eyes twinkled as he handed her the wine. From under his red headscarf, his brown curls ringed his face. His one gold hoop earring caught the sun's rays and sparkled as much as his perfect white teeth.

"Tell me about your childhood here on Grand Terre," she said, wanting to know everything there was to know about Geoffrey Lafitte.

"I had a wonderful upbringing. Sailing, learning the worth of cargoes, and gambling.

I remember the first time I shinnied up the mizzenmast. I was like a kitten. I climbed up easily enough, but when it was time to come down, I couldn't. I was petrified and clung to the mast like a barnacle to a ship's keel." He chuckled at the memory while breaking off two pieces of bread and offering her one. "When I looked down at that choppy sea, I was so frightened I couldn't move a muscle. Dominique yelled at me to climb down, and all Gambi did was roar with laughter."

Afraid the wine might cause her head to spin, she refused his offer of more. At Cypress Manor she was used to wine mixed with water. This red wine was too potent to drink undiluted. "What happened?" she asked. "Were you able to climb down all right?"

"Uncle Jean rescued me. He didn't come after me and carry me down. No, he climbed the mainmast and instructed me to follow what he did, so I could come down by myself. I watched him and slowly clambered down. Because of his guidance, my fear vanished. He was a great teacher. Since I came down from the mast alone, I didn't suffer the teasing I would have taken if I would have had to be carried down on his back."

"You must be fond of your uncle," she said gently.

"I am, but sometimes I think Gambi is right. Not in making prisoners walk the plank — I'd never do that. It's just that Uncle Jean is a little too soft and has released prisoners who would have given us a rich profit."

Looking at him askance, she said in a bantering way, "You're not upset because he's sending me back without a ransom demand, are you?"

He looked indignant. "He'd better not ask Captain Verlaine for ransom. You're special to me, Danielle . . . and I think you know it." His eyes softened as he took her hand, brushing the fingertips with his lips.

"Geoffrey." She leaned toward him, deciding to trust him. If you couldn't trust the one you loved, then who could you trust? "My father and mother have a priceless cameo collection. Gambi stole it and didn't tell Jean Lafitte. I don't want you to tell him, either. The stones are worth a fortune and are hidden under an old oak where we landed."

Geoffrey nodded. "I know the cove."

"Would you dig them out and bring them to me when I leave, so I can return them to my parents?"

"A whole box of cameos?"

"Yes, they're important to the Verlaine family. They may be needed to rebuild Cypress Manor."

He held her hand tightly. "I'll have them tonight and keep them in a safe place for you. It wouldn't do to keep them in your room. Lupé and Gambi are too friendly."

"I knew you'd help me, Geoffrey." She gave his hand a squeeze.

For a brief moment, he leaned toward her,

then jumped to his feet, pulling her up. "What a beautiful girl you are. Those blue eyes."

She felt heady looking into the depths of his eyes. He swept her against him and kissed her. Despite the cool day, she felt flushed, and responded to his kiss in a way she never had to Paul.

"Danielle," he whispered. "I love you."

"I love you, too," she murmured. Again he kissed her.

She withdrew and said shakily, "Geoffrey, I ... Please. I want to go back."

He laughed. "Of course. We'll return at once. But someday you will come into my arms and not want to leave. You will be my pirate queen."

When she lay in bed that night, the words *pirate queen* kept repeating themselves in her mind. She pictured herself in cutoff trousers, a full-sleeved blouse, a saber in one hand, and a pistol in the other. Geoffrey stood by her side, delighted with his fighting companion, and he wasn't at all jealous of her fighting spirit and straight shooting. Suddenly, Paul's frowning image floated into her fantasy, and he was shaking his head disapprovingly. She turned over, replacing his image with Geoffrey's. After all, perhaps it wasn't such a wild dream after all. Geoffrey was in love with her, and she was in love with him, and here she was on an island with him as her constant guide for three whole days. What could be more idyllic?

Chapter Sixteen

THE next morning Jean Lafitte again left Geoffrey and Danielle to themselves to plan their day over another cup of coffee and a second slice of hot bread.

Geoffrey leaned forward excitedly. "I have the cameos," he said in a low voice.

She set her cup in the saucer. "I'm so relieved. That's marvelous. Were they exactly where I told you?"

"Yes. I'll keep them safely hidden for you until Friday. Gambi doesn't suspect a thing." Geoffrey grinned, proud of retrieving the cameos.

"He doesn't suspect anything yet, but when he discovers the stones are gone, he'll come after me with a knife."

"Leave Gambi to me. Don't be afraid," said Geoffrey.

"I suppose you're right. I can't be concerned about him, too." She reached over and touched Geoffrey's hand. "I'm so worried about my mother. The British are still encamped at Cypress Manor. Did you hear if they are planning to evacuate soon?"

"I haven't heard a thing about their leaving," Geoffrey said with concern, "but there was to have been a prisoner exchange the day after the battle. Sixty-three prisoners were to have been traded."

"I hope my mother was one of them."

"Sixty-three American prisoners were all that the British had taken. The Americans had captured hundreds of British, but Jackson insisted they were to be traded man for man So you see, your mother is bound to be one of the Americans."

"I hope that's true. If it is, she and Father will be reunited by now. The next thing is to promote harmony between your uncle and my father. Once that is accomplished, the future will look much happier." She rubbed her brow.

"What's wrong, chérie?"

"Oh, it's Gambi. I know I should put him out of my mind, but I can't. When he finds the cameos are missing he'll . . ." Her voice trailed off. "I'm frightened, Geoffrey."

"Gambi won't do anything to you. He's one of Jean Lafitte's pirates, and if he disobeys my uncle, he knows what will happen to him. The same thing that happened to his lieutenant a long time ago. He'll be shot," he said simply, "so don't fret. Gambi likes life too

much to endanger his own by taking yours."
Geoffrey laughed. "Besides, he certainly can't
complain to my uncle that the cameos are
missing after he hid them away for himself."

Danielle remained silent, but she thought
of Jean Lafitte's brand of justice. He certainly didn't give a person much time for an
explanation.

Lupé entered and Geoffrey finished his
coffee, not mentioning Gambi again.

As Lupé cleared the table, she said to
Danielle, "Your dress and stockings are clean
and laid out on your bed."

"I'm grateful." Danielle smiled at this
sober woman, but there was no answering
smile.

"Don't thank me. Thank the washer-
woman," she muttered.

"I will," Danielle promised.

Lupé eyed Danielle's simple garb. "You
look better as a corsair's lady than an aristocrat."

"I think she belongs on Grand Terre, don't
you, Lupé?" Geoffrey grinned at the taciturn
woman.

"Hmph! Depends on your viewpoint,"
Lupé said glumly. "There's too many women
on this island already."

"Lupé, there's only one woman to every
five men."

"That's too many."

Geoffrey rose and encircled Lupé's waist
with both arms and said in a teasing voice,
"You just want them all to yourself."

Lupé finally managed a half smile, and her wrinkled face looked as if it might crack. "Enough of your charming ways, Geoffrey. You prefer this little maid, even in her black dress."

Danielle lifted her hands in a helpless gesture. "I'll admit that my black dress is not exactly my favorite, but there wasn't much I could do. I had just returned from the front when Gambi and Dominique grabbed me."

Lupé winked at Geoffrey. "Bring her to my cottage at midnight and I'll show her another quaint Baratarian custom. "Tonight," she said in a hushed tone, "there will be a special ceremony."

Geoffrey arched his brows and helped Danielle to her feet. "If Uncle Jean finds out, he'll put a stop to what he calls 'superstition and nonsense.' "

"I would like to cast a spell over him at one of my rituals and then let him call it nonsense!" Lupé stacked up the dishes, and before she went out to the kitchen, she said, "Besides, he won't find out. Tonight's rite is a unique request." Her brows knit together, and she glanced at Danielle with a strange glint in her eye. "It's a request from an old friend of yours, Miss Creole Girl. This man crossed too many gold doubloons across my palm for a refusal. I had to accept."

"An old friend?" Danielle wondered who Lupé meant. Could Geoffrey be planning a love potion ceremony?

"We'll be there, Lupé." He motioned Danielle to follow him. "We have many things to do before this evening, though. Let's go, Danielle."

"Are you going to the target range?" Lupé asked.

Geoffrey grinned. "Right. I've seen Danielle point a pistol at me. Now let's see if she knows how to shoot it."

On the way out Danielle noticed Jean Lafitte in the library. She loved the small, book-lined room. As usual, he was sitting at his desk.

As they went by, he glanced up. "Danielle," he called, "Geoffrey. Come in here a minute."

Danielle entered the cozy room, breathing the aroma of rich leather. Books were stacked everywhere. The only wall without books had maps — maps of Europe, Louisiana, and New Orleans with its surrounding islands.

"Danielle, I want you to see my library. I've collected a number of books on shipping and geography." Jean Lafitte handed her a book. "You might enjoy this book on frigates. Wasn't that young man I met at the dock last fall on the frigate the *Carolina*?"

She nodded, giving Geoffrey a sidelong look, but he was staring out the window.

"What was his name?" asked Jean.

"Paul Milerand."

"Ah, yes. The *Carolina* was sunk. Was he saved?" Jean Lafitte continued.

"Yes, he was," she answered, wishing he wouldn't talk about it anymore.

Jean Lafitte sensed her discomfiture. "Go ahead, page through it."

She leafed through the parchment pages with the fine ink drawings of sails, masts, decks, and every part of a schooner. The illustrations were fascinating, and she sank down into a leather chair.

"Danielle, it's time to go to the target range," Geoffrey said impatiently.

"I just want to browse a minute."

"Browse as much as you like. You see," Jean Lafitte said wryly with a smile, "Baratarians can be civilized, too."

She smiled also. "I'd like to stay here and look at all your beautiful books. And" — she touched a model ship on his desk — "to study these model ships. What exquisite workmanship."

"A hobby of mine. I'm good with my hands," the pirate leader said. "Unlike Geoffrey." He contemplated his nephew blandly.

Geoffrey shrugged. "I'm handy with pistols and sabers. That's all that counts."

"Not always, my boy," Jean retorted softly.

When at last Danielle rose, Geoffrey was sitting in the opposite chair, brooding.

She went over several titles, plucking out a volume entitled *Plutarch's Lives*. The burnished brown leather with gold lettering was a rare treasure.

Geoffrey yawned and rose languidly to his full height. "If we're going to the practice field, Danielle, we'd better hurry. I'll teach you a few techniques that you haven't seen before. I can hit a target at twenty paces."

Reluctantly, Danielle replaced the book on the shelf. She could have been engrossed in this room all morning.

"Look, Danielle," Jean Lafitte said, pointing to a map above his desk. "Here's Barataria Bay, Grand Terre, Petit Terre, and the Chandeleur Islands."

She examined the elegant cartography. The map was lettered in gold and had green sea monsters plying the seas amidst miniature ships and intricate scroll writing. "You can see," Jean said dryly, "what a strategic position we are in to protect the Mississippi Delta. Was it any wonder that General Jackson accepted our offer?"

"None at all," Danielle murmured.

"The map was drawn for me by an old Italian cartographer." He ran his fingers delicately over the framed map. "Here's the *Pride,* my schooner, which he sketched in. It's the fastest ship in the whole Atlantic."

Geoffrey hastily took her arm. "Danielle, it's time to go."

Jean Lafitte frowned briefly, as if he were loath to let an appreciative audience like Danielle leave. Then the moment passed and he waved them out the door. "You'll never be a scholar, Geoffrey. Take her to the target range." After his curt dismissal, he turned back to his books.

"I hate that stuffy room," Geoffrey said as they walked arm in arm into the woods.

"Books are the one thing that Uncle Jean tried to foist on me that I hated. Now that I've turned nineteen, I think he's finally given up on me and recognizes me for a soldier and a privateer . . . the best in the area!" He puffed out his chest, and Danielle had to smile secretly at how Geoffrey viewed himself, but she had to admit that his swashbuckling airs were quite attractive.

As they came into a clearing, a large, round target had been set up on a distant tree, and Dominique and Cut-Nose were aiming and firing their pistols.

Danielle felt at ease here and watched as Geoffrey proudly went up to the white chalk line. From his belt he took a pistol etched in silver, and began to fire at the red circle. He hit a bull's-eye twice and came very close to the center with his other three shots.

"Ho, Geoffrey! That's good shooting!" Dominique said, striding to the target and assessing Geoffrey's marksmanship.

Geoffrey, pleased, handed her the pistol. "Would you like to try, Danielle? Just take your time and aim carefully," he advised.

Deliberately, she stepped to the line and lifted the gun. Taking a slow aim, she shot three times at the target and was quite happy with the results. However, when she glanced at Geoffrey for approval, he was frowning. Two more shots and she handed the pistol back to Geoffrey. "I don't think I did too badly, do you?"

"You know exactly how well you did," he said curtly.

Amazed, she stared at him. He had gone white around his set mouth, and he was actually glaring at her.

"Looks like you've been bested!" Dominique chortled. "But I'll check it out." Once more he strode to the target. "Four bull's-eyes!" he crowed. "And the other so close it's hard to call. Geoffrey, this girl is a better shot than you are. She could give us all lessons." His raucous laughter filled the air.

"Stow that talk," growled Geoffrey.

Danielle, bewildered at Geoffrey's reaction, didn't know exactly how to appease him. She was disappointed in his petty attitude, but perhaps he had other things on his mind. She certainly didn't intend to miss the target so he could win. She finally asked, "Shall we try again?"

Cut-Nose barked a laugh.

"No. I've had enough." Geoffrey appeared to smolder under the pirates' mirth.

Cut-Nose sidled over to her. "How about teaching me to hold the pistol, missy?" He cast a smirking glance at Geoffrey.

Without a word, Geoffrey picked up his pistol, tucked it in his belt, and stalked off.

Danielle was left with Dominique and Cut-Nose. Humiliated, she scarcely looked at the two pirates who were still discussing her good shooting. She didn't know where to go or what to do. Where had Geoffrey gone? She left the clearing and began to follow a path that eventually led to the beach. Walking along the shore, she observed a schooner at anchor. The water was calm with only a few gentle ripples lapping against the hull.

For hours she sat on the bank by herself, thinking about this morning. She clasped her hands around her knees and hummed a mournful tune, her heart hurting. Looking up, she glimpsed a distant sloop sailing gracefully into the bay, and suddenly she remembered Paul. She and Paul had competed, too, but his reaction was so different from Geoffrey's. One day in August, she had been astride Ebony. Paul was on Caesar, his white charger, and they decided to race. They started near the azalea beds on either side of the city road and set their goal at the first bend in the lane, where Paul had tied a ribbon between two oak trees. The race had been short and swift, but Ebony had edged out Paul's horse. Paul had laughed and wanted to know her secret, and later had even boasted to friends in town about her win. He wasn't ashamed of his defeat and didn't treat her spitefully because of it. How unlike this morning's competition. She shivered. The chill air finally made her uncomfortable. Slowly she walked, kicking at pebbles and small crab shells that had washed ashore. Why had Geoffrey acted that way? What had she done that was so wrong?

When she came back to the house, Geoffrey and his uncle were checking a ship's inventory, so she went directly to her room. The second day at Grand Terre was drawing to an end, and she had spent the entire afternoon without Geoffrey. There was such an empty feeling inside her. Perhaps it was time to go home. Perhaps she had outworn her welcome.

Lupé poked her head in the door. "Early dinner tonight. Six o'clock."

"I'll be ready," she replied unhappily, glad that Lupé had not stayed to talk.

Again she dressed in her black dress and black stockings. How welcome it would be to get back to Cypress Manor and to wear clothes that were stylish and beautiful. Tears stung her eyes. The real reason, of course, was to be with her parents and Paul, who were understanding and proud of her accomplishments. She tied the sash around her middle, but the bow blurred and she stumbled to a chair. "Geoffrey," she whispered. "Geoffrey."

However, at dinner, sitting with the Lafittes — Geoffrey, Pierre, and Jean — she found each of them gracious and warm. In spite of her astonishment at Geoffrey's unusual charm, Danielle remained composed and extremely polite.

"Tonight, Danielle, we have a full evening." Geoffrey's wide smile brightened his face. "We'll walk to the South Beach where Uncle Jean will hold a Divvying-Out."

"A Divvying-Out?"

"You'll see," he said mysteriously with a wink.

She managed a small smile. This time she wouldn't melt so easily under his charm.

Unabashed, Geoffrey took her arm and squired her to the beach, laughing and talking all the way to the shore. When they arrived, he hoisted her up and set her on the keel of an upside-down rowboat. Grinning, he said, "Now you're going to see something."

His grin was contagious. "I thought that Lupé's ceremony was the main attraction."

Geoffrey chuckled. "That's at midnight. What you'll see now is something very few visitors are invited to."

Danielle sobered. "Geoffrey, were you annoyed with me this morning?"

"Annoyed?" He wore a puzzled expression. "At target practice?"

"Oh, that! Of course not, sweet. I wanted to attend a wrestling match between Gambi and Strangler Simon. I bet on Simon and won a good sum, too."

Her smile was wintry. She wanted to say, "Then why didn't you tell me where you were going? Why did you leave me standing all alone with two pirates?" But she held her tongue. His happy-go-lucky personality had returned, and maybe she was overreacting. No one was perfect. Besides, it looked as if the festivities were about to start as the buccaneers came from all directions down to the beach. Several men were building a fire; others were finding a good spot in the circle. Everyone was in a jovial mood, and there was much good-natured bantering and joking that filled the night air. The orange-and-yellow flames shot up into the dark sky, and by the time Jean Lafitte arrived, the bonfire was roaring. Pierre followed the chief, carrying a large chest. To one side was an upside-down box that was used as a table.

With calm deliberation, Jean Lafitte unlocked the chest and flung back the top with a flourish. Danielle gasped. It was filled with gold. She had never seen so many gold coins.

The laughing and talk ceased. All were intent on Jean Lafitte, who carefully stacked the coins in piles of twenty. The Divvying-Out began as he doled out shares to each pirate, each of whom, in turn, went back to his place and recounted.

"Beluche!" Lafitte called out. The pirate hurried forward, reaching out with both hands for his share.

"Nez-Coupé!" Jean called out the French version of Cut-Nose's name.

The coins clinked into the saber-scarred pirate's bandanna, which he held like a small hammock and tenderly enfolded around his gold.

"Marie!" Lafitte called, holding out the few coins that were left to a middle-aged woman, who had been seated beside Cut-Nose. She eagerly held out her hand, but Cut-Nose brushed her aside. "I'll take care of my wife's share," he said with great ado, swaggering forward for the second time.

Marie's face fell, but she cowered back into her place.

Lafitte closed his hand over the coins, with-holding them from Cut-Nose. His eyes nar-rowed. "I don't think so, Nez-Coupé!" He inclined his head in Marie's direction. "Marie, I'll have a gold thimble made from your coins." He jerked his thumb toward Cut-Nose. "I don't trust that old husband of yours. He hoards gold as naturally as a squirrel grubs for nuts."

Marie's lean face glowed in the firelight as she nodded vehemently at Jean Lafitte's words.

Cut-Nose turned his back in disgust and stomped off toward the compound of houses.

After the treasure had been distributed, more rum was poured, and someone strummed a guitar and sang a freebooter's song. Some joined in the singing while others left the circle. Jean Lafitte had a cup of grog with his men and conversed quietly with Pierre and Dominique.

Suddenly Gambi leaped to his feet and shouted, "Our share of gold would have tripled if we had collected ransom money from Antoine Verlaine." He was shaking with fury.

"Stow your infernal griping, Gambi, or I'll take your share myself." Lafitte's tone was level, but there was no mistaking the icy menace underneath.

Gambi's contorted features were ugly with hate as he flung his rum into the fire. "Aargh! You always have the last word, Jean Lafitte, but this time you've gone too far." His venomous look was directed at Danielle. "I'm not the only one who thinks so, either." He spun around and strode away.

A sickening feeling washed over Danielle. Gambi's hatred of her was almost palpable.

"Don't mind him." Geoffrey reached for her hand. "Lupé will be expecting us."

Looking at Geoffrey, she lost her fear. Even though at times he was like a little boy, he was lovable and sweet, but best of all he was her courageous protector.

When they entered Lupé's cottage, it was dark except for an oil lamp with the wick turned low and the fireplace aglow with red embers. Lupé was dressed in a striking wrapper of white with a white turban. When Danielle's eyes became accustomed to the gloom, she recognized five or six pirates sitting cross-legged against the wall. Gambi was one of them, his oily face creased with lines of impatience as he waited for the ceremony to begin.

It was as if Lupé had been biding her time, waiting until Geoffrey and Danielle were settled before she began.

All at once she raised her arms, shut her eyes, and, in a strange incantation, began to sway back and forth.

In front of Lupé was a small altar containing a tiny, covered box with six blue candles on one side and six black candles on the other. Taking a long stick, she poked it in the embers and then lit the black candles, leaving the blue ones untouched.

Geoffrey leaned over and whispered, "The blue candles are for love, and the black candles represent death. Someone in this room has arranged a death rite."

Danielle shivered. She much preferred the love candles.

All at once, a steady drumbeat filled the fetid air, and for the first time Danielle noticed the drummer squatting in the opposite corner. The throbbing grew in intensity, and Lupé's body went rigid. Suddenly the woman relaxed with her head lolling to one side. As she moved toward the covered box, she emitted groans and weird sounds.

The drumbeat stirred Lupé to dance, her feet beating a rhythmic tattoo on the dirt floor. Several times she tantalized the audience by making a feint toward the box but not uncovering it.

After her jerky dance was finished and the drum had stopped, it was dark and silent. Danielle held her breath in the stillness.

Then, with a scream, Lupé lunged for the box's cover, throwing it to one side. With a quick movement, she plucked out a small statue and thrust it in Danielle's face.

The young girl flung up her hands to ward off the image that had pins penetrating its heart. Daring to peek at the doll, she almost fainted as she grasped Geoffrey's arm. The statue was a tiny replica of herself!

Chapter Seventeen

THAT night, when Danielle tried to sleep, she tossed and turned on her bed until dawn, reliving Lupé's ceremony. The doll in the black dress kept zooming straight at her, and the name *Gambi* repeatedly hissed through the air like a snake. Once during the night she woke, drenched in perspiration, and found herself sitting straight up in bed.

However, the morning light restored her confidence, and she was determined to make her last day with Geoffrey a pleasant one.

As Danielle brushed her hair before the mirror, she surveyed the hollows in her face, which were deeper, emphasizing her cheekbones. The dark circles under her eyes were gradually fading. Yes, there was no doubt about it, she was becoming a woman. A woman who could see things clearly and weigh the right course to take. And why shouldn't she be? In the past months she'd seen her mother captured, escaped from the British, served on the front, and seen a boy — no, a man — die. She'd been kidnapped by pirates, thrown in prison, and, most important of all, had fallen in love, really and passionately in love. Yes, she was a woman.

Thoughtfully, she walked to the window. She gazed unseeingly upon the live oaks and the bay, thinking about Geoffrey and Paul. She knew now that she would stand up to her father, no matter what the consequences, and make up her own mind as to her future. No marriage contract could bind her. She intended to go slowly, though, and not let her emotions rule over reason.

As she dressed, she thought of her mission at Grand Terre. If she were successful, the pirates would become respectable citizens, and that would mean Geoffrey could come to New Orleans anytime he wanted. Like Paul, Geoffrey could take her promenading or to fancy balls. It would make her choice easier if she could see the two men in the same environment.

Looking at her image, she buttoned her collar. As she did so, the black dress became transformed into a white muslin gown she had worn at her first ball last summer with Paul. The masked fete, on April 30, 1813, was held in commemoration of Louisiana's first full year as a state. It was a special evening. Not only was it her first ball, but it was the evening Paul had saved her life.

Flags, with their eighteen stars and eighteen stripes, were draped throughout St. Philip's Theatre. How elegant the ballroom had been with the thousands of tiny candles illuminating the parquet flooring that had been drawn over the auditorium for dancing. She lifted her black skirt and twirled about in a wide waltz step, pretending she was once more in Paul's arms. Her heavy dress was a far cry from the gossamer sleeveless gown she had worn at the ball. She had felt so beautiful with her heavy curls, done in the classical style, piled high in front and tied with a blue ribbon, allowing the rest of her hair to cascade down her back. The blue accessories brought out her azure eyes. Someday, she hoped Geoffrey would be able to see her in that elegant white dress. How good it had felt when it swished softly about her legs, and how nicely the ribbon about her middle emphasized her tiny waist. She wore a blue cameo on a narrow ribbon around her neck, and on her upper arm was her mother's gold bracelet. Her feet were shod in scarlet sandals with thongs that laced around her ankle almost to her knees. Her turquoise eyemask matched her fan, and she remembered how nervously she had fluttered it in anticipation of meeting New Orleans society.

Paul, a calming influence for her excitement, had appeared bold and gallant in his dark navy uniform with brass buttons that caught the candlelight. How proud she had been of her tall blond escort, deeply tanned from the sun on the sea. What fun it had been to ride off in the carriage with Paul. Naturally, her parents followed close behind in their rig.

She twirled about once more in a graceful circle, reliving that shimmering, heavenly evening. Paul was a marvelous dancer with the natural grace of an athlete. When he swept her around the dance floor, she heard their names admiringly repeated several times. One remark she had overheard was "What a strikingly handsome couple they are."

The exhilaration of the evening and the fun of the dance had soon overcome her trepidation. Chivalrous Paul, always attentive and the gentleman, made certain her entire dance card was written in. She hadn't missed a dance.

When the ball was over, she had gone outside to wait for Paul, who had turned to get their carriage. While she was chatting with her mother, she heard screams, and people rushed to empty the street. She had jerked her head around and was thunderstruck. There, charging down upon her, were a pair of runaway horses. For a moment, she couldn't even scream. It was as if her feet were rooted to the wooden planks.

In an instant, Paul had spun about, racing alongside the frightened, careening horses and, with a lunge, had seized the bridle and managed to clamber on their backs.

Danielle, finally able to move, wheeled

about and found the theater entrance jammed with people, making it impossible to get out of the way.

Paul, pulling sharply on the reins, at last brought the terrified horses to a standstill, inches from her frozen body. The wondrous evening could have ended in tragedy. She owed Paul her life. She knew, however, that a marriage shouldn't be built on gratitude alone, and it was to his credit that he never mentioned the episode in order to hear her say, "Yes, I'll marry you."

He was special, but more and more she was beginning to believe that a marriage should be built on a racing heart, the way she felt about Geoffrey.

Lupé opened the door, and for a startled moment, Danielle had forgotten she was still on Grand Terre. In a flash, she remembered all too clearly the night before and again saw Lupé in her white wrapper and turban. Today, however, the spare woman appeared as taciturn as always.

"Lupé," she said evenly, trying not to betray her discomfort, "I know I'm late."

"Yes, they wait breakfast for you," Lupé said reproachfully. Her eye, with its mocking light, pierced Danielle, almost as if trying to observe how the aristocratic Creole miss had withstood the previous night.

Danielle, aware of her scrutiny, smiled pleasantly and said, "I'll be right there, Lupé." She would not show the abject terror the woman had caused her last night.

Before going downstairs, Danielle looked one last time in the mirror, pinched her cheeks, giving them a pink glow, and was ready for her last day on Grand Terre.

The morning went fast, for while Geoffrey readied a small sailboat so that they could take a turn around the island, she went into the library.

She was examining a miniature likeness of the *New Orleans,* a steamboat that had been built four years before. She remembered seeing the boat for the first time on the Mississippi. The chimneys had belched black smoke and sparks, and she had backed away from the bank. Now, however, the boat merely intrigued her.

"She's not as beautiful as a sloop, is she?" Jean Lafitte had entered quietly and come beside her to pick up his model. "It might not have the grace, but this snub-nosed steamer can go at least ten miles an hour against the current. Remarkable, isn't it?"

"It is," she responded. "I've heard what wonderful service there is on these steamers and about the long waiting list for the trip between here and Pittsburgh." She continued to study the two paddle wheels and the upper and lower decks. "They even serve 'tea with meats' plus three regular meals. Think of the sights you'd see. Someday soon I hope to see what the northeastern states are like."

"I think you'd find it fascinating," he said. "You would find excitement no matter where you travel, Danielle," and he gave her a fleeting smile.

She was pleased that Jean Lafitte thought so highly of her. She'd had no idea of his opinion because he was a strangely quiet man.

He turned back to the steamboat. "You even take an interest in my models. Very few do on this island," he added dryly.

"Why wouldn't I? These little ships are works of art." She, too, studied the boat. Compliments did not trip lightly off either of their tongues. "I've heard," she said, "that the steam and engine noise are major complaints on steamboat trips. I don't think it would bother me."

"I'm sure it wouldn't. By the time you take a trip east, I think they will have smoothed out a lot of the discomforts." He moved the paddle wheel around. "It won't be long before you can set your watch by the boat docking at each port along the Mississippi and the Ohio."

He settled himself in the leather chair and observed her. "Well, Danielle, what is your verdict? Do the Baratarians pass the test for citizenship?"

She left the model and sat across from him. "Yes, you pass the test." She smiled at his sober face. It was nice to think he wanted her views, but she wondered if she would actually be listened to back in New Orleans. Nonetheless, she proceeded with her explanation. "I've been treated fairly, except for Gambi and Dominique's kidnapping, and I've seen no slaving or smuggling or any of the things my father was so upset about." She cleared her throat nervously. "But, please, Jean Lafitte, don't expect miracles. My father is a man whose mind is hard to change once it's made up. Grand Terre is a lovely island, and I think you've made it a good place to live."

Jean Lafitte, his brown eyes boring into her, said nothing.

His penetrating eyes unnerved her, and she jumped up. "I almost forgot. Geoffrey is taking me for a sail around the island."

Jean Lafitte, too, rose. "I couldn't ask for a better ambassador. Just report what you've seen. By the way," he said, chuckling, "I doubt if you'll make it all the way around the island. Have a good time." He turned away in dismissal.

She traced a circle on the desk, reluctant to leave. Finally she said, "I must admit I'm ready to go home. I'm concerned about my mother and father. My mother was captured before Christmas, and I haven't seen my father since just before the battle."

A bit of his coldness returned, and she knew she shouldn't have broached the subject.

"You can be sure the Verlaines will be given special treatment, and I imagine your mother is in New Orleans right now, at your aunt's. Your father is, no doubt, with Governor Claiborne, telling him why we Baratarians don't deserve citizenship. Is he as stubborn with you as with other people?"

She wanted to retort sharply but decided to give him a reasonable answer. She thought of the marriage contract with Paul and her father's obstinate refusal to listen to her, but she wouldn't condemn him before Jean Lafitte. "At times," was all she said.

"That's too bad. You're a high-spirited girl and deserve better treatment." His smile returned. "You must frustrate him when he tries to tame you."

She laughed aloud at this, and they were both back on the easy footing on which they had been before. "Yes," she admitted, "I've seen Father angry more than once, and I've given him plenty of reason to be." She sobered. "But he is a man of principle, and I wouldn't try to fool him."

Lafitte's lips twitched in amusement. "Never would I fool Captain Verlaine. He's someone I haven't been able to win over, no matter what I do." He gazed past her at one of his wall maps. "And I imagine it will be men like your father who will eventually drive me out of New Orleans."

"I hope not," she said impulsively, doubting if anyone could force Jean Lafitte away from his island.

He grinned. "If only your father were as accepting as you are."

She wanted to tell him that her father was probably one of the most accepting men in all New Orleans when it came to fair play, but he wouldn't stand for wrongdoing or slaving. Anyone who practiced, or who had once practiced, those things didn't have much chance of redeeming himself.

"I thought I'd find you here," Geoffrey said, arriving at the doorway and smiling. "Are you ready for our sail?"

She saluted. "Aye, aye, sir."

"Run along, both of you." Jean Lafitte paused over his account book. "Danielle, early tomorrow we'll return you to your aunt's home."

"I'll be ready," she said. On the way to the boat, she reflected on her two-and-a-half days on Grand Terre. The time had been filled with adventure, and the only reason she wanted to leave the island was to see Aunt Madeline, her father, and hopefully her mother! To embrace each one of them would be sweet, indeed. And Paul, too. However, when Geoffrey slipped his hand into hers, she forgot about Paul. She was gloriously happy.

They sailed the two-masted sailboat several miles around the island's west coast and back again. The chill day, the salt spray, and pale sun against her face with Geoffrey at her side had been exhilarating. Danielle viewed the return to the compound with mixed feelings, for it meant that in a short while she would be going home.

The wonderful day came to a close under the stars. She and Geoffrey sat beneath the three oaks with his arm casually draped around her shoulders. The comfort of his arms and his closeness reminded her that this was her last night on Grand Terre. Together, they watched the swift-moving clouds obscure the silver moon every few moments.

"I'm going to miss you, Danielle," Geoffrey said, running his forefinger along her cheek and over her lips.

She glowed at his touch and looked at him. "Will you come to Cypress Manor?" she asked, studying every angle of his handsome face and wondering when she would see him again.

He grinned. "You won't be able to keep me away. That is, if your father won't bar my way with his saber."

"When you become a citizen, things will change, you'll see," she said with more confidence than she felt. Old prejudices against the pirates might change for most New Orleanians, but she'd be surprised if her father would change. Here it was the nineteenth century, and still he considered marriage contracts binding. Why, oh, why did he have such control over her life? She would never be free! The memory of herself as a small child came back to her. She had caught a chameleon and put it in a box. The small green lizard had constantly skittered around the box's side, trying to find a way out. She had finally let it go free. She smiled ruefully. Now she was the one who was hopelessly trapped, but there was no one to let her escape.

A pirate came running toward them. "Geoffrey! Your uncle wants you right away. Captain Ronsard has docked, and the cargo inventory needs to be checked." With a wave, he disappeared, going toward the beach.

Geoffrey groaned softly. "I don't want to leave you, darling Danielle. Not on your last night here." He hit his knee with his fist. "Checking an inventory list takes hours." He looked at her and leaned toward her, softening. "I just want to stay here with you . . . forever."

Her heart raced, but she responded sensibly. "You go ahead, Geoffrey. Jean Lafitte won't be put off." Inside, she, too, felt a pang of frustration. She, too, wanted Geoffrey by her side on this magic night. Her throat constricted, and she could barely get the words out. "There will be other times."

With a lithe movement, he rose to his feet and pulled her up with him. "You're right, Danielle. There will be other times." He entangled his fingers in her hair and pulled her toward him, kissing her. "And soon, I hope. You're my love, my pirate queen." He stepped back. "Are you coming to the house with me?"

"Not just yet, Geoffrey," she said with a tremor in her voice. "I want to stay for a while longer, alone with the moon and stars." She paused, gazing at him with open admiration. He appeared like a dazzling Greek god. "Alone, with my thoughts of you, Geoffrey Lafitte."

Pleased, he grinned, showing his even, white teeth. With his bold stance, he did look like a Greek god . . . Apollo, she thought.

"I'll see you in the morning, then." He touched his lips and held out his hand toward her. Then, abruptly, he wheeled about and strode in the direction of the great white house.

Sinking back down, Danielle sat with her back against the tree trunk and observed a star that sparkled more than the others, and made a wish. "I hope that each and every pirate, except Gambi," she whispered, "becomes a citizen." If her wish came true, Geoffrey would meet her father, and the two of them would become fast friends. It could happen. The war had changed many things. She had come to realize that life was too precious to waste on custom, and settled convention. She didn't intend to stay at home and have babies and do needlepoint for the rest of her life. If Geoffrey wanted her to go with him, she would be his fearless companion.

She knew pirates' lives were filled with danger, especially when they raided Spanish ships, but she could handle it. She could handle anything with Geoffrey at her side. She could almost hear her heart pound at the shining adventure before her. She was ready to throw off all restraints and to leave New Orleans in order to see the world. Hadn't Father broken the Creole tradition when he married an Englishwoman? He never mentioned that fact when he discussed her destiny with Paul. It was time she was given the same free choice that he had made.

She didn't know how long she dreamed of her future, but she suddenly realized that all was quiet, except for the murmur of voices. Two men were talking, and as they neared, she froze, sweat breaking out on her forehead, for she could identify one of the voices as Gambi's. She stiffened her back against the rough bark and listened.

"Jean Lafitte isn't fit to lead us anymore. He ain't no pirate chief. He's trying to become a New Orleans gentleman," sneered Gambi.

The other man's muffled response was unintelligible.

"Me?" boasted Gambi. "I'm a pirate. A bloodthirsty pirate and not ashamed to admit it. I've murdered enough men to fill a graveyard." He paused. "Cut-Nose, I have a proposition for you."

"Well?" Cut-Nose prodded.

"I'll organize my own pirate band on my own island. We'll have our own fleet and sell slaves. We'll be rich men within six months. What do you say, Cut-Nose? Are you with me?"

"Aye," growled his companion. "Did you see what he did last night with my share of the gold? He gave it to my wife, and to make sure I couldn't take it away from her, he's having Toma, the blacksmith, mold it into a thimble." He slapped his hands together emphatically. "Aye, old Cut-Nose is with you. Jean Lafitte will learn Cut-Nose don't forget insults." He repeated, "I'm with you, Gambi."

Gambi laughed softly. "Our first chest of gold will come from our first prisoner, Miss Danielle Verlaine. Jean Lafitte won't hold her for ransom, but he'll find Gambi ain't so squeamish."

"Huh?" grunted Cut-Nose.

"Don't you see?" Gambi asked. "We'll take her after midnight when everyone's asleep. We'll bind and gag her, and no one will even know she's missing until morning when they go to return her to her father." He laughed again, and a chill went down her spine. "Captain Verlaine will blame Jean Lafitte and come after him with the militia. We'll take Danielle to Petit Terre. I've talked to Dominique and Beluche, and they've vowed to join us. We'll rival the best of Jean Lafitte's fleet. Smuggling. Slaving. Raids on any ships, even Americans. We'll own the Caribbean Sea. Not only that, Cut-Nose, but we'll take our prize and sail to Petit Terre in the *Pride*." He snorted. "Can't you just see Jean Lafitte's face when he realizes his ship, the girl, and some of his men are gone?" He hesitated, as if wondering if he should tell Cut-Nose. At last he blurted, "I've got a treasure that will buy us two of the finest ships on the Atlantic." Danielle dug her hands into the sandy soil. The Verlaine cameos. So he didn't know they were missing yet.

A sudden wind erupted, bending the

branches and rustling the leaves. The quick gust stirred Danielle, and her heart trembled with the breeze. Gambi was going to capture her and take her to his own island. He was actually leading a mutiny against Jean Lafitte!

Well, she had no intention of sitting there and letting Gambi hunt her down. She stole a look toward the house, and caught a glimpse of the light in the library. Geoffrey and his uncle were so near and yet there was no way to skirt around the two pirates and warn Lafitte of Gambi's plot. Desperately, she cast about for a plan to escape. The bay was to her side, the swamp ahead.

Chapter Eighteen

FOR once Danielle was glad to be wearing her inconspicuous black dress. She sat as motionless as possible, every once in a while peeking around the tree. The library light had long since gone out, and Gambi and Cut-Nose were going up the stairs to her bedroom.

However, she knew, once they discovered she wasn't in bed, they would come flying down the steps in a fury. They would scour the island and track her down like hounds after an opossum, if she didn't find a special hiding place. Whether she could remain safe until the first light might save her life, for then she would be able to reach Jean Lafitte and tell him everything. How great it would be to see Gambi clamped in irons! But the hours that she had to stay hidden stretched ahead interminably. She fervently hoped she could outwit them long enough to see daylight. Was she never to be rid of Gambi?

If she ran to the beach, the moonlight on the white sand would make it easy for them to spot her. She thought of the rowboats lined up on shore, but that would be one of the first places they would search. If she were found at the bottom of a boat, she would be hopelessly trapped without a chance to flee. She thought of pushing one of the heavy boats into the water and rowing away, but she dismissed that idea as suddenly as it had come into her mind. She could never outrow two burly pirates. If she could only transform the boats into horses! That would be a different story. On a swift mount, she could outrace and outdistance either one of them.

In the few seconds she had before they reappeared, she sped toward the swamp. It was her only chance of not being seen. True, there was only a small morass on Grand Terre, but it had all the treacherous pitfalls of the larger swamps around Cypress Manor.

As she ran toward the marsh, the two pirates came bursting out the door, taking the steps two at a time. As they ran in her direction, she gasped. Had they seen her? Gambi's next words reassured her.

"Cut-Nose, go back and wake Beluche and Dominique. We've got to find the witch before dawn."

"Aye, aye." Cut-Nose was off to do his new leader's bidding.

"I'm heading for the swamp," Gambi called after him.

Danielle frantically clawed at the giant ferns that ringed the swamp, pushing them aside. Once she had fought her way through, she followed the narrow lane. Cattails caught at her skirts, and her feet became mired in the spongy soil. She moved quickly, becoming further enmeshed in the swamp. She wondered where the path led, but she had to follow it, for to step off could mean sinking into the quagmire or drowning in the murky waters.

There was a thrashing behind her. Had Gambi discovered her trail already?

A bat came sweeping out of nowhere, flapping its wings low over her. She quickly lowered her head and covered her hair with her hands. "Keep away from me, bat," she whispered between clenched teeth, peeking out between her fingers. The broad wings could be heard beating on the heavy air as the bat made another pass, but it flew away when she ducked beneath a cypress tree.

When the moon went under a cloud, she stood very still in the total darkness, not daring to move. Finally, the moon reappeared, and she was able to glimpse her mysterious surroundings. She caught her breath at the silver fairyland of dripping moss and fallen trees that confronted her. Where in this swamp could she conceal herself so that Gambi couldn't find her? She ransacked her brains for a ruse but could think of nothing. The only thing to do was plunge ahead. She ran lightly along the path, deeper and deeper into the center of the swamp. A fallen cypress tree blocked her way, and she hurriedly examined the half-submerged tree, its abundant leaves providing a good cover. This might be the perfect hiding place. The trunk was grotesquely twisted with its branches reaching out across the shadowy black surface. If she climbed along the wide trunk, no one could see between the rows of dripping moss that cascaded down from the upper branches.

The silence was shattered by a snapping twig. Gambi was close behind! Without a moment's hesitation, she climbed up on the broken tree and crept along the trunk until she was above the water. The Spanish moss engulfed her like mosquito netting. She was well hidden, at least for the time being.

Lying flat along the trunk, she was almost afraid to look through the lacy network that enclosed her like a shroud. Surely Gambi must hear her heart, which pulsated in her ears. The pale light filtered through the leaves and shone on a thick spiderweb. She shuddered and hoped the hairy spider that lived in its depths wouldn't crawl out.

"Gambi!" yelled Cut-Nose. "Where are you?"

"Over here — to the left of the path."

Not daring to shift position, she heard Cut-Nose's loud gasps for air. "Wait," he panted. "I need to catch my breath."

"We don't have time to rest here all night. Do you want to catch the girl or don't you?"

"All right, all right. Lead on," Cut-Nose groused. "Have you seen any sign of her?"

"Not yet," Gambi snapped. "But she can't have run far. Where's Beluche and Dominique?"

"Searching the beach. Beluche is keeping an eye on the house so that she can't double back and reach Lafitte."

Gambi spat. "They're wasting their time. I know where she is."

Shaking, Danielle hugged the trunk and wished she could become part of the bark. Was he coming up after her now?

"But let 'em search," Gambi said. "See this?"

She strained to see through the thick branches, but it was too dismal.

"It's a fresh-broken branch," crowed Gambi. "She went this way, all right, and when I get my hands on her scrawny throat, she'll wish she hadn't run away!" All at once he cupped his hands to his mouth and shouted, "Danielle! Danielle Verlaine! I know you're in the swamp and close to me!"

If you only knew how close I am, she thought.

Gambi continued to warn her. "We're coming in after you. If you come out," Gambi wheedled, "we'll show you some gold and give you part of it." Then his tone became threatening. "But if we have to find your hiding place, you'll get the beating of your life."

Danielle didn't take a breath.

"This way," Gambi ordered, clambering over the fallen tree stump directly at the foot of where she lay. *Oh, God, don't let them see me,* she prayed to herself.

Once she heard them on the path beyond the tree, she took a deep gulp of air. That was a close call. She continued to remain on the wide tree trunk, cautiously moving her cramped muscles. Suddenly, there was a splash beneath her. Peering through the gloom, she could make out the dark snout of an alligator, and watched as the leathery reptile glided to the opposite bank.

Once the two men had rushed off through the undergrowth, she wiped the cold perspiration from her forehead. She must think fast. It wouldn't take them long to traverse the small swamp, for it wasn't more than the length and breadth of a sugarcane field.

She pressed her fist against her mouth. When the men returned and again passed over this fallen tree, she was certain they would study it and realize what a fine hiding place the branches were. They must know she couldn't get off the path and wade into the water, so they would be able to figure out that she was either hiding in the oyster grass along the side of the path or someplace up in a tree.

On hands and knees, she carefully crept

backward to seek a new hideaway. With every movement, she was terrified they would hear her or that she would brush against a deadly water moccasin or some other snake.

She dare not go back to the house, for Beluche was watching. Perhaps she should head in that direction and hide in the ferns until daylight. In this way, she could watch the house, and if Beluche left, she'd make a run for it.

The hoot of a night owl startled her and she spun about. Two unblinking yellow eyes peered down upon her. Another creature rustled in the fronds and she half-turned. Was it an alligator? Her pulse quickened. She began to run blindly until she came to a fork in the path. Which way to go? Suddenly, the moon went behind a cloud, and the darkness descended over her like a mantle. She walked first one way and then another. Her throat closed. She was lost. She didn't know how to get out of this terrible bog. She hadn't remembered a fork in the path before. She ran more swiftly. Surely she could find her way out if she followed her intuition. Where were Gambi and Cut-Nose? Were they near? Another crackling in the brush caused her heart to almost stop and her lips to quiver. She couldn't get caught. Not now. Not when it would soon be morning! The path narrowed, and the undergrowth became more and more tangled. She had to sweep away hanging moss and vines from her face.

The moon reemerged, outlining the sunken

oaks against the gray sky. On one side of the lane, the water was shiny and black, while on the other it was thick with algae. The heavy, smooth, green surface looked solid enough to walk across, but she knew better than to touch that moving silent mass of living growth. She was breathing hard but determined to go forward. She stumbled and almost fell, but in trying to keep herself upright, her foot slipped off the path. She screamed with horror as she felt her foot being sucked into the quagmire. Down and down her foot was pulled, dragging her into the deadly pit. Quicksand! A sob tore from her throat. Was this to be the end? Unbalanced, she had been dragged in and was up to her knees in the liquid, thick, pulling sand. Trailing vines above her head were tantalizingly close overhead.

With a gigantic lunge, she firmly grabbed a vine and, with more strength than she knew she possessed, hauled herself hand over hand back onto the path. Her shoes were missing, but she was safe. She sprawled, gasping for breath, but knew she couldn't rest long. She must go on!

After what seemed like hours of running, she came to a small clearing. Exhausted, she sank down against a tree. Had Gambi and Cut-Nose given up? Unlikely. Squinting through the leaves, she saw the glimmering of pink streaks in the sky. Dawn. There was still hope of finding a way out and of reaching Jean Lafitte. She glanced around the clearing. She'd seen this bend in the path before, she was positive. Had she been going in circles? She'd never get out of this maze. She was hopelessly lost, and Lafitte's house, probably only yards away, might as well be on the next island. She shut her eyes briefly and felt the silence.

She knew she couldn't sit any longer. Wearily, she put her hand on a tree root to rise when, to her horror, it became alive in her hand. She snatched her fingers back and stared in terror as a water moccasin slithered off into the marsh. Stifling a scream, she leaped to her feet and bolted in the opposite direction. How close she had come to being bitten by a poisonous snake! Her heart pounded at the thought, but she kept running. This time the crackling behind her was unmistakable. The breaking branches and the swearing men sounded only a few feet away.

She moved swiftly and silently now, more determined than ever to elude her pursuers. When she came to the fallen tree across her path, her heart leaped with hope. She was heading in the right direction. Everything was in gray shadows, and she could dimly make out leaves, water, and alligator grass. Dawn was breaking.

Swiftly, she scrambled over the tree. Her dress caught on a branch, and in her frantic haste to wrest it free, the material ripped and part of her black dress was left behind.

When she glanced around, she almost collapsed, for she caught sight of Gambi's red shirt!

"Cut-Nose. Look! A piece of her dress. Hurry up before she gets out of the swamp," Gambi said excitedly.

"I'm coming, but I just ran a sliver under my nail," Cut-Nose said querulously.

"Forget it and run!" Gambi barked.

Danielle hurried on as fast as she could. *Please*, she thought, *don't let them catch me now*. She could see the beach and Jean Lafitte's house in the distance. She called on every ounce of strength. With a burst of energy, she ran even harder. The trembling leaves and crackling branches, directly upon her heels, reverberated in her ears.

Suddenly, her arm was grabbed and her heart sank. To think she had been so close to Jean Lafitte and safety.

"I've got her, Cut-Nose," Gambi crowed. "I've got her!"

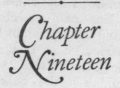

Chapter Nineteen

SHE tried to wrench free, but Gambi's fist had closed on her arm like an iron vise.

"At last we have the vixen!" Gambi heaved a sigh of relief. His greedy eyes glittered.

She turned her head from his sour breath and matted beard. Again she tried to pull free and at the same time yelled, "Help! Help!" Immediately, Gambi's big hand clamped over her mouth.

"Don't be too rough with her," Cut-Nose warned. "She's worth more alive than dead."

"She'll be alive when we toss her back to Captain Verlaine." Gambi snickered. "Barely alive." Whipping off his bandanna, he gagged her and shoved her along the path in front of them.

Although the scarlet, round sun would soon become golden rays, it was bright enough to see each of the cottages. At this early hour, no one was awake. Danielle was dragged swiftly along the beach to the boats.

She dug in her heels, and Gambi gave her a rough prod.

Beluche was waiting in the rowboat, and she was thrust into his outstretched hands. The boat lurched, and so did her heart. She had lost the deadly game of hide-and-seek.

"Where's Dominique?" growled Gambi.

"He said he wanted no part of our plan, that Danielle had been kidnapped once and Lafitte had given his word to return her." Beluche scratched his head. "He won't leave Grande Terre."

"Fine. Let him stay here and rot. Dominique always was yellow-livered." Gambi's big fists bunched and opened.

"Let's get out of here," Beluche urged.

"Aye, set the oarlocks and I'll be back in five minutes."

"Five minutes," whined Cut-Nose. "Someone will see us."

"No one will see us. Besides, I'm going after a treasure that will set us up on Petit Terre." Gambi turned to leave.

Danielle knew he was going to dig up the cameos, and dreaded his reaction after he discovered they were missing. There would be a thundering scene.

Beluche eyed her suspiciously. She lowered her lashes, not wanting to antagonize him. She was drained and bone-tired, but her brain was alert. She wished he would remove the gag. Her throat was dry, and the bandanna prevented her from swallowing properly.

Gambi returned, taking running strides. He pushed the boat off the sandbar and jumped aboard. "Start rowing!" he commanded. Before he sat, he glared at Danielle, reached over, and gave her a backhand slap across the face. "Where are the cameos?" he said between clenched teeth.

She felt her cheeks flaming. Tears welled in her eyes, but she only stared defiantly into Gambi's furious eyes.

Grunting, Gambi tore off the gag. "Well?" he stormed. "Where are they?"

She moved her jaw back and forth and swallowed, stalling for time.

Gambi repeated loudly, "Where are the cameos?"

"I don't know," she lied. "Remember? Dominique knew where they were, too."

"Dominique would never double-cross me." His laugh rumbled deep in his throat. "He knows what would happen to him if he tried!" But Danielle noticed his voice had a doubting, violent edge.

Beluche and Cut-Nose didn't talk. They only bent to the oars in a fast, efficient rhythm.

"Who did you blab to?" She flinched at Gambi's menacing glower, afraid of being hit again.

"No one. No one." If he suspected her of

lying, there was no telling what he would do to her.

He rubbed his chin with a speculative look. "Dominique wouldn't dare . . . yet I wonder." Then he turned back to her, lashing out. "Your father will pay double the ransom for this, you witch."

When they reached the ship, they forced her to mount the boarding ladder to the upper deck while they followed close behind.

"Unfurl the sails," Gambi directed, "and set the compass for Petit Terre."

Danielle gazed dully at the blue, rolling sea. She should be on her way home instead of being captured by mutinous pirates. The mainsail, unfurled overhead, cracked and billowed in the wind.

"Hoist the anchor," roared Gambi. "We're on our way!"

"I don't think so," said Jean Lafitte, stepping forth from behind a cannon.

Gambi wheeled about, eyes popping and jaw dropping. Then, retrieving his senses, he lunged for Jean Lafitte, at the same time yelling, "Beluche, Cut-Nose!"

Danielle's eyes widened as all at once, pirates tumbled out from every hiding place on the ship: belowdecks, the cabin, rowboats, and from behind coils of rope. They charged the rebel pirates with yells and brandishing sabers. Quickly they surrounded the mutineers.

Gambi's head moved from side to side like a bear's.

"Drop your weapons," Jean Lafitte rapped.

The three men grudgingly let their pistols and knives clatter to the deck.

"You rebel scum should all be hanged from the yardarm, but I'm going to be generous and give you a second chance." Lafitte looked bitterly at the ringleader. "You've been against me for years, Gambi, always creating dissension whenever you could. Well, this time you won't get off so lightly. This time I'm going to be rid of you for good."

Gambi sullenly stared at the deck, but there was nothing he could say in his defense.

Jean Lafitte motioned to his men to escort them to the rail, not so much as casting a glance at Cut-Nose or Beluche, whose heads also hung low and shoulders sagged.

Lafitte leaned against the rail on his elbows. "You wanted to set up a stronghold on Petit Terre? I will help you get there. There's the rowboat." He jerked his head at the bobbing little boat below. "Not exactly the ship you meant to sail in, eh?"

Dominique came forward, confronting Gambi. "You manhandled Danielle once too often, and went against Jean Lafitte. I had no choice but to turn you in."

As Gambi climbed down the ladder, he shot Dominique a look of hatred, snarling, "I'll come back and get you for this."

"If ever," Jean Lafitte said in measured tones, "you dare to come back to Grand Terre, there will be a reward for the man who turns you in, and this time I'll personally see to it that you walk the plank!"

With a growl, Gambi was gone. Danielle watched as he swung down the ladder. Was she done with him at last? She rubbed her cheek where he had slapped her, and took a deep breath of relief.

Geoffrey hurried to her side. "Thank God you're all right," he said. His eyes were warm with concern. "If Gambi had escaped, we might never have gotten you back." He ran his hand through his thick curls. "Gambi has a reputation for holding prisoners for ransom, and once the money is paid, he kills them." His eyes narrowed and his chin jutted out. "I'm glad he's off Grand Terre. He's been against Uncle Jean as long as I can remember."

She smiled tremulously, delighted with Geoffrey's obvious caring.

Jean Lafitte walked over to them and casually dropped a hand on Danielle's shoulder. "You're fortunate that Dominique took a liking to you, my dear. It was while you were in the guardhouse that he developed an admiration for you. . . . So, you see, your stay in the guardhouse wasn't all bad." His half-mocking smile disappeared, and his expression became serious. "I'm relieved we can take you back to New Orleans as we planned." He gave her a gentle pat on the shoulder. "Are you ready to return?"

"Oh, yes," she said in a low voice. How

quickly her future had been changed. From being at the mercy of Gambi, who loathed her, to going home with Geoffrey, who loved her.

"Come," Jean Lafitte said kindly, taking her arm. "A ketch is waiting to take you back."

She nodded, her heart too full to say anything. Everything had happened too fast.

Later, before she boarded the two-masted ship with the bright red wingsail, she turned to Dominique. "Without your help, I wouldn't be going home now." She held out her hand to the grizzle-faced pirate.

He hunched his shoulders and gave an embarrassed laugh. "You were a brave girl. I took a liking to you."

"You know something, Dominique? I like you, too. You helped me when I needed it the most."

"Good-bye, Danielle." Dominique waved and cast a knowing look from her to Geoffrey. "I think you'll be back for a visit before too long."

She, too, looked at Geoffrey, smiling. "Perhaps you're right, Dominique."

Geoffrey tucked the box of cameos under the boat's seat. "These are Danielle's peasant clothes," he explained, looking directly at Pierre, who merely shrugged.

Danielle saw the precious box and heaved a sigh. She wouldn't be going home empty-handed.

Sailing on the ketch with Geoffrey and

Pierre Lafitte, she was content, feeling the cool salt breeze blow against her skin.

"Are you happy to be going home?" Geoffrey asked.

"Yes," she said, gazing at him wistfully. "But sorry to be leaving you."

"We'll see each other very soon, I promise you. You can't escape me that easily." His eyes danced. "The next time I come to New Orleans, I'll call on you at Cypress Manor."

When they reached the docks of New Orleans, her anticipation heightened. She would soon see her mother and father. She wanted to leap out of the boat and fly to them, but there was nothing to do but curb her impatience.

Pierre, who hadn't said much the entire trip, allowing her and Geoffrey to talk, now spoke. "I'll stay with the boat, Geoffrey. Maybe I'll find a food stand along the docks and eat me some shrimp jambalaya. You come back before dark, Geoffrey." His crossed eyes were serious.

Geoffrey agreed, raised his hand, and dashed off with Danielle to find a carriage to take them to Rampart Street.

The sun was low in the sky when they reached Aunt Madeline's, and Geoffrey took hold of the cord on the bell. The clapper resounded. Geoffrey, with the cameo box tucked under his arm, glanced at her to catch her reaction.

Danielle stood with her fingers over her mouth. Who would answer?

The door flew open, and her father held out his arms, embracing her. "Danielle, Danielle! How we worried." A final hug, and he swung her about, beaming. "Look who's with us again! Danielle!"

Her mother, bathed in sunlight, stood by the window, her blond hair turning to gold. Danielle opened her mouth, but no sound came out. Tears coursed down her cheeks as they ran into each other's arms. Danielle clung to her and they kissed, her tears mingling with her mother's. Captain Verlaine joined them, and the three family members held each other for a long moment. Finally, tearfully, they broke away.

Aunt Madeline, waiting patiently, eyes shining, hugged her niece in turn. "Welcome back, chérie."

Danielle, still clinging to her aunt, half-turned. Laughing, then crying, she indicated her buccaneer escort. "This is Geoffrey Lafitte, Jean Lafitte's nephew. This is my mother, Adelaide Verlaine."

Geoffrey stepped forward and kissed her hand. "My pleasure, madame. Now I understand why Danielle is such a beauty."

She acknowledged his graciousness with a half-amused smile playing about her lips.

"And here, madame, are the cameos," Geoffrey said simply, offering her the box. "They were stolen by the two kidnappers."

Adelaide uttered a sharp cry. "Antoine! Our treasure is back!"

"Bon, bon," he said, addressing Danielle.

"I'm glad you retrieved them for us, chérie. We may have to use them."

"You can thank Geoffrey Lafitte for digging them up," Danielle replied. She went to her father, tucking her arm through his, and proudly said, "Geoffrey, meet my father, whom you've heard so much about." Her eyes twinkled at Geoffrey. "Meet Captain Antoine Verlaine."

"Sir, it's a pleasure." Eagerly, Geoffrey held out his hand.

For a moment, Antoine stared disdainfully at this young pirate.

With dismay, Danielle said, "Geoffrey helped me throughout my stay on Grand Terre and has brought me back."

Captain Verlaine reluctantly shook hands. "Geoffrey Lafitte," he acknowledged coldly. "Anything you've done for my daughter, I appreciate. Will you have a glass of wine with us?" It was obvious he wanted to keep this a close family reunion and not share it with an outsider — especially a Lafitte.

Geoffrey glanced at the dining room in the background, which was set with china and silver, and then looked back at Antoine's rigid stance. "I'll not stay," he said pleasantly. "Uncle Pierre waits for me on the ketch, but thank you, sir."

Antoine's brows beetled. "The pirate who broke out of prison?" He nodded as if that was all you could expect from a Lafitte. To break the law. To escape prison. To smuggle. He eyed Geoffrey with distaste.

"Sir," Geoffrey continued with his usual charm, "if I could return at a later date for that glass of wine and pay a formal call on your daughter, this I would consider as the greatest of favors." He smiled into Antoine's frowning face.

Antoine observed him without a word.

The awkward pause was broken when Madeline said quickly, "I'll bring in the wine." She hurried from the room.

Adelaide, in a shimmering green gown, tilted her head slightly and said sweetly, "Geoffrey, we would welcome you at Cypress Manor." She glanced at Danielle. "We should be back on our plantation by the end of the month."

"Thank you," Geoffrey said, again kissing Adelaide's hand. "Then it's good-bye. Your daughter was a cherished guest." With a meaningful look at Danielle, as if to say, "Soon, my darling, soon," he waved, opened the door, and was gone.

Her father's attitude would be hard to change, Danielle thought, eyeing him. Already his jovial smile had returned now that Geoffrey was gone. She would need to work out a strategy later to make him see how wonderful Geoffrey was. Now, however, all she wanted was to eat something and go to bed. She hadn't slept for twenty-four hours, and even though the happy reunion had sparked enough energy to talk to her family, she was tired enough to drop. At any rate, why was she surprised at her father's reaction to Geoffrey? She should have known he would bristle at the name Lafitte. Yet she had hoped her father would have softened toward her protector, even treating Geoffrey with respect and some warmth.

Madeline brought in the crystal goblets filled with sparkling burgundy.

As she lifted her glass to toast her family being together once again, she gazed fondly at each one of them. How she had yearned for this moment, yet the cool reception given Geoffrey had chipped away at her happy spirit.

That night, before Danielle went to sleep, her joy at being back wouldn't be dampened. Things would improve, she just knew it. Even her father would fall under Geoffrey's spell.

The next day, refreshed, she sat over breakfast, talking with her mother. Her father had left for a meeting, and Aunt Madeline had gone for an early-morning horseback ride with Captain Ellinger.

Danielle faced her mother. "Was it terrible?" she questioned gently. "Being a British prisoner, I mean."

"No, it wasn't terrible, but it wasn't the most pleasant experience, either." Her mother's expression was sad and a bit grim.

"I — I saw Colonel Thornton slap you, and when they tied you up, you don't know how much I wanted to run to you and help you."

Adelaide laid a hand over her daughter's.

"I knew what you were thinking, my darling, believe me. I was so afraid that you'd come charging down the stairs and attack the whole British regiment." Adelaide's eyes sparkled. "But thank heavens you didn't follow your usual daredevil ways. Fortunately, you kept a clear head and managed to escape to warn General Jackson." She wiped her mouth with her napkin and leaned back in her chair. "The British untied me that night, but I was their house prisoner. When the wounded began coming in, there was plenty to do. I couldn't keep up with the hundreds of men who were brought in every day." Her eyes had a faraway look. "I did what I could. The wounded were kept downstairs, and filled every inch of space. Outside, tents were pitched on the grounds." She gazed at her daughter with admiration. "But you helped, too, didn't you, dear? I heard you were at the front, tending the wounded just as competently as some of the more seasoned nurses. I'm so proud of you, Danielle. War is terrible, isn't it?"

Danielle thought of Christopher and the dazed British soldier. "Yes," she agreed. "War is awful. I was glad I could help, though. On the front, I met all kinds of people. One of them was Betsy Summers, an American who was such a great worker and had a great sense of humor. I want you to meet her someday soon."

"I'd like to," her mother replied.

"I had never really spent any time with

Americans before and found them warm, outgoing people." From beneath her lashes, she glanced at her mother and changed the subject, asking casually, "What did you think of Geoffrey Lafitte?"

Her mother, with a quick look, arched her brows. "He seems like a charming youth." She studied Danielle. "Maybe I should ask you the same question. What do *you* think of this young man?"

"I — I don't know," she stammered, gripping her hands together in her lap. "I'm confused, Mother." She jumped up from the table and moved to the window. "I only know I don't want a marriage contract hanging over my head like a sword. I know Paul is wonderful and comes from a good family, but —" She stopped, facing her mother, and threw out her hands in a helpless gesture. "Father won't listen to me. Once his mind is made up, I just can't talk to him. What am I to do?"

"You are not going to do anything," Adelaide said quietly. "You've just returned from Jean Lafitte's stronghold where I'm certain everything was all very exciting, including Geoffrey. I know he was attentive and you found yourself attracted to him."

If you only knew how much, Danielle thought.

Adelaide went on. "You have the Verlaine name and tradition to live up to. You mustn't be foolish or headstrong. Your father and I want only your happiness. That's our only wish for you. You'll have time to sort things out when we return to Cypress Manor." She rose and stood alongside Danielle, putting her arm around her shoulder. "Give your emotions time to settle down. Promise me you won't run away or refuse Paul without at least talking to me first."

Danielle hesitated. How could her mother read her thoughts? "I — I don't plan to run away," she answered halfheartedly.

"I'm sure you don't mean to do anything drastic, but . . ." she cautioned, giving Danielle's shoulder a small squeeze. "If a dashing pirate came sailing up the bayou to sweep you in his arms, you just might be taken in for a brief moment and throw away your father and me, Cypress Manor, and your future. Please don't ever do that."

Danielle stared out the window, her eyes glistening. She watched as Aunt Madeline and William rode up, dismounted, and kissed tenderly. She had found a love like that, too. She wouldn't lose it.

Her mother seemed to guess her inner turmoil about Geoffrey. "Will you promise that you'll talk to me first?" Adelaide repeated gently.

"I promise," she whispered, hoping by everything she held dear that she could keep that promise.

Chapter Twenty

THE next day when Danielle awakened, it was almost noon. Her sleep had been deep and dreamless. She felt happy and optimistic, remembering the plans her father had told her about over dinner. Tonight was the city's formal celebration of the victory over the British, and later there would be a dance. The Verlaines were invited to the gala to honor the hero of the day, Andrew Jackson.

The British should be leaving their camps south of New Orleans soon, and Danielle's family could then return to Cypress Manor. As she pulled her morning wrapper around her, she wondered what they would find on the plantation. Certainly, it would be hard work to put everything back in order, and she only hoped there wouldn't be too many things destroyed.

She was excited, for she was to meet Paul

at three o'clock that afternoon at the Napoleon House. He only had a few free hours, as he was involved with the military honor guard that night, but he would be her dance partner. She hadn't realized how much she had missed Paul and longed to see him.

After a leisurely lunch and chat with her mother and Aunt Madeline, she dressed. How gleefully she had thrown her black dress in the rag bag. And how luxurious it was to have a selection of a few dresses. She decided on a deep red gown trimmed with black collar, cuffs, and wide hem.

When she arrived at the Napoleon House, she bypassed the delightful courtyard with the outdoor tables, which were all empty because of the chill in the air, and went inside.

Her heart skipped several beats when she glimpsed Paul, who jumped to his feet and strode quickly to her side, taking her arm.

"How I missed you, Danielle," he said, his brown eyes shining with pleasure.

He looked broader and more mature, and she was a little taken aback at her reception, half expecting that he would sweep her into his arms and kiss her. Disappointed, she pouted prettily and gave him a sidelong glance. "Paul, don't I even rate a hug?"

His thick brows lifted. "Danielle Verlaine! A hug? In public? Where are your manners?" he asked mockingly. Then, with a laugh, he took her head in his hands and gave her a lingering kiss.

When they parted, she was breathless.

"Paul," was all she could murmur.

"I have a surprise for you," he said.

Her pulse had settled to a steady beat, and she joked, "A surprise? I don't need any more surprises than I've had in the past week."

"This is a surprise you'll enjoy." He held the door ajar for her, and they began to walk along Toulouse Street.

"You'll see," he added mysteriously. "It's not far. Tell me about your stay on Grand Terre," Paul said, searching her face for telltale signs of what had happened. "Was it bad?"

She told him about the Divvying-Out, the midnight ritual, her frightening pursuit in the swamp, and Gambi's subsequent capture by Jean Lafitte. However, she conveniently omitted the moonlight walks with Geoffrey, their boatride, and their long conversations.

"Are you still stationed on the *Louisiana*?" she asked.

He nodded. "I'll be on board until I take my examination and graduate next month. You know I'll be nineteen then, and that makes me eligible to become a first lieutenant. Commodore Patterson assures me I'll be up for a quick promotion because of the way I handled the artillery in the first salvos against the British. When I receive my rank, I may sign on with a frigate in the U.S. Navy in the Carribean Sea to wipe out pirates." He glanced her way. "If I do, I may be away for a long time."

She said nothing, nor did she dare look at

him. She was afraid he might offer the emerald ring again and expect her to wear it. But as they passed a garden, the memory of another day and what he said came back to her. He would never offer the ring unless she asked for it. That day when they had kissed in the garden was all too vivid. She had been afraid Paul had drowned when the *Carolina* had been sunk. When he turned up alive, they had talked a long time in a garden with the statue of King Louis XIV listening to them. Paul had wanted her to wear his ring on a chain, but she had refused. When he had asked if there was someone else, she remembered how her heart had almost stopped! She had been able to put him off by saying they would discuss it when things were back to normal. Well, the fighting was over. Should she tell him about Geoffrey? She glanced at his happy face and decided to inform him later. She mustn't delay too long, though. It wasn't fair to Paul or to Geoffrey.

She drew a deep breath. No, she needn't worry about Paul offering the ring. The memory of their conversation came back clearly.

She had said, "When I'm ready I'll ask for the ring."

Paul's rather abrupt reply had been, "Good. Because I won't offer it again." She had been surprised at that.

Now, as they wandered through the market, the stalls were being shuttered for the day. A food seller, taking down the long strings of garlic hung around his open stall, had yet to move the red-pepper plants inside. The strong odors permeated the air.

Nearing the city stables, she stopped and stood rooted. "Please. Tell me this is where you're taking me, Paul."

"You guessed." He laughed. "Yes, Ebony waits for you inside."

"What a wonderful surprise! Ebony!" She grasped Paul's arm. "Is he all right?"

"He's in perfect condition."

At these words, Danielle broke into a run with Paul racing after her.

She tore open the stable door, flying past the astonished stable boy, searching from one stall to the next.

Ebony, sleek with his black coat shining, was in the middle stall. She threw her arms around his neck and nuzzled his mane. "Ebony. I missed you so. Did they treat you well?"

The horse, ears pricked forward, danced and bobbed his head up and down.

Paul held the bit as Ebony stamped and snorted. "Is the excitement too much for you, old boy?" He looked from Ebony to Danielle. "The horse is cleared for you to take him riding whenever you desire."

"Oh, Paul. This is the best present you could have given me." She impulsively flung her arms around his neck and kissed him. "How can I thank you?" she asked jubilantly.

He kissed her in return. "I can't think of a better way than this."

She felt her face flush and, giving a small laugh, backed away and once again turned to Ebony. She ran her hand along his withers, haunches, and over his rump, examining him. Ebony had been well taken care of, and she wondered what part he had played in the battle.

"I'll be outside," Paul said. "I saw a praline vendor. I'll buy us a treat."

"I'll be out in a minute, Paul. I just have to be certain Ebony understands I'm coming back for him."

After Paul had left, she looked around for the stable boy. He was standing by a post loaded with hanging bridles. However, Danielle noticed he wasn't a boy. He was about thirty with a straw blade drooping from his mouth. His narrowed eyes were set in a wide, fleshy face, and he was studying her intently.

"Stablemaster," she addressed him diplomatically. "Could you tell me who rode this horse in the battle?"

"Sure can. Captain Wilson. He's with Jackson's Tennessee frontiersmen."

"It looks as if my stallion had good care," she said, smoothing Ebony's forelock.

"We give all our horses extra special care, just as if they were highborn ladies." He paused. "Like yourself."

Danielle gave him a sharp look and decided it was time to leave.

As she edged past him, she moved quickly to the door but not quickly enough.

He caught her around the waist. "Let me

help you up on your horse's back, young lady. He'd welcome that, I'm sure."

"I need to leave," she said, struggling to unclasp his hands.

"Danielle?" Paul entered the gloomy stable. When he saw them, he clapped a hand on the stableman's shoulder. "Let her go at once," he demanded coldly.

The man spun about. "You leave me alone!" His temper flared, and his face turned purple. "Keep your hands off me, pretty boy in your fancy uniform." He scooped up a handful of sawdust and threw it at Paul. "I was only helping the lady up on her horse."

Paul shoved him against a post. "Stop it!" His order was rapped out in the clearest of officer's tones. He turned to Danielle. "Is what he said true, Danielle?"

Not wanting a confrontation between the two, she said shakily, "Yes, Paul. He only wanted to hoist me up on Ebony. Please, can we leave?"

Paul, with slow, deliberate care, dusted off his blue jacket and white trousers, giving the stableman a contemptuous look. He turned and followed Danielle out the door.

Despite her words of assurance that the man had meant no harm, he had had his hands on her. She wondered why Paul hadn't knocked him flat, but she doubted if Paul was much of a fighter. Geoffrey, with his fiery temperament, would have taught that ugly stableman a lesson that he'd never forget.

However, she wouldn't allow the incident

to mar her pleasant day, and by the time they reached Aunt Madeline's, she realized Paul's positive attributes far outweighed any niggling little criticism she had of his fighting prowess.

That evening Danielle dressed for the ceremony and the ball, reflecting on her good fortune. She had been chosen, along with nineteen other young ladies, as the loveliest in all New Orleans to take part in the parade. She fastened the train to the shoulders of the Empire waistline dress, and even though the same white gown would be worn by all of the girls, it was still lovely.

As she picked up her fringed shawl, she heard the victory cannon booming. The military dress parade was about to begin, and she didn't want to miss being in her place. The girls would have a prime spot to see the sailors from the *Carolina*, the military, and General Jackson astride his charger march directly before them. Before leaving, she took one last instant to look in the mirror and twisted several ringlets on her forehead. As she moved her head, her jade drop earrings flashed, and she was not displeased with the picture she made.

Her father had already left for the parade, and later her mother and Aunt Madeline would go in style in Madeline's coach.

Danielle left early so she could be in her place by six o'clock. She arrived at the Place d'Armes and walked through the flower-festooned Arch of Triumph that was supported by six columns all entwined with garlands and ribbons. She passed two young girls, representing Liberty and Justice, who were taking their stations in front of the Corinthian columns.

Danielle found her place; all of the other girls were already there. She took her position between the two de la Ronde sisters. Their white dresses fluttered in the breeze, and Danielle adjusted the small blue veil that was fastened in her curls with silver stars.

The young girls stood on either side of the street leading up to St. Louis Cathedral. Behind each girl was a lance stuck in the ground with a large shield of every state or territory. Danielle's state was Massachusetts with the state motto —"By the sword we seek peace, but peace only under liberty"— across the shield. Flowers and evergreen boughs were scattered everywhere, even across the entire avenue, covering the path in which the honored victory fighters would march. The balconies and rooftops were alive with people.

Danielle held her banner high, emblazoned with the name "Massachusetts." In her other hand, she held a wicker basket of yellow daisies. The band struck up "The Star-Spangled Banner," and a thrill of pride surged through her, such as she'd never felt before. She was an American, and part of a young, wonderful country that was growing every day with a new national spirit.

The churchmen, resplendent in their white

brocade, gold-embroidered robes, stood on the cathedral steps to welcome Andrew Jackson, who had especially asked for this mass of thanksgiving.

At six-thirty, the navy men passed in review in their dress blues, and Danielle's banner wavered when she spotted Paul, so upright and with eyes straight ahead, marching to the cathedral. She held herself erect and dared not look in his direction any longer, for she, too, was on display.

Following the sailors were Jean Lafitte and Pierre, plus several pirates pulling a cannon; then came the frontiersmen, the black battalions, and the generals. Even the prancing horses wore plumes and flowers in their chinking bridles.

Cheer after cheer resounded as one colorful regiment followed another with a flag guard leading each group.

Suddenly there was an artillery burst, signifying the arrival of General Jackson, the darling of all New Orleans. A lusty cheer for Old Hickory was heard from every side as the tall general, looking neither to the right nor left, rode toward the steps of the cathedral.

Abbé Duborg, along with Madame Livingston, waited on the cathedral steps for the general. Once Jackson had dismounted, Madame Livingston stepped forth and, with words Danielle couldn't hear, placed a laurel wreath atop his head. The tall, craggy-faced general, somewhat flustered, soon removed the honored crown and advanced inside the church.

Danielle, with the nineteen girls, closed ranks and, singing a hymn of thanskgiving along with generals, soldiers, wives, and citizens, filed into the cathedral. She found her place in a cordoned front section of the nave and sat back, her heart beating to the thrill she felt at the inspiring pageantry around her.

When the service was ended, Paul found her and, together with a select group of prominent New Orleans citizens, walked to the French Exchange for supper and the ball. The building had been decked out with flowers, red and green lanterns, and flags from every regiment. Signs, too, were part of the colorful decorations. The large banner as they entered the lower floor, where the supper was being held, read:

JACKSON AND VICTORY: THEY ARE ONE!

Creole men and women freely mixed with Americans, and the banquet tables were long and filled to capacity. General Jackson, with his plump wife, were at the head of the table, and as soon as he sat down, waiter after waiter began to carry in huge silver salvers of varied dishes. In the center of the red-white-and-blue tablecloth was a large roast boar surrounded by mounds of fluffy rice. The silver lids were lifted from the trays, presenting an elegant display of river shrimp, crab gumbo, tomatoes and onions, small peahens, rich pastries, and long loaves

of French bread, still steaming from the
ovens. The table sparkled with Bohemian
crystal, bone china, and silver service; and
all along the white linen tablecloth were
bottles of bubbling champagne.

Danielle and Paul were seated across
from Aunt Madeline and Captain Ellinger.
Danielle waved at her mother and father,
who were seated next to the Claibornes and
close to General Jackson. She looked about
for Jean Lafitte and Pierre, and saw them
seated by General Morgan. Jean Lafitte was
talking to Madame Livingston, and her smile
was radiant as she conversed with the
handsome pirate.

Her aunt glowed in a wine dress with a
low, wide neckline and dainty puffed sleeves.
So, as a matter of fact, thought Danielle, did
William, in his dark blue coat with the
stand-up red collar that almost touched his
ears. The brass buttons and gold braid shone
in the candlelight, and William toasted
Madeline before he took his first taste of
champagne.

Danielle looked fondly at both of them
and said, "Paul, did you know we'll be attend-
ing a wedding next week?"

"I knew it was coming, but I didn't know
it would be quite this soon," he said.

William grinned, taking Madeline's hand.
"Yes, we see no reason to wait until June.
We'll have a small wedding next Sunday, if
General Jackson lifts the curfew. Tonight is
a special dispensation, but tomorrow he will

reimpose martial law, and I'll have to report to General Morgan again."

"Yes," Paul said. "And I must go back on the *Louisiana* to be on duty by ten A.M. I don't mind so much, but some of Jackson's Tennesseeans are hopping mad. They want to go home."

"Some of them already have," Captain Ellinger said dryly. "If caught, they could be hanged as deserters." He obviously didn't want to go against the general's orders, but he, too, seemed disgruntled with the curfew.

A Creole merchant, overhearing their conversation, leaned over and said, "This means that my goods must stay in the warehouse. There's no way to move them out. For two years, my merchandise has sat there because of the British blockade, waiting for the war to be over. Now that the war is over, my cotton must still sit there. Jackson is a hero tonight, but he'd better change his policy tomorrow, or he'll be a low-down dog." The merchant turned to a man at his left, who also bemoaned his wares that couldn't be shipped. The two men, lost in their own animated conversation, turned away from William.

Danielle, reaching for a large grape, nibbled on it and said, "Back to the wedding. We've talked a little about it, but Paul doesn't know that I'm going to be a bridesmaid and my mother will be the matron of honor."

Madeline smiled at Paul. "Naturally you're

invited, Paul. It's a small home wedding, and Antoine will give me away."

"I'm going to be transferred to Boston," William said, taking a bite of the melon and creamy cheese on his dessert plate.

"Boston!" Danielle said, almost choking on a grape.

Aunt Madeline sipped her champagne, the sparkling liquid playing against the beads of her dress.

"I didn't want to mention it until we were certain." Her aunt's big eyes studied Danielle. "You know how you always wanted to travel, Danielle. Maybe you and Paul will sail up to Boston Harbor and pay us a visit." She stopped, noticing Danielle's crestfallen face. "Dear, Boston isn't the end of the world. Aren't you happy for us?"

Danielle managed a smile, but how she would miss Aunt Madeline.

Captain Ellinger said comfortingly, "Remember, as an army man, I could be transferred back here in a few years."

"But to leave New Orleans," Danielle said, uncomprehending. "You've lived here all your life, Aunt Madeline."

"Yes, and it's time to see another part of this country with my husband. They say Boston is a very cultured city, and it will broaden my outlook on the United States."

"I'll miss the Verlaines, too. They're my new family," William said, smiling. "I've become very fond of all of you."

"And we won't let you be apart from us

for long," Danielle retorted, matching his jovial mood. "The Verlaines will follow you to Boston for a visit."

"You're originally from Boston, aren't you?" Paul asked of Captain Ellinger. "Do you have family there?"

"I have a married sister whose husband imports tea and spices. They have two sons, Jeremiah and Amos." He squeezed Madeline's hand. "So my new bride will have someone to help her settle in." His dark, handsome face was pleasant. "I have mixed feelings about leaving this area. I grew up in Boston and attended West Point, but New Orleans is a place I've fallen in love with"— he glanced at Madeline —"along with a vivacious brunette from Rampart Street who stole my heart."

Their conversation was interrupted when Governor Claiborne stood and said, "General Jackson, will you say a word to the assembly, please?"

Jackson unbent his long legs, and his sober features broke into a smile. "I'm deeply touched by the adulation I've been given." He cleared his throat, and his penetrating eyes darted from one face to another. "When I entered the hall, I noticed a sign —'Jackson and Victory.' Perhaps it should read 'Hickory and Victory.'"

There was polite laughter.

Jackson half turned toward the olive-complexioned woman on his right. "I want to salute my wife, who has recently arrived from Tennessee to be with me."

Danielle craned her neck for a better look at Rachel Jackson, who had caused a scandal by divorcing her husband to marry Andrew Jackson. She looked with such adoring eyes at Jackson that Danielle thought he was a lucky man, indeed.

Jackson faced the people again, with a second toast. "And to the citizens of New Orleans, who have been brave and strong. Without their courage, I never could have defeated the British, who, by the way, are even now on their boats, heaving their anchors up and leaving Louisiana." He downed his champagne while everyone applauded and cheered wildly.

Jackson shouted, "On to the dancing!"

When Danielle and Paul walked upstairs into the ballroom, there was already a lively tune being played by the fiddlers. Jackson and Rachel led the pas de deux, and Danielle joined in the clapping. She laughed to see the long-limbed general bobbing opposite his rosy-cheeked, short wife. When the two dancers sprang up in the air, Danielle gasped with delight. She'd heard that Mrs. Jackson was very religious and had made derogatory asides about New Orleans, saying that it was a city of pleasure with too many theaters and coffee houses. But seeing Rachel Jackson dance, you'd never know she had made such stuffy remarks.

After the Jacksons had started the festivities and others began dancing, she and Paul moved onto the floor and danced the gavotte and the waltz.

When it was almost midnight, she and Paul enjoyed a glass of punch at the refreshment table. Danielle was pleased to see Jean Lafitte and Governor Claiborne talking and laughing. She would go over and speak to Jean Lafitte after he had finished talking. To think that not long ago Governor Claiborne had tried to arrest Jean Lafitte! Yes, Danielle thought, the war had brought different people together who wouldn't even have shaken hands before. Perhaps she could even introduce Jean Lafitte to her father. The pirate chief hadn't seen her yet, and as she impatiently waited for Governor Claiborne to depart, she sipped her punch. When she looked up, she saw the governor beckoning to General Coffee, Andrew Jackson's brother-in-law, to join them.

She sighed. The ball would be over before she could talk to Lafitte. Finishing her drink, she set the glass down and listened as Governor Claiborne introduced General Coffee to Jean Lafitte.

General Coffee appeared not to hear and turned his back. All at once, Jean Lafitte grasped the general's shoulder, spinning him about and shouting, "My name is Jean Lafitte! Lafitte, the pirate!" Then he wheeled about and, without another word, strode from the ball.

Chapter
Twenty-one

THE next day, as Danielle packed her belongings to return to Cypress Manor, she relived the previous night's awful moment, when General Coffee had insulted Jean Lafitte and the pirate stormed out of the French Exchange.

Everyone had been buzzing over Lafitte's abrupt departure. Even when General Coffee had run after him to apologize, the pirate leader wouldn't listen.

Danielle shook her head. There went any hope of gaining her father's support in Lafitte's search for citizenship. It was unlikely now that Lafitte would pursue his ambition to be a citizen of Louisiana. She was sure he wanted nothing to do with New Orleans society. She wondered what effect this act would have on Geoffrey's wish to call on her. "Damn!" she swore under her breath, stuffing a pair of shoes in her valise. Why couldn't General Coffee have been polite to Jean Lafitte? The evening would have gone smoothly, and as a result she might have been able to see Geoffrey. There was still a chance. After all, Geoffrey had returned her safe and sound from Grand Terre and had been the perfect gentleman . . . well, almost perfect. The memory of the beach and his kisses even now brought the blood racing to her cheeks. She hadn't exactly been the perfect lady, either. But that was something her father didn't have to know. The only thing she had done wrong was to kiss a pirate, but that would be enough to set off her father's mercurial temper.

"Danielle," her mother called. "Are you ready to go home?"

How good those words sounded. To go home—at last! "I'll be right there," she answered. She clamped shut the valise and ran downstairs.

As they drove in the carriage, with Ebony behind, she savored every bend in the drive home. The trees and hedges were beautiful. As they came up the lane to Cypress Manor, however, she noticed that the shrubbery and bushes had been trampled. Chances were that no flowers would bloom this spring unless replanted. She saw her father already hard at work with a contingent of soldiers, using the sugar mules to haul away trees the British had chopped down. She gazed at the plantation with a quickening pulse. There was an upturned cannon in front of the pillared porch, and scattered over the area were bandages, broken guns, hats, pots and pans, and a few lopsided tents.

Adelaide gripped her daughter's arm. "Things will be different inside, so be prepared, dear. Remember, the British were in every corner of the house except your bedroom. That was my room, and Colonel Thornton gave orders that no one was to enter without my permission." Adelaide smiled grimly. "He did give me that privilege after I helped with the wounded."

Danielle steeled herself as she stepped warily across the threshold and into the large hall. She fully expected to see wrecked and broken furniture, slashed drapes, and marred walls, but as she looked around, the only change seemed to be that the tables, chairs, and settees were all pushed against the wall. No doubt this was to make room for rows of beds. The rugs were rolled up and the drapes flung back. On the whole, however, it wasn't nearly as bad as she had anticipated.

Josephine, the house servant, back from Baton Rouge, was polishing the staircase, and when she saw them, she came flying downstairs to hug first Danielle and then Adelaide.

They shared their war experiences before the short and lively Cajun girl went back to work. Her husband, Etienne, was outside with Danielle's father, removing logs from the premises.

Danielle hurried upstairs to see her room. It was as she remembered. The blue-and-white chintz was a cheery welcome. The canopy over her bed, the drapes, and her personal things were all in their proper places.

Unpacking the white porcelain cat, she returned it to its rightful place on the mantel and stepped back to admire the dog and cat, together once again.

That evening as she sat on a footstool and pulled off her father's boots, she was content to stay quiet at his feet before the fireplace. How she had longed for this moment when she could be at home with her father and mother!

Captain Verlaine leaned back in his chair as Adelaide polished a small table with linseed oil, trying to remove the deep scratches.

"Well, Danielle," her father said dryly, "you'll be happy to know I saw a copy of the letter that President Madison sent to General Jackson. It seems the president has granted the pirates on Grand Terre their citizenship." His face darkened, but he didn't launch into a tirade.

Danielle tried to hide her quick elation.

"Yes"—her father gave his daughter a shrewd look—"in spite of anything I could do, Jean Lafitte is a citizen. I think the president's words went something like this: 'Because of the inestimable service of Jean Lafitte and his men in the Battle of New Orleans, the United States is proud to grant them American citizenship.' "

Antoine clenched his fist. "Now we give the right to vote to smugglers and killers." He stared into the fire, lost in thought. "Yes, Jean Lafitte is a citizen, although after he was snubbed last night, I doubt if he gives a damn. I rather imagine he'll leave his island. Times have changed. Lafitte had asked President Madison for restitution for all his buildings and goods that had been destroyed by the American ships before the battle, but the President showed good sense and at least didn't pay the pirates for their stolen merchandise. Lafitte will probably go someplace else, where his piracy on the high seas is viewed with more tolerance than around these parts."

A stab of fear went through Danielle. The pirates might leave Grand Terre. That idea had never entered her head. And Geoffrey? What would his plans be? Would he follow his uncle? She sat back and clasped her hands around her knees, watching her father. He must never suspect what inner turmoil his news caused her.

Her father, fatigue lines across his forehead, looked warmly at Danielle and Adelaide. "It's good to be home again, the three of us together once more."

Adelaide sat back on her heels, examining the round table. "It is good, my darling. What a contrast to have had the British in these rooms and now have my family here where they belong." She rose and moved to the back of Antoine's chair, kissing the top of his black hair.

He reached back and patted her hand, which was resting on his shoulder. With his other hand, he caressed Danielle's cheek. A muscle rippled along his jaw in the firelight. "I hope we'll never lose our close family love and that we'll always be together." He smiled. "Even if you visit Aunt Madeline in Boston, we'll still be near to one another."

Danielle rested her cheek on her father's knee. She wanted to make her mother and father happy, but all she could bring them was sadness. Someday soon there would be a terrible wrenching apart. How she dreaded to leave them, but she had to go on seeing Geoffrey. Nothing or no one would separate them. Should she ruin this sweet moment and ask if Geoffrey could call? Perhaps now, when her father was filled with affection and contentment, was the right time after all. She lifted her head and looked at her father, feeling defensive from her lower position on the footstool. "Father," she said, risking his anger, "Geoffrey Lafitte asked if he might call on me at a later time." Her hands were clammy, and she swallowed hard as she noticed a visible stiffening in her father's body. She rushed on. "He helped me on Grand Terre and interceded in my behalf more than once. Do you think?..."

"Does this pirate know you are spoken for?" her father interrupted in an icy voice.

"Well, I haven't told —"

"You haven't told him about Paul, is that it?"

"There's nothing to tell," she said defiantly. The words came tumbling out before she could stop them. "Father, you champion other men's rights and won't associate with anyone who has ever dealt in slaving, yet you treat me like a slave. I'm expected to do your slightest bidding."

Not giving her father a chance to speak, she jumped to her feet. "What's the use! You don't understand . . . you never will." Blinding tears blurred her way to the staircase. She stumbled up the steps.

She fell and heard her mother say, "Danielle is going through a difficult stage, Antoine. She needs time. You only fan her romantic notions when you forbid her to see Geoffrey Lafitte. I think once she really got to know him, she'd come back to Paul of her own free will."

She scrambled to her feet. Her mother didn't understand, either. She dashed into her room, not wanting to hear her father's reply. A sob tore from her throat. She didn't need to. His answer was always the same. Slamming the door, she flung herself headlong across the bed, muffling her sobs in her pillow.

About midnight, she got up, filled the washbasin, and splashed cool water over her swollen eyes. Well, she had met Geoffrey secretly before, and she could do so again. Undressing, she slipped between the sheets, determined to find Tulci and give him a message for Geoffrey. She hoped the war hadn't forced the old swamp man from his hut on the bayou.

The gray morning light stirred her. Despite the comfort of her own bed, she had slept poorly. In her imagination, she had been at the helm of a ship with Geoffrey's arms around her as their schooner plowed the waves like an Arabian charger plunging over sand dunes.

She skipped breakfast, letting her mother and father think she was still asleep. First she would write Christopher's parents, a task she had put off far too long. She went over to her small table and, pulling open the drawer, placed paper and pen in front of her and began writing:

Dear Mr. and Mrs. Rollins:

Your son asked me to write to you just before he died. I was with Christopher and want you to know he didn't suffer from the British soldier's bullet in his chest. I knew Christopher severel days before he was brought into the hospital tent where I helped tend the wounded. Christopher taught me how to throw a knife. He loved Tennessee and his family very much. I think of him often. You can be proud of how he died for his country.

Your son's friend,
Danielle Verlaine

Putting her quill down, Danielle gazed out over the field of sugarcane stubble but saw only Christopher's happy grin in his freckled face, topped with fiery hair. How full of life he had been.

Suddenly, she spotted her father entering the field, followed by several soldiers. He pointed to an upside-down cart and some debris close by the wooden fence, and the men set to work. The Verlaine plantation was considered a military target; therefore, General Jackson had authorized a two-day cleanup detail. The soldiers had worked well, and the plantation grounds would be in good shape when they pulled out tomorrow. Her father, too, would be returning to his unit. Glumly, she watched as he kicked at a sugar vat and wished she could run down and talk to him before he left. She shook her head, knowing that was a foolish idea. They had had their talk last night. His reaction was just as she knew it would be. She folded the letter and tucked it in the envelope. When she dripped wax on the closed flap, it seemed so final. The chapter on Christopher was closed. How sad death could be. And life, too.

Life wasn't worth much if she couldn't see Geoffrey. How she yearned to talk to him, but it was certain now that he'd never be invited to Cypress Manor. There was no one she could express her feelings to about Geoffrey. Should she find Tulci and send Geoffrey a message? She had to see her love again. Perhaps she should search out Betsy

Summers. She was always ready to listen and could be impartial, too.

That's what she'd do. She'd seek out Betsy.

Quickly, she fastened in her tightly coiled braids two silver clasps that matched the buttons on her wheat-colored riding dress. Flinging her cloak around her shoulders, she hurried downstairs where her mother was carefully returning each cameo to the show-case, a glass-topped table.

"Danielle," Adelaide said in a puzzled tone. "There are two cameos missing."

"There are?" she asked blankly. "I can't imagine what happened to them unless Gambi went back and dug up several for him-self. It was Geoffrey who retrieved them for me and kept them safe until I left Grand Terre. That's something else he did," she said, becoming breathless in his defense. "Without Geoffrey, we wouldn't have had *any* of our cameos returned."

"I know, Danielle." Adelaide placed an onyx cameo in the case and turned. "The missing cameos are special — your baby cameo and my jade."

"Oh, no," she groaned. "Why would Gambi steal those? Mother, Gambi was so ugly and mean. It's as if he knew that stealing those two would hurt us the most."

"He must have terrified you so," her mother said sympathetically. "I'm so glad you're out of his reach." Adelaide sighed, polishing an amber cameo and placing it neatly on the black velvet. "I'll have to tell your father about the missing cameos tonight."

Danielle frowned. "It will give him another reason to hate pirates."

"Perhaps not." Adelaide smiled. "At least the plantation is in good enough order so that no major repairs need to be done. None of our cameos have to be sacrificed."

"That's good news, at least," Danielle answered.

"Where are you going in your smart riding suit?"

"I need to post a letter. I finally wrote to Christopher Rollins' parents. Then I'll make a brief call on Betsy Summers. Is that all right?"

"Certainly, dear. Just be back early. Josephine is roasting duck with orange sauce tonight. It's your father's last evening at home until Jackson lifts martial law."

"I hope it's soon. At the ball I heard two merchants grumbling about the trade embargo."

Adelaide pushed the cameo inventory to one side. "Your father feels bad about losing his temper with you last night."

"I do, too," Danielle admitted, feeling a sting behind her eyes but vowing not to shed any more tears.

Adelaide smiled. "Why don't we forget all about the pirates tonight and think only of making your father's last evening at home a pleasant one."

"I'll try," she said with biting calm.

"Good. Then please be back by six. I've invited Madeline and William, and we'll have a lovely evening. We need to do lots of planning for the wedding. Next week Madeline wants us to meet her in town so we can shop for our gowns."

Danielle smiled but inwardly wondered if the shopping expedition was meant to keep her mind off Geoffrey. *Well,* she thought grimly, *it will take more than a new dress for that.*

"I'll be back late this afternoon," she promised. "Earlier if I can't locate Betsy Summers quickly."

"I hope you find her. I know you'll have lots to talk about."

She looked keenly at her mother. It was as if her mother knew Danielle had to talk to someone about Geoffrey. You couldn't talk with anyone in this family about a new gentleman caller. Only one gentleman caller was permitted at Cypress Manor, and his name was Paul.

Riding Ebony was sheer ecstasy. She started her stallion at a trot down the familiar lane, then, when they reached the City Road, broke him into a canter and finally a gallop. The stones sparked beneath his hooves. Her skirt billowed around her, and she breathed in the fresh country air.

Slowing Ebony to a walk along Chartres Street with its palm trees along each side, she finally arrived at the wharf. The smells of fish and shrimp wafted over her from every direction. In the distance, shrimp boats bobbed quietly at the docks, instead of sailing out in the Gulf, as most of the fishermen were still in the militia.

She noticed a crusty old man seated on a post mending a fishnet, and rode up to him. "Do you know where Betsy and Jeremiah Summers live?" she asked.

He rubbed his beard. "Third cottage on the waterfront." There was an avid interest in his squinting eyes. "You a friend of theirs?"

She nodded, smiling, but didn't elaborate on who she was.

"We don't get many Creoles on Old Levee Street. You must have known the Summers in the war?" He arched his bushy brows.

"That's right," she said cheerily, riding on.

"Jeremiah ain't home," the fisherman shouted after her.

The door was open, and Betsy, a heavy shawl around her broad shoulders, was shelling shrimp.

"Hello, Betsy," Danielle said, silhouetted in the doorway.

The plump woman looked up. Seeing Danielle, her whole face lit up. "Danielle Verlaine! What a pleasant surprise! Come and set yourself down. I'd give you a hug, but I'm all fishy-smelling."

Danielle perched on a stool next to Betsy. How good it was to see this big, warm American woman. "Let me help," she offered.

"You'll dirty that beautiful wool gown and

those dainty hands." Betsy smiled broadly. "It's good to see you."

"Then let me help you clean shrimp," Danielle said, laughing. "Please. Everyone along the docks stared at me as I came down Old Levee Street, as if to say, 'Here comes a rich Creole girl. Pretty but useless.'" Danielle dipped into the bucket and plucked out a shrimp. "I just want to prove I'm good for something." She grinned, and Betsy grinned, too.

"Be my helper." Betsy chuckled. "Glad to have you. It's too bad you can't meet Jeremiah, but he's guarding the streets of New Orleans, as if there were still some danger." She pressed her lips together. "Why Jackson continues the curfew I don't know. Well, the general is going to be hauled before the United States court for his high-handed treatment of the citizens here."

"A court trial?" Danielle echoed in disbelief. "For Jackson?"

"Certainly a court trial. Why should we have to suffer martial law?" Betsy asked as she viciously snapped the head off a shrimp. "After all, we did win the Battle of New Orleans. The war is over."

"Maybe General Jackson is afraid the British will return and attack us?"

"Hmpf. Unlikely. The British are halfway across the Atlantic Ocean by now."

"But Andrew Jackson shouldn't have to face a judge. He's the one who saved our city."

"There's lots of folks who are grateful to him, too," Betsy said, "but Jackson has to realize that the enemy is gone and he's keeping the city from trading and the fleets from fishing. Our shrimp boats will be idle until the men come back from the militia. I'm only cleaning these little devils because the old men took out two boats this morning." She broke the shrimp shell with her thumb and forced out the meat and then threw the pink flesh into a pot of brine swimming with red and green peppers.

Danielle knew how to clean shrimp but watched Betsy's method so she wouldn't do it wrong. Her fingers flew as she put pressure on the shrimp, sliding the meat out. "Jackson is stubborn," she said. "He'll only impose a stricter law if citizens defy him."

Betsy slid her bulk off the stool. "But enough of our problems. You came here for a reason, Danielle, I'm sure of that." She laughed. "Best I put on the kettle, and we'll have a cup of tea."

"Betsy, have you heard of Jean Lafitte's nephew, Geoffrey?"

"I heard mention of him." Betsy set two cups on the table. "Why?"

"I know him."

"I understand you know him quite well," Betsy said, removing the boiling water from the wood stove.

"You know about it?" Danielle asked.

Betsy chuckled. "When we were at the

front, a soldier told me. Said he'd seen you out by the well talking to Geoffrey Lafitte." She winked. "And it looked like serious talk, too."

Danielle stopped shelling and moved to the table, observing Betsy's florid face. Could she trust her? Sinking into the chair, Danielle knew she had to confide in someone or burst.

Betsy set a plate of scones in front of Danielle. "Freshly baked this morning."

Danielle reached for one of the pastries. "I am hungry," she said gratefully, remembering that she hadn't eaten breakfast. Besides, it would be much easier to talk over a cup of tea rather than pinching heads off shrimp.

After Danielle had drunk half her tea, she said abruptly, "I'm in love with Geoffrey Lafitte."

If she had expected Betsy to stare at her with mouth shockingly agape, she was mistaken. Betsy calmly finished her scone and poured a second cup of tea. "I thought as much."

"I'm supposed to marry Paul Milerand when I'm eighteen."

"And how old are you now?"

"Fifteen. I'll be sixteen in March." She set down her cup and pushed the scones away. "I don't know what to do. My parents want me to fulfill this marriage contract, and I want to make up my own mind about my own future."

"Sounds like you've already made it up." Betsy grasped Danielle's knee, shaking it to and fro. "You have, haven't you?"

"I only know I won't be held to a marriage contract that was made when I was six years old." She dug her fingernails into her wrist, not wanting to cry. She had shed enough tears over this situation. Now it was time for action.

Betsy shook her head. "I don't say you shouldn't see Geoffrey. Love is very important. I just think you should slow down." She rose, clearing the table.

Disappointed, Danielle closed her eyes for an instant. "This is supposed to be the land of the free. What happens to Creole girls like me?" She watched Betsy closely, not wanting to be lectured. Betsy, of all people, should agree with her and not tell her to slow down. Americans didn't cling to Old World customs. She had been certain Betsy would have been the first one to advise her to flee with Geoffrey, and hang tradition.

"You know, when I was your age, I was in a similar situation." Betsy leaned on the table. "But I was a clever young girl. Clever, just like you, Danielle. Jeremiah Summers was a fisherman, and I came from a family of British textile workers. No daughter of the Winthrop family would have anything to do with a fisherman. No, indeed! When I introduced Jeremiah to my mother and father, they told him to stay away from me. But he kept coming around, offering to help load cotton bales on ships. Father was impressed with Jeremiah's attitude toward hard work. My father didn't know much about fishing." With her elbow, she poked Danielle in the ribs. "So Jeremiah took my father out cod fishing. It got so that on his days off, my father would beg Jeremiah to take him out on the boat." Betsy shrugged. "My fisherman became part of the family. Everyone was fond of him. It was a wedding both families attended, and it brought Jeremiah and me happiness, not to mention a solid base for our marriage, which by the way, has lasted over twenty years."

"Your situation was different," Danielle said. "At least fishing is an honorable trade. My father views pirates as cutthroats and murderers."

"Introduce Geoffrey to your parents. If he's half the man you say he is, he'll prove the mettle he's made of. I'll bet your family will eventually welcome him into the Verlaine clan."

Danielle's heart sank. Betsy didn't understand, either.

Chapter
Twenty-two

AS Danielle walked along the bayou, the sun played hide-and-seek with the branches overhead. The water, dark and still, reflected the trees and her shadow. There was a mystery in the beauty surrounding her.

It had been several days, and yet she hadn't heard from Geoffrey. Was he patiently waiting for an invitation to Cypress Manor? Perhaps he felt the first move should be on her part, and he didn't want to be forward and come calling without being asked. A good thing, too, she thought glumly. She wouldn't be surprised if her father would greet him with a musket ball. She skirted a snakeskin that had been shed last summer along the moss-covered path.

She came to a clearing where the bayou waters widened, and in the distance, mallard ducks were sitting, others swimming in and out of the bulrushes. She saw Tulci's shack on stilts, nestled in a grove of mangrove trees with its shaggy palmetto roof and peeling paint. His pirogue was pulled up close to the front steps.

She pulled out the note for Geoffrey, scanning what she had written:

Dearest Geoffrey:
Things at Cypress Manor are still not back to normal. I wanted to invite you (and hope to, soon) but in the meantime I will be coming into town Saturday and will be in the vicinity of your warehouse about noon if you should care to meet me.

                    With affection,
                    Danielle

Going up the steps, she knocked on Tulci's door, feeling the hairs prickle on the nape of her neck. Even though she'd known Tulci for years, he was a rough swamp man whose ways were strange. He liked his privacy, and it was seldom that any visitors called on him.

She knocked again. Still no answer.

"Tulci," she called. "It's Danielle. I want you to deliver a message to Grand Terre."

The door opened a crack, and Tulci peered out with one bushy brow quirked. "What time is it?" he asked, opening the door wide and scratching his head.

"Lunchtime."

He yawned. "I was up most of the night

skinning rabbits." His eyes narrowed. "What message is so important that you came through the swamp to see old Tulci?"

She held out the envelope. "Will you deliver this to Geoffrey Lafitte?"

He slyly peeked at her from under his grizzled brows. "You two young'uns are still seeing each other, eh?"

"Yes, Geoffrey and I are still friends," she said, not daring to meet his eyes.

"Friends?" he echoed. "Sure, sure." Tulci tucked the envelope in his buckskin shirt pocket and laughed. "*Good* friends, I'll wager."

She blushed from her cheeks to her throat, not bothering to answer his insinuation. She glanced about his one room and noticed a rumpled pallet and dirty dishes on the table.

"I'll deliver it for you," said Tulci. "I'm going to The Temple this afternoon, anyway. I know Geoffrey will be at the auction."

"Has Jean Lafitte started his auction already?" She tried to keep the alarm out of her voice. Jean Lafitte should realize how unpopular smuggling had become to the authorities, since all of his activities had been brought out in the open in his bid for citizenship. Now that it had been granted, one would think he would be more law-abiding, at least until the rumblings had died down from people like her father.

"Jean Lafitte doesn't have much merchandise left to auction, but he aims to sell what he has. You know that pirate will do anything that will bring him a profit. He lives high." Tulci chortled, observing her. "But you should know that, you saw his mansion on Grand Terre."

"Yes," she agreed. "He lives like a prince." She didn't intend to voice her concern to Tulci. If she could see Geoffrey, perhaps she could tell him the feelings of most New Orleans citizens about Jean Lafitte's smuggling.

"Yup." Tulci grinned. "Jean Lafitte not only lives like a prince, he acts like one, too. If anyone would dare to interfere with his high style of living, I wouldn't be surprised if he'd up and leave here."

She took a quick intake of air. Jean Lafitte mustn't leave Grand Terre. Her hand trembled slightly as she slipped a silver dollar into Tulci's palm. "Thanks for delivering the note." Placing a finger to her lips, she said in a low voice, "Remember, this is just between the two of us. Right?"

"Right. Right." Tulci nodded vigorously.

Her heart was still beating hard as she hurried away. She was convinced Jean Lafitte would be leaving soon. This was the second time she'd heard such a rumor. She must see Geoffrey.

What if she went to the warehouse and he didn't show up? No, Geoffrey would never do such a thing. If he couldn't meet her, he'd get a message to her somehow. She knew he would. Yet suddenly, she was afraid. If Governor Claiborne tried to close The

Temple after General Coffee's insult, she knew Jean Lafitte would burn his new buildings and sail away with his fleet. Where could he go? She knew the pirate chief quite well, and he wouldn't tolerate any meddling in his affairs. Earlier, he had laughed when Governor Claiborne put a price on his head, and most of the city's citizens had laughed with him. But the war had changed men's and women's outlooks on his behavior. Most of the authorities were Americans, and Americans were heroes now. New Orleans citizens were Americans, too. Whatever the government wanted was all right with them.

Arriving at Cypress Manor, she was surprised to see her father dismounting from his war charger. Was martial law lifted? Why else would he be home?

"Father!" She broke into a run.

"Danielle, dear." He gave her a quick hug. Releasing her, he put his arm around her. "Come into the house, I have some news."

She was relieved he didn't ask where she'd been. His news must have put all other questions from his mind.

Once in the parlor, Antoine pulled off his gloves and threw them on a small table.

Adelaide joined them, wiping her hands on her apron. "Antoine. You're home. Anything wrong?"

"No, no, darling . . ."

"I should wash my hands. I've been helping Josephine peel apples," Adelaide said.

"Come, sit down." Antoine looked at both

of them. "Good news. New Orleans is no longer under martial law."

"You mean Andrew Jackson has lifted the curfew?" asked Adelaide.

"He had to," Antoine replied grimly. "The peace treaty has been settled at Ghent, Belgium. The news came in by packet boat today."

"The peace treaty is signed?" Danielle repeated, her mind racing ahead as to what this would mean for New Orleans. Theaters would reopen; trade would resume. Life would be happier again.

"It was signed and sealed in Ghent, Belgium, on December 24, 1814."

Danielle did a brief calculation. Stricken, she stared at her father. "But that was two weeks before the Battle of New Orleans was fought."

"That's right. The battle for our city wasn't necessary."

Danielle's heart turned over. All she could think about was Christopher. He had died uselessly.

She dully repeated her father's words in the form of a question. "You're saying the battle wasn't necessary?" She grasped the chair arms until her knuckles whitened. "The poor soldiers who died," she whispered. "For what?"

"Don't think that way, Danielle," Antoine remonstrated. "They died to help this country grow up. After this, the United States will be treated as an independent country!"

Fine words, thought Danielle bitterly. But Christopher would never again go hunting squirrels in his beloved Tennessee hills.

"Have the British agreed not to take any more American sailors off our ships?" asked Adelaide.

"Impressment wasn't mentioned," Antoine said sheepishly. "About the only thing that came out of the treaty was the cessation of hostilities."

"Impressment was the whole reason for fighting the war!" Danielle exploded. "It sounds as if nothing was accomplished. I can't believe it. We win the war, and the British are the ones who dictate the terms."

"Now, now, Danielle. Rest assured our negotiating team has top-notch men, including Henry Clay and John Quincy Adams. They know what they're doing."

Adelaide smiled, and her porcelain beauty made the room glow. "I only thank God the conflict is ended and we can return to everyday living. No more British troops, no more hospital tents." She gazed fondly at her daughter.

"Yes, both sides are sick of this conflict," Antoine agreed, gazing at the sugarcane fields before him.

There was a silence as the three contemplated what peace meant. Danielle knew her parents' thoughts were very different from hers. She couldn't help remembering Christopher and the thousands of British who had been killed. The memory of the gallant General Pakenham waving his sword and shouting words of encouragement to his soldiers was another vivid picture that remained with her. She wondered if General Pakenham's body had completed the final journey to England. She'd heard he was being shipped back home in a vat of rum. Preserving bodies in rum was a common enough practice, but this image of the dead general saddened her. She sighed. Christopher and Pakenham, two dead soldiers, were both so different and yet so noble. They would never let her forget the futility of war. She rose and joined her father at the window. She loved him and hoped the days ahead would be brighter. She didn't know what was ahead of her, but she prayed Geoffrey would be part of her future.

Antoine spoke, breaking the quiet. "There's a lot of work ahead of us. Furrows need to be dug along the south acreage, the sugarcane needs to be cut, and the stalks laid in the furrows. Hopefully next summer we'll have a good crop."

Adelaide came over, and the small family seemed closer than they had ever been. Danielle, in the middle, slipped her arm first around her father's waist, then around her mother's. If only it could always stay like this.

Adelaide said, "Once the fields are cleared, I know we will have a profitable season. We'll need to ship in more sugar vats, though, for the British used most of them in their defensive line." She leaned against Antoine. "It's so good to be home with my husband and daughter. For a while I was beginning to doubt if I'd ever see either of you again." She laughed, a sprightly, tinkling sound. "But enough love and emotion. First thing you know, I'll have myself in tears." She pulled away. "The baked apples should be finished. Who would like one?"

Danielle shook her head. "Thanks, Mother, but I'm not hungry."

"Then I'll take them out of the oven, and if you want one later they'll be there." She left to go back to the kitchen.

Danielle kept her arm around her father. "We'll make Cypress Manor the most beautiful and most profitable plantation in New Orleans." She meant it, too. She was filled with resolve, and determined to roll up her sleeves and help with the cleanup of their home.

"Yes, if we work together it can be a showplace." Antoine seemed pleased at Danielle's observation. "And now, dear, I'll change out of this uniform into the clothes of a planter." He laughed. "How good that will seem."

She enjoyed hearing her father laugh. For a long time there had been very little cheer in this house.

The next day was one of pleasure. She and her mother met Aunt Madeline for a day of dress and accessory buying, but the rest of the week was lost in work.

Exhausted, she fell into bed each evening.

Every floor, every wall, every dish and pot had to be scoured and scrubbed.

When Saturday came, she eagerly rode to the city to meet Geoffrey. She had told her mother she needed new slippers to match the peach-colored gown she had chosen for her aunt's wedding. She was prepared, however, to wear her brown sandals and to tell her mother that she couldn't find any shoes the color she needed.

As she rode down Dumaine Street, she galloped past the small shops and the St. Louis Hotel, which was almost hidden by the palm trees in front of each column. She waved to the liveried doorman at the double-doored entrance with its carved grillwork.

Her heart matched Ebony's hoofbeats on the cobblestones, and she urged him to go even faster as they approached the warehouse.

When she arrived, Geoffrey was leaning against the building's oak door, arms folded, patiently waiting. He wore a short black cloak with red-and-white striped trousers and gleaming leather boots.

She wanted to cry out his name but restrained herself. However, when she neared the hitching post, she jumped off her stallion's back and flew into his waiting arms.

"Darling," he said. "I've missed you." He kissed her and then gazed into her eyes. "*How* I've missed you!"

A breeze ruffled his curls, and his cape blew out behind him. "I've missed you, too,

Geoffrey." A cold wind caused her to shiver in her wool cloak, and she pulled it closer around her.

"Cold, my sweet?" he asked solicitously. "Let's go inside."

She hesitated, not trusting her emotions. "We'd better stay out here," she said timidly, teeth chattering.

"Nonsense, Miss Prim and Proper." He held up his hands. "I promise to be good."

She laughed. "Then lead the way, my bold buccaneer."

They stepped inside. The warehouse floor was bare except for a few empty boxes. "Where are all the crates?" she asked, puzzled.

"Everything was confiscated by the authorities." Geoffrey shrugged. "My uncle is wealthy but he's retained Grymes and Livingston to get back what is rightfully his. He's suing the city to retrieve money for his burned buildings and for all the goods that were taken. He wants his fleet returned, too. He has only eight sloops left."

"Do you think he has a chance?"

"I doubt it. The city is already planning to auction off his goods before the government can make a judgment. Grymes and Livingston are the best lawyers money can buy, and Jean Lafitte intends to be paid for everything that was stolen from this warehouse." Geoffrey walked about, his boot heels making a hollow, clicking noise in the cavernous building.

He paused and glanced in her direction.

"The Baratarians have been given their citizenship, but that's where the people's generosity ends." His tone was bitter. "No reimbursement for smuggled goods, they say." He snorted. "They were eager enough to buy them before the war." He faced her, hands on hips. "Even if my uncle wins the case, he has made plans to leave Grand Terre."

"Leave? Oh, no," she gasped. "Would you go, too?"

"Naturally." Geoffrey grinned. "Jean Lafitte has the ships and men. How else can I make my fortune? Besides," he added, "I love my uncles."

I love my parents, too, she reflected, *but I'm ready to give them up for you.* But she said nothing.

"Jean Lafitte knows when he's no longer wanted," Geoffrey continued. "They've put a price back on his head, and the other night at the ball he even had to shake hands with the Spanish consul. That means that the United States has recognized Spain in these waters, and he no longer has a free hand to board their ships. That, plus stealing his goods, has given him all the reason he needs to find a more hospitable place."

Stolen his goods! Danielle marveled at how Jean Lafitte could look at his situation. He had stolen those goods in the first place. She wanted to respond, but she was sure Geoffrey wouldn't understand, either. Instead she asked, "Where will you go?"

"Maybe along the Texas coast. My uncle has mentioned Galveston. If you study a map, you can see that's as good a location as Grand Terre."

"Galveston! It — it seems so far away." She could hardly get the words past her closed throat.

Geoffrey took her hand. "We won't be apart, Danielle. I promise I won't let that happen."

She gazed at him through bright tears. His image blurred. "Oh, Geoffrey," she said.

He pulled her forward, and she came into his arms. Then, holding her head, he kissed her long and hard.

"I love you," he said softly.

"I love you, too," she murmured, filled with such yearning.

Gently, he undid the clasp in her hair, letting it fall thick about her shoulders like a curtain of sunlight.

When his fingers tenderly touched her cheek, she had never felt such love. She moved even closer into his arms. Suddenly, she stiffened and took a step backward, holding her clenched fist to her mouth. "Geoffrey!" she cried in a choked voice, staring in horror at the glinting necklace around his neck.

"What's wrong!?" Geoffrey exclaimed, gazing at her in astonishment.

Her voice was fierce and perfectly clear. "You're wearing my mother's jade cameo!"

Chapter
Twenty-three

Y OU stole cameos from our collection!" she gasped. Backing away, she bumped into an empty crate. Her throat was dry, and she couldn't speak — only stare blindly at Geoffrey.

Puzzled, Geoffrey advanced. He touched the oval cameo at his neck. "What's wrong, darling? Are you upset because I took this cameo?" He whisked the chain up and over his head. "Here! Take it." He held out the lovely piece of jade, which dangled from a golden chain before her.

Danielle held out her hand, and the pirate dropped the necklace onto her palm. "Why? Why did you do it, Geoffrey?"

"Why?" He threw back his head and laughed. "I rescued the Verlaine treasure for you, remember? There must have been several hundred gems. I didn't think you would

mind if I had a small reward for my trouble."
He held out his arms. "Least of all, you,
sweetheart."

She stood rigid, refusing to move into his
outstretched arms. "And my blue cameo?"
she asked, amazed that he could treat his
thievery so lightly. Perhaps he really thought
he'd done nothing wrong. She remembered
that he had said Jean Lafitte was too lax
about certain prisoners and should be more
like Gambi. Did Geoffrey imitate Gambi
rather than his uncle? She stole a look at her
love. He could never be that callous . . . he
just couldn't. He simply didn't realize how
wrong his actions were. Why was she making
excuses for his wretched behavior?

He dropped his arms when he saw how
serious she was and became sober, too. "Hon-
estly. I didn't know you'd be upset." Geoffrey
appeared so stricken that she almost believed
him.

Helplessly, he threw out his hands. "Please
forgive me, darling." His apologetic smile
was appealing. "Look, I have the blue cameo
at Grand Terre. I'll look for it and bring it
next time we meet." He winked. "And for
good measure, I'll bring back the black pearl
necklace. I'd still like you to wear it, you
know. Will you?"

"Just return my cameo." Her words were
slow and measured. "It means a great deal
to me." She flung her cloak around herself
and wheeled about. It was obvious he didn't
see anything wrong with what he had done.

The sudden draft that swept through the barren warehouse was not the cause of her shivering.

"Are you so angry we can't talk about this?" Geoffrey asked quietly.

"I'm not angry. I'm just" — she searched for the right word — "disappointed."

"I'm sorry. I didn't think you'd mind two stones. From all the cameos in the box, what's one or two?" He paused, and she could hear his light breathing. "Danielle," he coaxed, "please look at me. The cameos are yours for the asking." He gently took her by the shoulders and turned her around to face him.

She lowered her eyes, not daring to look at him. "I'm leaving now, Geoffrey."

"May I give you the cameo next week? Same time, same place?"

"Yes, I'll meet you here," she said in a resigned voice. She was certain she wouldn't have the same eager feeling she had felt when she had ridden like a fury to meet him today.

He smiled at her and his eyes danced. "Forgive me?"

She managed a tight little smile. "You're forgiven . . . only, Geoffrey, I wish you'd think before you take other people's property."

"I promise that I'll never do such a thing again." His voice was solemn.

"Good-bye, Geoffrey." She turned on her heels and hurried out the door.

Geoffrey ran after her, taking hold of her upper arm. "Danielle, sweet, I don't want you to leave like this. I said I was sorry. I made a mistake."

She half turned. "It's all right . . . really." Her heart felt heavy, but when she gazed into the depths of his dark eyes, she relented and blew him a kiss. "Until next week," she said in a breaking voice.

His lips parted, and then he smiled as if reassured of her constant love.

On the ride home, she opened her hand and looked at her mother's cameo. The delicately carved face on the green stone was exquisite. She was happy she'd be able to give it back, but how would she explain Geoffrey's action?

While she brushed her hair at bedtime, she placed the jade cameo in her shell-trimmed jewel box. She'd tell her mother next week after her blue cameo was in her possession. By that time, she might feel better about her pirate love, too.

In the meantime, she would think lovely thoughts of tomorrow's wedding between Aunt Madeline and Captain William Ellinger. She wished the two of them would be stationed in New Orleans for at least another year; but Captain Ellinger's orders had come through, and the newlyweds would be leaving on the steamer, directly after the wedding luncheon. Dear Aunt Madeline. How Danielle would miss her. She hoped William would be good to her. He seemed to be such an upright, honest man. Honest! The word pierced her heart like an arrow.

That night she dreamed she was chasing lost cameos that Geoffrey dangled in the air, just out of her reach.

Danielle was happy to see that the day of the marriage was sun-sparkling. Rain would mean bad luck on the honeymoon.

With care, she donned her chiffon Empire-style gown. The pale apricot tint brought out her eyes and coloring to good advantage. Her brown sandals, embroidered on soft satin, looked striking with her dress and white stockings. She stood before the mirror, and plucked up her puffed sleeves. Finally she put on her large-brimmed hat, trimmed with turquoise ribbons, and arranged the ringlets around her face into an attractive frame. The straw was too summery for February but, after all, this was a wedding. Paul would accompany her. After the wedding, they would all lunch at the St. Louis Hotel and then see Madeline and William off on the *New Orleans*. When ready, she picked up her small satin purse and her ruffled umbrella and went downstairs.

Her father and Paul, conversing in the parlor, were patiently waiting.

"Beautiful!" Paul exclaimed when he glimpsed Danielle. His eyes were filled with love and admiration as he hurried over to kiss her hand.

"Yes," Antoine said dryly, as he slipped into his green jacket. "I've always said I've reared the loveliest daughter in all Louisiana." He placed his hat on his head and gave the top a snappy pat.

Danielle laughed and, with the tip of her umbrella, touched her father's beaver hat, which gave him the appearance of being as tall as Paul. "The two of you aren't so bad-looking yourselves."

Paul, his midshipman's hat tucked beneath his arm, placed her moiré shawl about her shoulders.

Antoine picked up his ivory-headed cane. "Let's go out to the carriage. Even though we're the only wedding guests at Madeline's wedding, it would be bad form to be late. Ah," he said as Adelaide swept into the room, "here's *my* lovely bride."

He hurried over and kissed her hand.

Adelaide laughed and brushed his cheek with her lips. She looked about. "Paul, how nice to see you." She moved to her daughter's side, lifted a corner of Danielle's flowing skirt, and nodded approvingly. "How regal we all are." She carried a wool-fringed shawl, looking elegant herself in her green silk gown. Atop her blond hair she wore a white lace cap adorned with feathers. It was small enough to show off the shining blond chignon she wore coiled on the nape of her neck.

Adelaide slipped her arm beneath Antoine's arm, and the two led the way to the stable where Etienne held two prancing horses. Captain Verlaine held open the door to the black-lacquered carriage, then he climbed in the driver's seat with Paul next to him.

Danielle breathed in the crisp air. They were off to the city and a marvelous wedding. What a perfect day! And how splendid they all looked, she thought, settling back on the horsehair cushions. She smiled as she recalled a line she had read last week in Sheridan's *The Rivals*:

"Dress doth make a difference, David. 'Tis all in all, I think."

She disagreed with the sentiment. Dress wasn't everything, but your appearance certainly helped in how others viewed you. She remembered her first meeting with Geoffrey. He had been so dashing in his black shirt, trousers, and boots. She smiled at their furious battle. How their relationship had changed — perhaps not for the better. She moved uncomfortably and gazed at Paul's straight back. He had such grace and poise. He always had, but once he shed his midshipman's uniform at his graduation next week, his new lieutenant's uniform with its braid and gold trim would make him even more impressive.

When they arrived at Aunt Madeline's, the front door was festooned with garlands. Inside, the parlor was even more gala. The room had been decorated with boughs of greenery and magnolia blossoms. The fireplace was aglow with a bright, crackling fire, and long tapers, flames flickering, clustered on the mantel.

Pots of crimson azaleas were on either side of the solemn reverend, a rotund little man garbed in white, who waited before the tapestried wall for the bride and groom. Behind him was a cross of shining gold.

The ceremony began when the couple took their place before the reverend. Aunt Madeline, in flowing blue, looked especially radiant, and William especially handsome.

The opening of the wedding ceremony began with the reverend's words, which filled the hushed parlor: "Dearly beloved, we are gathered together here in the sight of God and in the face of this company to join together this man and this woman in holy matrimony...."

Danielle was behind Aunt Madeline, who stood quite still with her large eyes fastened on the reverend's face. Danielle looked at Paul. He gave an imperceptible nod, and she realized he must be thinking ahead to the fulfillment of their marriage contract. She had to tell him about Geoffrey — and soon. It wasn't fair to go on deceiving him. Not Paul, who didn't have a dishonest bone in his body.

She shifted her weight uneasily. It would be difficult to hurt him, but it was something she must do. She focused on the ceremony.

After William had placed the ring on Madeline's finger, the beaming reverend said, "I now pronounce thee man and wife."

The bride and groom tenderly embraced, and William's kiss was a lengthy one.

Next Antoine strode up to Madeline, tapping William on the shoulder. "My turn, captain."

After a sweet kiss, Antoine stepped back and said, "It might be a long time before I see my sister." He held Madeline's heart-shaped face between his hands.

Madeline gave her brother a loving glance. "Come to Boston next summer." She reached for Danielle's hand. "Your daughter has always desired to take a steamer trip."

"I think that might be arranged," Adelaide said as she, too, kissed Madeline. The two women clung to one another, for Adelaide was more than Madeline's sister-in-law. She was her close friend.

After the congratulatory hugs were over, William and Madeline ran to the carriage amid a hail of rice and ribbons.

Everyone adjourned to Royal Street where the manager of the St. Louis Hotel had prepared a lavish table for six. Peach-colored roses ringed the centerpiece, a swan bowl filled with white orchids. The sumptuous luncheon, impeccably served, consisted of pheasant under glass, fresh strawberries, potatoes lyonnaise, and a marvelous crème caramel for dessert with café au lait.

Aunt Madeline, vibrant in her silk dress and blue-flowered headdress, nodded graciously as Antoine proposed a champagne toast to the newlyweds. Her pearls glowed lustrously against her olive skin. Danielle wished Madeline were wearing their wedding gift to her, an onyx cameo trimmed with tiny diamonds, instead of pearls, for pearls symbolized tears . . . and a wedding was no place for tears.

Sipping the champagne, Madeline's eyes found William's over the crystal rim of her goblet.

Their transparent love sent a thrill of happiness through Danielle. When she examined Madeline's ring, her aunt slipped off the wide gold band and handed it to her.

Danielle held the engraved ring between her two fingers and read the inscription: "Love is All. February 27, 1815." She grasped her aunt's hand. "Oh, Aunt Madeline, what a lovely sentiment."

Madeline leaned over, whispering in her niece's ear, "It will be your turn soon, dear."

Danielle smiled at her aunt. If she only realized how confused her emotions were at this moment.

The luncheon over, they boarded the *New Orleans* and had an hour before the luxurious boat departed. She and Paul took a few minutes to walk the deck, passing the dining salon with the plump velvet chairs and red drapes.

They stopped at the rail. The Mississippi River, wide and muddy-green, lapped against the levee. Cotton bales were being loaded.

"Paul," she began hesitantly, knowing that

this was the time for honesty. "There's something I must tell you."

He lifted his brows, and his steady gaze didn't falter. "Yes?" he prompted. "What is it?"

She took a deep breath and said quickly, "I — I met someone . . . I mean . . . I . . ."

Paul's gentle eyes sharpened. "Who is he?"

"You don't know him. His name is Geoffrey Lafitte." Not able to look at his reaction, she lowered her thick lashes. "I met him even before I went to Grand Terre. I've been seeing him ever since, but no one knows. Only Tulci."

"And now me," Paul said flatly with a set to his angular jaw.

"And now you," she softly echoed.

Paul stared at the river. "I'm not surprised. I thought there was someone, but I had no idea it was a pirate."

She flared with anger. "Do you condemn him just because he's a pirate?" She paused. "Like Father?"

"I don't condemn him at all," Paul said brusquely. "I'm sure if you care for him, he must be special."

"You know," she said, her mouth softening, "the irony of this whole situation is that I think you and Geoffrey would like each other."

"Hmmmm." Paul was noncommittal as he walked to one of the hanging rowboats and ran his hand over the supporting ropes.

"Somehow I doubt if I'd like him much." He came back to her side. "How serious are you about him?"

"I — I don't know. I need time to sort things out. I only know I won't be dictated to by any marriage contract that was made when I was only six years old."

"I want you to know one thing," Paul advised, his dark eyes flashing. "I'm not giving you up just like that!"

She felt a stab of pity for him. She said gently, "You need someone who will love you for yourself. Someone who's not as stubborn as I am. Someone who will wilt in your arms and obey you."

"That's exactly the type of girl I don't want," he snapped.

They looked at one another for a long moment. Paul's blond hair ruffled in the wind, his face a golden bronze. "And as for forgetting you, that's something I could never do." He pulled her to him. His kiss was hard and fierce. Abruptly, he released her and spun about on his heels, leaving her alone.

She stayed at the rail, watching the slow-moving water, as melancholy as her thoughts. She had deeply hurt Paul, but aside from that, she wondered why her confession hadn't brought her more relief.

When her father came to tell her the crew was almost ready to lift the gangplank, she quickly wiped her moist eyes.

After tearful embraces, they left William

and Madeline. From the dock, they watched as the paddle wheels churned and roiled the water, moving the three-decker steamboat out into the main river channel.

That evening, her father was in an expansive mood. "Adelaide," he said, "I like your idea of a Boston trip." He turned to Danielle. "What about you, dear? Would you enjoy a steamboat ride?"

"Very much," she said, but her feelings didn't match her words. She wondered where she would be next summer.

Her father didn't seem to notice his daughter's preoccupation. "Yes," he went on, "we haven't been away from New Orleans for a long time."

"I've been checking our accounts," Adelaide said, "and if our sugarcane crop is as good as last year's, we'll have extra money for the journey."

Verlaine lit a cheroot and puffed contentedly, smiling at Danielle.

Risking his wrath, she decided that for one last time she would broach the subject of Geoffrey's visit to Cypress Manor. "Father," she began tentatively, "I'd like very much for Geoffrey Lafitte to call on me and introduce him to you and Mother." She dared to look at his face, half expecting his features to darken into a thundercloud, but he remained calm. "Geoffrey was good to me on Grand Terre and . . ." Her voice trailed off, not sure how she could convince him of Geoffrey's worth.

At first, Antoine didn't reply. He watched the smoke spirals curl upward.

"He — he saved our cameos, too," she urged, not mentioning the two Geoffrey had filched.

"All right, my pet." Antoine sighed with resignation. "Bring this pirate into our house. However, this call is only to pay his respects, and it will be the first and last time." He looked knowingly at Adelaide. "Perhaps this visit is what you need to get Geoffrey Lafitte out of your system"— he examined the tip of his small cigar —"and to get Paul Milerand back in."

Ignoring Paul's name, she said, "Thank you, Father. I know you will like Geoffrey when you meet him." She leaped to her feet, gave him a big hug, and ran upstairs.

As she slipped into her nightgown, she was puzzled. This was what she had wanted all along, and now that Geoffrey was at last coming to the plantation, the elation she thought she'd feel didn't materialize.

Chapter
Twenty-four

DANIELLE, awakening to the sound of a chattering blue jay and a dazzling sun that poked through the slats, stretched. After the previous night's heavy rain, the sun was a welcome sight. She stared at the ceiling, not quite ready to get up. It had been such a busy week that she couldn't believe it was Saturday already. Geoffrey was coming to Cypress Manor today . . . the day that she had long awaited. She hoped her mother and father would be taken in by his charm. She smiled, throwing back the quilt and swinging her feet onto the cold oak floor. "Taken in" weren't exactly the words she'd meant to use. A better choice of words might be "captivated by his personality." Briefly, she wondered if she had been "taken in" by Geoffrey's dashing ways. She moved to the window and ran her fingers through her hair. She didn't care if she had. He was a wonderfully bold pirate, and she loved him.

She watched as a graceful egret circled the bayou and finally came to rest in a cypress tree. The large bird's white plumage reminded her of the white plumes on the naval officers' hats yesterday, at Paul's splendid graduation. He was now a full lieutenant and would soon captain his own schooner. The ceremony had been held aboard the *Louisiana,* and even Andrew Jackson had attended. The general personally shook the hands of the eight graduates.

After a blare of trumpets, Commodore Patterson made a brief speech and then the cadets divested themselves of their short jackets and donned the naval frock coats with tails. With shouts and yells, the midshipmen sailed their ribboned tams out over the river waters and were then each given a three-cornered hat. Paul had set his navy hat squarely on his head, grinning at Danielle all the while. The band had played, flags fluttered in the breeze, and the festive occasion was topped with champagne and fresh shrimp.

She and Paul had promenaded about the deck, and it was as if he had forgotten that she had told him about Geoffrey. Paul wasn't one to sulk. In fact, he had treated her with his usual gracious attentiveness. Of course, he had also vowed to win her back.

Yawning, she stretched again, arms reaching for the ceiling, and turned to her armoire to choose a dress. Her green riding gown would be appropriate, she decided, for she wanted to look her best. If yesterday was spectacular, today would be even more so.

Geoffrey would be here directly after lunch to take coffee with them before her father went out to the fields again. She hoped the two would become friends. Who wouldn't like Geoffrey? Her mother, she was certain, would absolutely adore him. Of course, Adelaide seemed to have more of an open mind than Antoine.

A sinking feeling returned when she thought of the Lafittes and the possibility that they might leave Grand Terre soon. What would she do then?

After breakfast, she helped her mother add up the hogsheads of sugarcane to be sent to St. Louis. She was gradually learning about the ledgers her mother kept for Cypress Manor. She was pleased her mother trusted her and complimented her on "her good head for figures."

When they finally finished their accounts, her mother looked pointedly at Danielle. "Don't be disappointed if your father isn't too cordial with this Geoffrey of yours," she warned. "After all, it was quite a concession for Antoine to allow a Lafitte on our grounds." She smiled, looking striking with her blond hair about her shoulders and her velvet dressing gown the same color as her emerald-green eyes.

Danielle stood and ran a hand along her mother's shoulder. "I realize it was hard for

Father to agree to meet Geoffrey, but I know he'll relent and be glad he did when he sees how wonderful Geoffrey is." She dug into her pocket and brought out the jade cameo. Now was as good a time as any to confide in her mother. She took a deep breath. "Geoffrey gave this to me last week," she said shyly as she gave the jade stone to her mother.

Adelaide's eyes widened at the reappearance of her precious cameo, but she said nothing. She waited patiently for an explanation.

Danielle continued softly. "I was trying to think up a good explanation of what Geoffrey had done, but I just couldn't, so I'll tell you straight out how he happened to have your cameo." She faced her mother and said abruptly, "Geoffrey took two cameos as a reward for returning the Verlaine treasure to me." She paused, lowering her eyes. "I thought at first it was Gambi, never dreaming Geoffrey was the culprit. He promised to return my cameo today." She bit her lip, hardly daring to glance at her mother.

Adelaide rose, her face emotionless and pale. How different her mother's reaction was to her own, she thought, remembering how she had stared at Geoffrey in horror. At least her mother didn't seem to be shocked at the news.

"I'm happy to have my cameo back," Adelaide said simply, gazing at the magnificent stone, one of the most expensive in the collection. Calmly, she went on, "I would have thought more of Geoffrey if he would have returned the whole set of cameos in the first place, without expecting a reward."

Her quiet words hurt more than a tirade would have.

"I know, Mother. So would I." She looked up and hastened to add, "But Geoffrey was contrite and promised never to do such a thing again. He didn't realize what he had done and why I was so upset."

"He didn't realize?" Adelaide's brows shot up. "I find that difficult to believe."

She could only nod dumbly.

Adelaide reached for Danielle's hand. "I'm glad you told me. I know it wasn't easy for you."

"You won't tell Father, will you?" she blurted out. She felt embarrassed for Geoffrey. Why did he have to put her in this position?

Adelaide shook her head. "Your father doesn't need to know every household secret. Don't worry. My lips are sealed." She smiled again.

Her mother's smile lit up the whole room, and Danielle felt as if a heavy weight had been lifted from her shoulders.

"Today," Adelaide said happily, "is for Geoffrey Lafitte, and we're going to enjoy his company." She eyed her daughter appreciatively. "You look very pretty. I like your hair that way, caught up in back with a clasp. Casual but nice." She touched her flowing hair, laughing. "I'd better do up mine and change clothes, or Geoffrey will wonder what

kind of a hoyden you have for a mother." She
waved her two hands in Danielle's direction.
"Now run. We'll have lunch early."

"Mother" — her voice caught — "thank
you for being so understanding." She left
quickly before the tears could surface.

As she walked the length of the veranda,
she stopped and placed her hands on the rail-
ing to quiet their trembling. Her mother had
such insight about most things, but despite
her kind words, there was no doubt she had
difficulty in understanding Geoffrey's theft.

At one o'clock, Geoffrey rode full tilt onto
the grounds. He was right on time. How
straight and tall he looked dressed all in
black. Dismounting with grace, he glanced at
Etienne, who was adding pebbles to a hole in
the road. "Come over here and see to my
horse," Geoffrey barked.

Etienne continued to empty the stones into
the deep rut, and Danielle was dismayed to
see Geoffrey stride over to Etienne and grasp
his shoulder, spinning him about. "Didn't you
hear me?" he shouted. "Tend to my horse."

Etienne's leather-lined face gave Geoffrey a withering glance as only a Cajun could
do. His eyes flickered in Danielle's direction.
She gave an imperceptible nod.

Etienne carefully placed the bucket by the
side of the road and slowly moved to Geoffrey's horse. The pirate, furious, kicked the
loose pebbles, some of them hitting Etienne's
legs, but the proud servant didn't look back.

Geoffrey shook his head in disgust and turned to meet Danielle. His mood quickly changed. "Danielle!" With swift strides, he was at her side, scooping her into his arms and grinning down at her.

"Geoffrey," she said reproachfully. "There was no need to speak to Etienne that way."

"Don't worry about a servant," he said, pressing the blue cameo into her hand and giving her a hurried kiss.

She stared at him, almost seeing him for the first time, and clutched the dainty stone tightly. "Thank you, Geoffrey. I knew you wouldn't forget."

"I don't want my one true love unhappy with me," he said half mockingly, raising one eyebrow.

Slipping the cameo into her pocket, she wondered why he still didn't take his theft seriously and why he treated Etienne with such contempt. She lifted her chin and tried to put everything out of her mind except this moment. She wanted to present Geoffrey in the best possible light.

"I hope your father had a good lunch so he won't bite me," Geoffrey teased.

She took his arm as they walked up the steps, and could feel the muscles beneath his silk shirt. "Don't worry about Father. He can be as sweet as the sugar he grows when he wants to be."

"Ha!" Geoffrey responded. "I've heard he's an ogre who would throw all pirates in the drink if he had half a chance." He grinned, and his tanned face and dark brown hair appeared splashed with sunlight.

"Come," Danielle urged. "I know he'll like you enough to invite you back."

Geoffrey shook his head. "I won't be coming back," he said lightly. "At least not to see your father. The pirates on Grand Terre are leaving Monday for Mobile. Jean wants to sail there and perhaps to Florida before heading for the Texas coast. He's checking several locations before he decides on a particular one." He looked at her for a long moment. "I'm going along."

"Geoffrey, no!" Her emotions were in a turmoil again. Just when she had forgiven Geoffrey and when he was allowed to call at Cypress Manor, he was leaving. He was disrupting all her dreams. Didn't he love her enough to want to stay here?

"It will be fun to see someplace different. Besides, I want you to come to Mobile with me."

"Please," she said, laughing. "Be serious, Geoffrey. We'll talk about this later." She pulled away. "Right now, prepare to meet the ogre."

As they entered the parlor, Antoine Verlaine was standing stiffly by the harpsichord.

Danielle's mother, hair neatly done and wearing a crisp white blouse, came forward, hand extended. "How nice to see you again, Geoffrey."

Beaming, Geoffrey swept his arm across his chest, then brushed her fingertips with his lips. "Madame Verlaine. You're as fresh and lovely as a flower."

He faced Captain Verlaine. "Sir. How nice to see you once more. It's a pleasure to be here. Cypress Manor is a beautiful plantation."

"We've worked hard to make it that way," Antoine said, not unpleasantly.

The conversation was casual with comments about the Battle of New Orleans, the crops, and the weather; but before the time was up, Verlaine abruptly terminated the "coffee hour." He stood and reached for his wide-brimmed hat. "I need to supervise the field hands." He held out his hand. "If you'll pardon me." Not once had he mentioned Geoffrey Lafitte by name.

The two men politely shook hands, but Danielle could feel her father's inward disapproval of Geoffrey. The magic meeting was over, and it had not been terribly successful.

She walked with Geoffrey to his horse, and when he wrapped his cloak about her and kissed her, all her reservations about him were forgotten. How she loved him!

He released her and stepped backward. "Ah, Danielle, how I wish I could stay here with you." He loosened his mount's tether. "But my uncle expects me in New Orleans within the hour to help dismantle his town house."

The pirate placed a foot in the stirrup and

lithely swung into the saddle. "Come with me to Mobile. I'll be back tomorrow for your answer."

"Geoffrey, I can't —"

He held up his hand to stave off an answer. "No decision now." He reached down and placed his hand against her cheek. "Don't make a hasty choice. There's a whole new world waiting for the two of us out there. You mustn't say no to our exciting future together." He blew her a kiss. "Until tomorrow afternoon at the same time. I'll meet you at the stable." He kicked his horse in the ribs, goading him into a swift canter.

After he had disappeared beyond the ferns and mangrove trees, Danielle stood for a few moments, gazing at the empty lane.

Her heart thumped painfully as she walked to the stable. Another dilemma. It seemed Geoffrey was good at creating dilemmas for her. But what was there to think about? Of course, the whole idea was preposterous: She couldn't go running off with Geoffrey.

Saddling Ebony, she led him out of the stable down toward the riverbank. She clung to her stallion as they galloped along the river shore. The sunny day, the breeze, and even the mud splattering her dress and face felt wonderful.

She rode for almost an hour and finally brought her lathered horse to a shuddering halt. She was covered with mire but didn't give it a thought as she patted Ebony. "Come, boy, I'll lead you. First, however," she murmured, "I'll take off my shoes and stockings."

The cool silt oozed between her toes. As she plodded along the bank, her feet made a squishing sound. The waters lapped gently against the shore, and once she saw a water snake gliding over the surface but paid little heed, for her thoughts were on Geoffrey. How could she leave Cypress Manor and go away with a pirate? Although she had to admit the idea was a thrilling one. It might be her one and only chance of ridding herself of the infernal marriage contract. At any cost she must free herself of that.

Mobile Bay. The name sent a shiver of delight through her. She knew that it was a natural setting for pirates. To be able to see a new city and a new bay dotted with islands, which Jean Lafitte would choose as his headquarters, would be a once-in-a-lifetime chance. An opportunity to sail to the west coast of Florida awaited her also. She'd heard tales that the oranges grew as large as cannonballs and that gold was as plentiful as fish in the Gulf. It would be thrilling to see the land where Ponce de León had searched for the Fountain of Youth. She picked up a twig and tossed it in the river. It floated a short distance, then a whirlpool dragged it under.

A flatboat floated by, manned by three flatboatmen. One of them, dark and burly with his sleeves rolled up, spied her and waggled his push pole in her direction. "Halloo," he yelled, cupping one hand around his mouth. "Come with us to St. John's Landing."

She gave him a friendly wave and grinned but didn't reply.

The men laughed and began poling the large barge faster upriver. One of them stomped his foot three times and broke into song. The others lustily joined in.

When the boat rounded the bend, their lively tune became faint, then faded out of earshot completely.

She pulled the cameo from her pocket. The ice-blue background and the white, carved profile was hers once again. She clasped it tightly to her breast, glad to have it back. Dearest Geoffrey. Maybe she could teach him certain things that he seemed oblivious to. He was eager to please.

As she walked, her feet became cold and she stopped. Looking at her muddy feet, she decided not to put on her shoes and stockings.

Remounting, she sat atop Ebony for a long time, surveying the muddy yellow waters. How many childhood memories she had along the river and bayous, especially at Slippery Cove, which was directly ahead. The happy times she had had there with her mother and father were too many to count. How she had loved it as a small girl when she, on a pony, and her mother, on her roan, rode out on a late summer day to Slippery Cove. A picnic hamper was lashed to the rump of the roan. Spreading out the cloth, they waited for her father, who rode in from the fields to join them. They had a leisurely dinner and would sometimes go barefoot along the river's edge hunting soft-shell crabs. The three of them had met like this for years — ever since she'd been old enough to sit a pony. On her tenth birthday, she'd been given Ebony, the most marvelous gift she had ever received.

As she had grown up, they hadn't met as frequently at Slippery Cove, but though the times were not as often, when they did meet they were all the sweeter. Last August, they had their supper while overlooking the river and the small island in the center. They had talked about the imminent war with the British and future plans for Cypress Manor. Danielle wearily wheeled Ebony about and wondered if they would ever meet there again.

The horse's slow walk back was at a very different pace from the wild gallop earlier. She reached down, stroking Ebony's neck. There would be no room for him aboard a sloop. No room at all. There she was, thinking of Mobile Bay again, knowing that she would never dare leave.

The westering sun streaked the sky with bright pinks and yellows. Had she really ridden for hours? She had resolved nothing in her mind. She only knew she would be sixteen in two weeks, and it was time to spread her wings and fly, not have them clipped and settle into an arranged marriage.

She reached overhead and plucked a leaf from the magnolia tree. The tiny buds meant an early spring this year.

It was almost time for dinner. She must hurry and bathe and change clothes.

After she led Ebony into the stable, she brushed and curried him, removing most of the dried mud from his stomach and withers.

Toting her shoes stuffed with her cotton stockings, she cautiously opened the back door and peeked in, hoping to slip upstairs unseen, but she was unlucky. Her mother and father were in the kitchen drinking coffee.

"Danielle!" Adelaide exclaimed, jumping to her feet. "Just look at you. Barefooted, your beautiful suit filthy, and mud in your hair. Whatever are you thinking of!"

"I'm going to bathe right now," she promised, the words fairly tripping over each other.

Her father, frowning, stepped forward, hands on hips. "I don't think you'll ever grow up, Danielle. Why would you come into this house with bare feet and looking like a raga-muffin?"

"Father, I couldn't help it. I was lost in thought and before I knew it I" — she glanced helplessly down at her splattered riding suit — "I was covered with mud." She brightened, hoping to soften their anger. "It was so beautiful at Slippery Cove. I was remembering our picnics."

"Danielle," Adelaide said quietly but firmly. "Go straight to your room and clean yourself."

Danielle hurried, hoping to slip past them without another word.

"Just a minute, young lady," her father said firmly. "I did you a favor by allowing your pirate friend to enter Cypress Manor. Never again. From now on, you're to behave like a lady. No more socializing with pirates. No more wild rides. Now do as your mother says and take your bath. Dinner is at seven sharp."

"I'm not hungry," she said defiantly, sweeping around her father and dashing up to her room. She angrily strode to the window. She hated it here. The winding lane, the moss softly swaying in the breeze, all seemed to beckon to her.

Suddenly, she knew what she must do. She'd run away! She whirled about and fetched her valise from the bottom of the armoire, threw it on the bed, and snatched a few clothes to fill it. Her lower lip trembled, and tears made a blur of the dress she was hurriedly folding. There was no point in staying where she wasn't wanted and where she did everything wrong. *Steady, girl,* she reasoned. *Be fair.* It wasn't true that she wasn't wanted in Cypress Manor. She knew her mother and father would be frantic when they discovered she was missing. Furiously, she brushed a salty tear from her lips. They had driven her to this. She didn't want to leave, but she must.

A plan began to take form in her mind. She would run away with Geoffrey tomorrow and sail as far as Mobile with Jean Lafitte's crew. Once in Alabama, she could make her way to Boston. Her beautiful cameo would pay the passage by river and coach. Why couldn't things go smoothly? Why did Geoffrey have to leave now? Why did her parents have to treat her as if she were five years old? It was all so confusing, but if she could get away and stay with Aunt Madeline, she'd find a job in Boston. Given time, the future might become clearer.

Not eating any dinner, she crawled into bed, exhausted. As she stared into the darkness, she thought, *This is my last night at Cypress Manor. My last night in this room. My last night in this bed.* Her parents had left her no alternative. She seldom flinched when they scolded her about her reckless ways, but when it came to her life, she was determined to lead it the way she saw fit. With a stab of sorrow, she realized she would never see Paul again. Her sweet naval officer and staunch friend. He would be disappointed in her running away. He'd see her escape as not facing up to her own problems. However, Paul didn't know what had happened here today.

A ragged sob tore from her throat, and she buried her head in her pillow.

Chapter
Twenty-five

THE morning had dragged along interminably. Danielle was as nervy and as skittish as a river water bug, trying to avoid her parents as much as possible. She didn't have to worry about Etienne and Josephine, for on Sundays they were free to do as they pleased. They usually went to church and then stayed for the afternoon social. Would her parents ever leave? They were supposed to drive into town to meet the buyer of Aunt Madeline's town house, where they would have lunch and give the man the keys. Well, she thought grimly, she wouldn't be here when they returned. Her valise was under the bed, and she was dressed for travel in a long-sleeved dark cotton print with leather boots and a wide leather belt. Geoffrey might arrive early, and she intended to be ready. Nothing must interfere with her plans to leave Cypress Manor.

"Danielle," Adelaide said, coming into her room. "We're leaving now. We should be home by three o'clock. Are you certain you don't want to come along?"

Danielle sat at her dressing table and returned her mother's look in the mirror. "I'm sure," she answered. She brushed her hair, letting it fan out around her drawn face. She tried to keep her voice light when she said, "I plan to go over the accounts with the abacus to recheck the figures."

"There's no need to do that," Adelaide said, giving her daughter a long look.

"I know," Danielle answered, "but I want to do a comparison with this year's and last year's shipments." She hoped the lie sounded convincing.

Adelaide placed her hands on Danielle's shoulders, then leaned down and hugged her about the neck. "Let's forget yesterday afternoon." She sighed quietly. "Ah, Danielle, growing up is painful, and I know you think your father and I are constantly criticizing your every action." She smiled, patting her daughter's arm, preparing to leave. "It's not that at all, you know." Her wide-set eyes gazed at her gently. "You do so many more right things than wrong. It's just that you were covered with mud, and your father and I had been talking about a special party we were planning for you."

"A special party?" she echoed blankly.

"Your sixteenth birthday! We're planning a gala for your debut." Adelaide laughed.

"And then you came in looking like a swamp girl. I must admit it upset me more than it normally would have."

Adelaide half turned with her hand on the doorknob. "We love you, Danielle."

Impulsively, Danielle jumped up and ran to hug her. This might be the last time she'd be able to embrace her beautiful mother. Her eyes were filled with a brimming brilliance.

Her mother patted her on the back, as if soothing a small child. "We'll be back soon and have a pleasant evening together. Your father would be so pleased if you showed him how much you loved him, too."

She broke from her mother, feeling the tears on her thick lashes. If Adelaide only knew that she would never have that chance. Danielle swallowed away the lump of sorrow clutching at her throat, and managed to say, "Have a nice luncheon."

"Yes, Mr. Pearson will enjoy taking possession of Madeline's lovely home." She blew Danielle a kiss. "We'll see you soon." Adelaide softly shut the door.

No, not soon, Danielle reflected sadly. She wondered if she'd ever see her mother and father again. She sank down on her bed and brushed at her teary eyes.

She stayed in her room until she heard the front door close. Hurrying to the window, she watched her mother mount the carriage steps and seat herself beside Antoine. Because of the hooded cloak she was wearing, Danielle couldn't see her face. At any rate, she had

said her good-byes to her mother. She concentrated on catching a glimpse of her
father's face. His top hat was set at a rakish
angle, and he was smiling at Adelaide. After
he had flickered the whip over the horses'
rumps, setting them at a trotting pace, he
settled back on the cushioned seat and slung
one arm around Adelaide's shoulder. Danielle
craned her neck until the carriage disappeared from view. "Farewell," she whispered.
"I'll miss you."

Slowly she left the window, gazing about
at her cheery room. She was determined to
leave it spotless. She straightened her remaining clothes in the armoire, lined up the
four pairs of slippers, and evened the three
bonnets on the top shelf. How exquisite they
looked; the pink tulle with green velvet
leaves, the red with the black satin bow, and
the blue ruffled one. She had no place for a
bonnet on a pirate ship, and when she traveled
to Boston, she'd use the hood of her cloak.
That would be good enough.

Once her clothes were all in order, she
next went to the quilt chest at the foot of the
bed. She would fold the quilts neatly and then
be ready to go downstairs.

Kneeling, she opened the chest and found
the quilts were already neatly folded. As she
was about to close the lid, however, she
noticed a small leg protruding from beneath
the feather comforter on the bottom. Pulling
the limb free, she saw it was attached to an
old doll she had played with as a tiny child.

She sat back on her heels and held the small figure at arm's length. The baby's porcelain face had a rosebud mouth and a rouge patch on each plump cheek. The round head was topped by a mound of painted black hair, and the former white kidskin body with its many joints had yellowed with age. "Baby Louise" was what she had named the naked girl doll. She wondered where Louise's long lace petticoat and dress had vanished. How long ago she had dressed and undressed Louise. As she cradled the doll in the crook of her arm, she had a dim recollection of a tea party she'd held under the three oak trees on the front lawn. She had propped Louise against a tree trunk as her guest. Danielle breathed deeply. As a small child, she had to play at make-believe games by herself; however, she had never missed having playmates. Her parents had taught her independence at an early age. Well, today, she was doing the most independent thing of her life.

Carefully she tucked the doll back amongst the bedding and stood up. It was almost one o'clock.

She lugged the valise from beneath the bed. To think one bag represented all her possessions! Her pulse quickened. The time had come. She pulled on her riding gloves and draped her cloak over one arm. With a last glance around the room, she opened the door and went haltingly down the steps. The house was so silent, she could almost hear her thumping heart.

Out into the bright sunlight, she resolutely strode to the empty stable. She would have time to bid a sad adieu to Ebony before Geoffrey came riding up the lane.

Cooing tenderly to Ebony, she stopped when she heard the sound of hoofbeats. At last Geoffrey had come to take her away. With trepidation, she reached for the pitchfork and threw down plenty of fodder, but Ebony only pricked his ears forward and stamped nervously as if he knew there was some mischief to be played on him today.

The stable door creaked open and there, with the sun behind him, Geoffrey stood, all burnished gold. Her Greek god, whom she had so admired months ago, had come to free her. Smiling, she ran to meet him and he opened his arms.

They embraced for a long moment. Then he stepped back and grinned. "Does this mean you're going with me?"

"Didn't you see my valise by the door?"

"My eyes could see only you." He laughed, squeezing her tightly. "You're going with me," he said gleefully. "Danielle, we'll have such good times together. Adventures. New lands. New seas. Soon I'll get away from my uncle, just like you're getting away from your mother and father, and we'll be on our own — just you and me. You're my lady. How perfect it's going to be."

For a moment, she had a fleeting doubt. She wasn't anyone's "lady" . . . she was her own person. Wasn't that why she was running away?

But when Geoffrey held her close like this, all uncertainties were erased. She'd follow him anywhere.

He kissed her lingeringly and she responded warmly. Shakily, she freed herself from his encircling arms. "We should go, Geoffrey."

"We don't need to hurry," he said lazily. "Your parents won't be coming home for a while, will they?" He pulled her back to him, he kissed her again, and his lips were as sweet as a piece of sugarcane.

She stepped backward. "I think we should go, don't you?" she repeated uneasily.

Geoffrey smiled laconically. "We have all the time in the world. The ship is packed, and my uncle waits for us on the *Pride*, off the docks of New Orleans."

"Then he's left Grand Terre?" she questioned incredulously, expecting to have to make an arduous sail into Barataria Bay.

"Uncle Jean left the island yesterday, bringing three treasure chests with him." Geoffrey grinned. "A nice start for a new place, eh?" His grin broadened. "If I'm careful to please Uncle Jean, I might inherit one of those chests very soon."

"I can't imagine Jean Lafitte giving you a whole chest of gold."

"My uncle is generous. If we marry, my sweet, it could be our wedding present." His fingers made little tracks up and down her arm. "We can be back to New Orleans by the time he has the rest of his town house possessions loaded, and in time for a dinner aboard the *Pride*."

So, if they married, Geoffrey might gain a gold treasure. Was this why he wanted her? She dismissed the notion as soon as it entered her head. Geoffrey loved her for herself! "How many pirates are accompanying Jean Lafitte?" she asked, masking her doubts.

"Only twenty-three. The rest of the band are staying on Grand Terre or becoming respectable businessmen in the city." Geoffrey laughed derisively. "Imagine! Even Dominique is remaining in New Orleans to run a warehouse."

"I was hoping to see Dominique once more," she said wistfully. "He saved my life. If it hadn't been for Dominique, I would have been sailing on the *Pride* under very different circumstances." She shuddered at the memory of Gambi and his terrible ransom plan to spirit her away to his own island. Jean Lafitte was lucky to still have his favorite ship, his gold, and his loyal buccaneers.

"Come, Danielle, we can stay here for a while longer," he said, reaching for her.

"I don't think so, Geoffrey."

He frowned briefly, then smiled leisurely. "You just won't let yourself enjoy this moment." He gathered her in his arms and kissed her again.

"Please, Geoffrey." She surveyed him with

new eyes. "I'd really like to go now," she said firmly.

He stepped back but didn't release her completely. Holding her hand, he laughingly pulled her to him. "In a minute," he vowed.

He cupped her face with his hands. "I love the way your hair surrounds that beautiful face." He lifted a thick strand, letting it fall back over her shoulder. He bent to kiss her again, but now she had become alarmed at his insistence.

She pushed him back. "No. I want to leave, Geoffrey."

His eyes shot flinty sparks, and then he teased lightly, "A pirate queen must learn to obey her pirate chief."

For a heartbeat, she stared at him in disbelief. Panic rose in her throat, and she furiously yanked herself free. She made a rush toward the door, but with a sudden lunge Geoffrey caught her.

He said triumphantly, "You don't know how lucky you are, Danielle. I could have a dozen girls with one whistle."

Angry, she whirled around and pushed him with all her strength. He lost his balance and toppled over into the pile of straw.

Amazed, he stared up at her. Several blades of straw stuck out of his thick curls.

She felt beads of perspiration spring to her forehead. Was this the man she was trusting her future to? Many things he had done, that she had overlooked or excused, stirred in her memory. His temper tantrum when she had bested him in target practice, his obvious distaste toward learning, even if some show of interest would have so pleased Jean Lafitte. But more important, she thought of his questioning his uncle's too-lenient treatment of prisoners, his theft of the cameos, and his treatment of Etienne. His warning that she should obey her pirate chief infuriated her. How could she have been so blind? So stupid?

"Geoffrey," she advised calmly. "Have a care."

"You little tease." Geoffrey chuckled, unhurriedly getting to his feet. He moved close to her, and his hand darted forth, catching her wrist. "Just one more kiss." Roughly, he pulled her against him. She struggled but was no match for his firm grip.

"Geoffrey, stop it!" she demanded.

The door opened, and a shadow fell across her face. Suddenly, Geoffrey was spun about.

"Let her go!" demanded a familiar voice.

With a sense of relief, she saw Paul confronting Geoffrey with menacing sparks in his eyes. One strong hand stayed planted on Geoffrey's shoulder.

With a snarl, Geoffrey twisted free. "Who the hell are you?" he exploded.

"The name is Paul Milerand," he answered with an edge to his light tone. "I'm a close friend of Danielle's and take exception to her being manhandled by you!"

Danielle flung up a hand as if to ward off the inevitable fight. *Poor Paul,* she thought.

He's no fighter, and Geoffrey will maul him unmercifully.

"Paul," she advised calmly, "Geoffrey and I are leaving. Please don't try to stop us." She faced Geoffrey. "Are you ready?" She couldn't disguise the note of desperation in her voice. At any cost, she must get Paul away from Geoffrey and prevent an unfair fight.

"We're not leaving just yet," Geoffrey said, spacing his words far apart. He ran his eyes contemptuously over Paul's neat uniform. "This 'cabin boy' needs to be taught a lesson!" He placed a fist on a narrow hip. "When I'm through with you, you'll crawl aboard your ship like a rat in the hold." All at once he placed both hands on Paul's chest and viciously shoved him backward.

Paul staggered, fell, and scrambled to his feet.

With an abrupt laugh, Geoffrey advanced, shoving Paul harder and slamming him against a post, sending bridles and harnesses clattering to the ground.

"Geoffrey, stop!" Danielle cried.

"No, I won't stop," Geoffrey said, his lips curling into a hard smile. "Your navy friend is too neat. He needs to be dirtied up a bit." With a short jab at Paul's face, he bloodied his nose. A spurt of crimson cascaded down Paul's smart uniform.

Paul wiped his nose on the back of his hand and lunged at Geoffrey, wrestling him about the waist. He hit the pirate in the midsection and, with a swift uppercut, caused Geoffrey's head to bounce backward.

Startled, Geoffrey stared for a brief instant at this tiger, who only moments ago had been a docile kitten. With a grunt of fury, he pounced on Paul, hitting him hard in the chest and on the cheek.

Danielle stifled a moan. Paul's blood was smeared over his face and hand, and bright drops had splattered onto the straw.

Geoffrey moved in to hit Paul again, but Paul leaped back and came at Geoffrey from the side, dealing him a hard blow below the ear. He moved in fast and struck a second time at Geoffrey's jaw.

Before Geoffrey went down, Danielle saw a look of surprise and fear.

Gasping for breath, Geoffrey glared at Paul. Suddenly, he jumped to his feet, and something sparkled in his hand.

Danielle gasped. A knife! She couldn't believe Geoffrey would actually pull a knife on someone unarmed.

She dashed at Geoffrey's back, pummeling him with her fists and screaming, "No, Geoffrey! No!"

With an obscenity, he whirled on her, shoving her so hard she went sprawling in the dirt. A whimper wrenched from her throat. Geoffrey intended to kill Paul. She bit her lower lip, tasting blood.

The two fighters, in a crouching position, circled each other warily.

Geoffrey feinted at Paul with his dagger,

the blade glinting in the sun's rays. Paul ducked, and while the pirate angled for a favorable position, Paul lashed out, kicking Geoffrey's hand and sending the dagger flying.

With a quick movement, Danielle snatched the knife and threw it in the hay mound, out of Geoffrey's reach.

Paul pressed his advantage and hit Geoffrey in the mouth. Geoffrey doubled over. Slowly, he collapsed to his knees, then fell on his side, groaning.

"Paul! Paul!" she cried, running to his side. "I didn't know Geoffrey had a knife!"

Rapidly, she fumbled in her pocket, drawing out her handkerchief. "You're hurt," she murmured sympathetically. Her heart went out to Paul as she wiped the blood trickling down his face.

Gently, he held her wrists and brought them down to her side. "I'm all right," he said dryly. "I suggest you tend to your friend." He glanced with disdain at Geoffrey. "I think he needs more help than I do."

Geoffrey, bunched up on all fours, was painfully and laboriously attempting to rise.

With dismay, she looked first at Geoffrey, then at Paul. For a long moment, her eyes and Paul's locked, then she lowered her lashes. She had to go to Geoffrey's aid. She had a few things to settle. For the first time, her thoughts were clear, and she no longer was confused or had any doubts about doing the right thing.

"Good-bye, chérie," Paul said tenderly, his brown eyes once again liquid-soft. He blew her a kiss. "I hope Geoffrey makes you happy." He wheeled on his foot and was gone.

She helped Geoffrey stagger to his feet. He leaned heavily on her shoulder. Propping him against the spokes of a coach wheel, she observed his swollen eye. "Geoffrey," she said grimly, "I need to talk to you."

But Geoffrey paid no attention to her statement as he examined his torn shirt and muttered, "I'll track that miserable navy cur to the bottom of the ocean if I have to." Grimacing, he touched the purple bruise that colored his cheekbone and carefully moved his jaw back and forth. "When I'm through with him, he'll be a dead sailor."

"I don't think that will be too easy to accomplish," she said, shaking her head, "considering what he did to you today." She paused. "Unless, of course, you have your dagger."

He shot her a baleful glance. "Let's get out of here," he said, drawing a ragged breath. "I'll fetch your valise."

"I'm not going with you, Geoffrey," she said simply.

His head jerked around. "What did you say?"

"I said I'm not going with you."

"What do you mean, you're not going with me?"

"It took me a long time to realize that

you're not the man for me. I should have known it a long time ago, but I guess I was confused by your charm." She smiled at him and said softly, "I'm sorry, Geoffrey, but as you said, there are a dozen girls after you." She glanced back to the empty spot where Paul had stood. For a moment, her heart stopped. She had half expected him to come back.

"That's fine with me," Geoffrey said, trying to swagger toward her. However, his stiff walk was more of a limp. "You don't think I ever really cared about a silly little girl like you. I only wanted to use the Verlaine name and prestige for whatever I could. *You* are unimportant."

His eyes glittered with rage, and Danielle felt her heart beat faster. He was capable of doing anything when he was angry. She knew that, and fearfully looked toward the door, her only way to escape.

Then Geoffrey shrugged, and that old, mocking smile played about his lips. "Good-bye, Danielle." He held open his arms to her. "A last embrace?"

But she scarcely heard him or saw his out-stretched arms as, with trembling hands, she lead Ebony from his stall, terrified of being stopped.

Outside in the radiant day, she leaped atop Ebony's back and dug her heels in his ribs, causing him to leap forward.

She had to catch Paul. She only hoped she

wasn't too late. Ebony's galloping hooves raced down the stony lane as she spurred him even faster, until she glimpsed Paul rounding a bend. "Paul!" she shouted. "Paul!"

Looking over his shoulder, Paul reined in his horse and patiently waited for her to catch up.

"Danielle," he said, coldly. "What are you doing here? Where's Geoffrey?" He gave her an icy look as he quietly waited for her explanation.

"He's gone back to New Orleans." She reached out to Paul. "Oh, I don't know where he's gone and I don't care!" She rushed on, "I must talk to you, Paul. I must!"

"I'm listening," he answered expectantly, watching her carefully.

"Please," she said, a catch in her throat as she scrambled off Ebony's back. She looked up into Paul's impassive face and tightly gripped his horse's bridle. Did she dare hope that he still loved her? "I've been wrong," she said humbly, the words coming out quickly. Now it was her turn to wait expectantly as she held her breath. The only sound between them was the fidgeting horses.

Looking at Paul, with the sun turning his hair to white-gold and his resplendent uniform into a bright glow, the agonizing thought pierced her heart that here was the man she loved. How late she realized this! She didn't know if it was the sun's dazzle or the tears threatening to spill over that caused her to blink. "Paul," she pleaded. "Please, dismount. I can't talk to you when you're up there."

He hesitated and then swung out of the saddle and jumped lightly to the ground. "All right, Danielle, what is it you're trying to say?"

He isn't making it easy for me, she thought as she eyed his cold, dark eyes. "I made a mistake," she blurted out. "I was infatuated with Geoffrey and discovered he was all dash and bravado." It was difficult to swallow, but she forced herself to go on. "He didn't know much about being kind or honest."

Paul said coolly, "You finally found him out?"

Nodding mutely, she lowered her lashes and clasped her hands in front of her. She longed for him to take her in his arms, but the silence only grew between them.

Finally, Paul reached out and touched her hand.

Their eyes locked. "Paul, I wouldn't blame you if you never wanted to see me again," she said softly. "You once said you'd never offer me the emerald ring again, unless I asked for it." She took a deep breath and plunged on, heedless of the tears that slipped down her cheek. "I'm asking for the ring now."

Wordlessly, Paul drew forth the small leather pouch from his upper pocket and shook the green jewel out onto his palm. "Danielle, I've waited a long time to hear that." Tenderly, he slipped the ring on her finger and bent his head close to hers.

Danielle's heart surged with joy as she closed her eyes in anticipation of his sweet kiss. She felt as if she had grown up very suddenly . . . that the girl who had yearned after Geoffrey, who had thought he was exciting and dashing, was not the same young woman who knew that Geoffrey was a child with no substance and that Paul — dear, loving Paul — was the man with strength. A man who was a match for her own spirit and need for independence.

As she returned his kiss, she could see their future together. A young woman and a young man, equally in love.

SUNFIRE™ ROMANCES

Spirited historical romances about the lives and times of young women who boldly faced their world and dared to be different.

From the people who brought you WILDFIRE®...

An exciting look at a NEW romance line!

Imagine a turbulent time long ago when America was young and bursting with energy and passion...

When daring young women defied traditions to live their own lives...

When heart-stirring romance and thrilling adventure went hand in hand...

When the world was lit by *SUNFIRE*...

SUSANNAH by Candice F. Ransom $2.95

Not since young Scarlett O'Hara has there been a heroine so spirited. SUSANNAH Dellinger had lived her sixteen years as a proper Virginia girl. But when her brother and her fiancé are called on to defend the South, she must fight for her own life, for her family, and for the secret love born in the flames of war.

ELIZABETH by Willo Davis Roberts $2.95

The Salem witch hunts of the 1600's is the frightening setting for ELIZABETH's story. When her friend Nell is accused of being a witch, ELIZABETH has to decide whether to risk her own life and defend Nell, or to remain silent and watch her friend die. Silence will win ELIZABETH wealthy Troy and safety. Crying out will bring her reckless Johnny and love.

AMANDA by Candice F. Ransom $2.95

With only a silk dress to protect her from the blazing sun, AMANDA embarks on the Oregon Trail. The hardships of life on a wagon train change her overnight from a spoiled pampered city girl, to a strong frontierswoman, who finds drought and death, beauty and joy, and a love that will last...forever.

An exciting excerpt from the first chapter of
JOANNA follows.

JOANNA

by Jane Claypool Miner

Chapter One

IT was harder to leave home than Joanna had imagined. In the weeks following her decision to go to work in the mills in Massachusetts, she'd thought only of the delight of seeing a city, learning new things, and having money of her own to spend. Now, standing in front of the dry goods store, watching the distant stagecoach draw closer, she could think of nothing but the people she was leaving behind. Her excitement turned to fear, and her pleasure turned to pain.

She turned to her father and saw his face through the haze of her tears. For a moment, the years of hard work on a New England farm were erased and he looked like a young man again. His deep blue eyes were covered with a mist of their own and his voice was rough as he said, "God be with you, Joanna."

He's seeing Mama, Joanna thought. Her lovely brown eyes, dark brown wavy hair, and oval face were all replicas of her mother's, she knew. The small portrait inside the locket that she wore around her neck was testimony to her resemblance to her dead mother.

Joanna leaned forward to embrace her father. He put his arms around her as though she were still a small child and said, "You do not need to leave your home, Joanna."

"I want to go to Lowell," she said and though she was already missing her family very much, she knew it was true.

Lowell, the very name was exciting. The first thing she would buy when she got to Lowell was a piece of fabric to add to the bottom of the dress she wore. She was fifteen now and too old to wear a little girl's short skirt. This dress came to the top of her high-laced shoes. Better yet, she would buy a new dress, perhaps one of the dark blue Merrimac prints that was so popular among the Lowell girls.

Joanna touched the gold locket that circled her neck and bit her lip to fight back the tears that were crowding her eyes once again. She turned to her father and said, "Good-bye, Papa."

The stagecoach pulled up in a cloud of dust. The driver opened the stagecoach door and motioned for her to get inside. She felt a sharp thrill of excitement and eagerness, and then the pain of leaving home closed in on her again. She leaned her head on her father's chest for one moment. The homespun tweed jacket smelled of wood-stove smoke and years of wear — but to her, it smelled sweeter than any spring flowers. It smelled of home — the home she was leaving, perhaps forever.

Her father pulled her from him and looked into her eyes gravely as he said, "You're fifteen and a sensible girl, Joanna. But you are not experienced in the ways of the world. Be careful and remember that you'll always have a home with us. If the work is too hard . . ." her father's voice trailed off.

"I want to go," Joanna said once again. Even though the parting was so difficult, she knew that Lowell was her own free choice. There was so much more opportunity for a girl like her in Lowell than in a small town like Putney or a smaller village such as Wainscott. The year 1836 had been the last of several bad farming seasons and many families were leaving New England farms for other opportunities. Joanna wasn't the only young person leaving home that year. Many would be setting out to the mills or, like Jed Robbins, to sea to earn their fortunes. She pushed the thought of Jed away. It was too painful.

Once inside the coach, Joanna squeezed into a small space between a very fat woman and a young woman who wasn't fat but seemed as large as most men. It was impossible for her to look out and wave good-bye, and she longed to ask her companions to trade places with her for just a moment. But the fat woman looked rather unfriendly and the younger woman seemed to be asleep.

As she settled herself into the small space, the fat woman complained, "Wouldn't hurt them to build these things a bit wider."

Joanna tried to make herself smaller, but she couldn't think of anything to say except, "I'm sorry."

She realized that there had been more room on the other side, next to two men who were probably brothers, since they were wearing the same sort of tweed jackets and looked something alike. They were older and smaller than Papa and not very interesting-looking, she decided. Of course, it would never have done for her to choose to sit by the men, even if there was more room. A respectable girl wouldn't do that.

As politely as possible, Joanna gazed at her fellow passengers, who didn't seem to be a very exciting group. She smiled at herself for her quick judgments and asked herself whom she had expected to meet on this trip to Lowell. Did she think every stranger was going to be as fascinating as the ones she read about in the novels she borrowed from Lucy Robbins?

Why not? Joanna asked herself. Wasn't she doing something as adventurous as anything she'd read about in those books? Going to Lowell, Massachusetts, all by herself was something most women would not have dreamed of until very recently. It was only in the last ten years that any of the girls in her village had had the courage to leave home and seek work.

"On your way to be married?" the woman on her right asked Joanna.

"I'm going to work," Joanna answered proudly. "In the mill at Lowell."

The fat woman nodded and said, "Had a cousin who worked at Cohoes for a while. She soon tired of the noise. Said it wasn't as nice as they wrote about it. I wonder your folks let you go off like that alone. In my day, no respectable girl was allowed to travel alone. But girls ain't respectable these days."

Joanna was torn between her desire to respond to this rude woman and a need to giggle at her old-fashioned attitudes. Either response would be unladylike, of course, so she bit her lower lip and looked demurely at her hands. They were strong capable hands with long fingers and nails that were cut straight across. Looking at her hands reminded her of Jed Robbins and that made her frown. Jed had held her hands between his when he'd come to say good-bye six months ago. His larger, rougher hands had fully enclosed hers and she'd felt warmth coursing between them. Then he told her he was going to sea.

She had not been able to hide her disappointment and hurt. She had always thought that someday she and Jed would marry. When he took her in his arms and kissed her deeply, Joanna put her arms around his neck and held him close to her. Then in a sudden rage, she pushed him away.

"If the sea means more to you than I do, you are not the man I thought you were."

"I'll be back, Joanna . . . and then, maybe. . . ."

Joanna turned her back on him. "Go away. I don't care if you come back or not."

Since then, his sister Lucy had received letters from him, but Joanna had not heard a word.

She shook her head, reminding herself that now Jed Robbins was a former neighbor, nothing more. The chances were she'd never see him again. Yet she couldn't help wondering what he'd think when Lucy wrote to tell him of her journey to Lowell.

"No doubt you're a good enough girl," the fat woman went on. "Probably planning to send all your money home so your brothers can get an education. Or pay off the mortgage?"

Joanna remained silent, resenting the woman's prying.

"Saving for your wedding? Got a young man?"

"No," Joanna said firmly. She thought

again of Jed Robbins. He was certainly nothing to her. If he could go off to sea and never even write, then he certainly wasn't important to her. So why did his laughing green eyes dance in her mind? She would never see him again and yet. . . .

Soon Joanna was hungry and she longed to know what time it was. She had a small amount of food with her but it would not do to eat it all the first few hours of the trip. Yet, when her stomach began to growl, she decided it was time to have a bit to eat. There was bread and cheese and six hard-boiled eggs. She opened the calf-covered bandbox that sat on her lap and took out one of the eggs. Cracking it against the side of the wooden band, she began to peel the egg slowly.

As she peeled the egg, she became aware that the younger woman on her right was watching her from beneath lowered, not closed eyes. Joanna was uncomfortable about eating in the presence of strangers without offering them anything. Torn between worry about her small store of food and her need to be courteous, she chose courtesy. She offered the peeled egg to the young woman who seemed to hesitate for a moment, then darted her hand forward and took the egg.

Joanna watched in amazement as the young woman ate the egg in two fast gulps. She was obviously very hungry, so Joanna offered her a second egg out of pity, knowing that she might be hungry herself by the time the trip was over. The young woman seemed to hesitate just a moment longer but then accepted the second egg and swallowed it even quicker. Joanna closed the lid on the bandbox without taking out a third egg for herself.

The young woman leaned over and whispered, "Eat your food. I have money to buy us something in the next town."

Joanna did not know what to say in reply to that. If the young woman had money, why hadn't she provided a lunch for herself? Joanna was too embarrassed not to obey the young woman's instructions. She opened the bandbox again and took out the third egg. This time she peeled and ate the egg as quickly as she could, in order to avoid having to look at the hungry girl's eyes.

When she finished the egg, she turned to her traveling companion with the idea of striking up a conversation, but the young girl's eyes were closed again. Joanna studied her carefully, as though there might be clues in her outward appearance to her strange behavior. She was a large, strong-looking girl with hair that was very light reddish-blond and with very large freckles. From the freckles, Joanna guessed that she was also a farmer's daughter and wondered if it was possible that she might be on her way to Lowell as well.

She wished the other girl would wake up so that they might pass the time with conversation, but there were no signs of that possibility.

Joanna longed for the trip to be more eventful. She had hoped for adventure, and hours of riding in the middle of a dark stagecoach wasn't exactly thrilling. In fact, after six hours on the road, Joanna was beginning to wonder how she would ever endure the next two days. When they finally pulled into a small town and stopped, Joanna was surprised that the girl beside her still did not open her eyes.

The fat woman gathered up her belongings and said, "You be a good girl, hear me," and got out of the stagecoach.

When the driver said, "You can stretch your legs here, we're changing horses," Joanna prepared to follow the two men who climbed out; but the girl put a large, strong hand on her arm and held her fast. The driver turned to ask, "You're not getting out?"

"We'll be right there," Joanna said. She wondered at her answer since she could not speak for the strange girl who was holding her arm.

"Here's money," the girl whispered. "Get as much food as you can buy. I'm starving." She held out a silver dollar to Joanna.

"Aren't you getting out?" Joanna asked.

"Please," the girl said. "Just buy the food! And if anyone asks you about me, say you're my sister. It's important."

Joanna's heart began to race. Here was excitement, after all! Was the young woman escaping from an unwanted suitor? Or was it more dangerous, more serious than that? Somehow Joanna could not believe the girl was a criminal. Her wide blue eyes were too honest and open. Joanna nodded in agreement and opened the stage door and slid to the ground.

She bought the food quickly, choosing a tin of crackers, some dried beef, and apples. As she paid for the food, the shopkeeper asked her, "You from New Hampshire?"

"No, sir, Vermont."

The shopkeeper was wearing eyeglasses on the end of his nose and he squinted as he looked at Joanna, then shook his head. "Man was here about half an hour ago looking for a runaway. You a runaway?"

"No, sir."

"I reckon you've got black hair, right?"

"Yes, sir." Her hair wasn't really black; it was a dark chestnut brown, but she thought it simpler to agree with him. Her heart was racing with excitement as she realized that the girl in the stagecoach might be the runaway the shopkeeper was talking about.

"Man said his girl was real tall and had yellow hair and blue eyes. Your eyes blue?"

"No, sir."

"You ain't so tall neither." He seemed almost angry that she wasn't the girl he was looking for.

Even in her excitement, Joanna couldn't resist a smile as she saw how plainly disappointed the man was because she wasn't tall and blond.

The two male passengers had apparently been hearing enough of the conversation to be curious and stepped closer. One of them asked the shopkeeper, "You say the girl is a runaway?"

"Not this one," the shopkeeper complained.

Joanna slipped away as the two men began to question the shopkeeper. She moved quickly back to the stagecoach, climbing in and handing the food and the remainder of the money to the hungry girl. She said, "If you're from New Hampshire and your father is searching for you. . . ."

The girl sat upright quickly and nodded her head. "Right, that's me. I'll thank you for the food and be on my way."

"My name's Joanna Adams."

"Best you don't know mine," the girl replied and then she smiled. "He's not my father. He's married to my aunt but he's no relative of mine. A wicked, angry, and stingy man, he is. I'll be gone now."

The girl slid out the door of the stagecoach carrying her bundle of food. She picked up her skirt and began to run as fast as she could, heading toward a group of trees that they'd passed just before entering town.

The two men returned to the stagecoach in a minute and seemed surprised that the other passenger was no longer there. "She told me she got off here," Joanna lied.

"I believe she might have been the runaway girl, after all," one of the men said to his brother.

The other brother shook his head and said, "I wonder what sort of mischief she'll get herself into. A young girl who runs away like that is ruined for life."

"Women need the protection of a man to survive." The other brother nodded his head up and down this time.

When the second brother began nodding his head up and down also, Joanna grew impatient with their conversation and asked, "Sirs, what if the man is cruel and heartless? Is it still better for a young woman to seek *his* protection?"

The men smiled at Joanna as though to indicate she was too young to understand.

Suddenly a man broke into the coach and asked, "You have a young girl here, don't you?"

"Only me," Joanna spoke up. She was not really frightened of the man for herself but she trembled for the blond girl when she looked at this man's face. He looked every bit as bad as his stepniece had described him and suddenly Joanna was very glad she'd warned the yellow-haired girl. She only hoped the girl's long, strong legs would enable her to escape.

"You seen my girl? Delia? Tall with light red-yellow hair?"

"We believe she may have been a passenger," one brother said reluctantly. Joanna wondered why there was doubt in his voice. Was it because he was unsure about helping this horrible man?

"Talks with a slow tongue," the man said. "Mark on her cheek, maybe." Then he growled, "When I get my hands on her, she'll have more than one mark." Then he seemed to realize that his brusque manner might offend the stagecoach passengers. He said, as though to explain his anger and eagerness to get her back, "Stole my money, she did."

Joanna caught her breath at that news. Delia was not only a runaway, but also a thief. What had come over her to lie for such a girl? And yet, when the man asked her directly, "You see that girl?" she shook her head no.

"There was a girl here," the one brother said. "But whether she was Delia, we have no idea. She slept the whole trip."

The man nodded his head solemnly. "That's the girl. Lazy, she is. Lazy and stupid. Where is she?"

He turned to Joanna and asked, "You, girl — where is she?" His manner was so threatening and bold that she understood he intended to catch her off guard.

"The girl who was here said she lived by the river. She walked toward that road, down that way." Joanna pointed in exactly the opposite direction from the one Delia had taken.

The man seemed angrier than ever as he turned away from the stagecoach and headed toward the river. At that moment the stagecoach began to move. Joanna leaned back, looking out the small window as the stagecoach rumbled and jolted down the road. Joanna was happy that she'd added a bit to Delia's chances of escape. She'd been on her travels for only a few hours and while it was true that she already told the only two lies of her life, it was also true that she had had an adventure. On the whole, she was more excited than remorseful, though she supposed it should be the other way around if she were to be a proper mill girl.

Her life was going to be exciting. She knew it. For a moment Jed's green eyes flashed before her and she remembered how his lips had felt on hers, but he was gone and her new life was ahead.

Move from one breathtaking romance to another with the #1
Teen Romance line in the country!

NEW WILDFIRES! $1.95 each

- ☐ MU32539-6 **BLIND DATE** Priscilla Maynard
- ☐ MU32541-8 **NO BOYS?** McClure Jones
- ☐ MU32538-8 **SPRING LOVE** Jennifer Sarasin
- ☐ MU31930-2 **THAT OTHER GIRL** Conrad Nowels

BEST-SELLING WILDFIRES! $1.95 each

- ☐ MU31981-7 **NANCY AND NICK** Caroline B. Cooney
- ☐ MU32313-X **SECOND BEST** Helen Cavanagh
- ☐ MU31849-7 **YOURS TRULY, LOVE, JANIE** Ann Reit
- ☐ MU31566-8 **DREAMS CAN COME TRUE** Jane Claypool Miner
- ☐ MU32369-5 **HOMECOMING QUEEN** Winifred Madison
- ☐ MU31261-8 **I'M CHRISTY** Maud Johnson
- ☐ MU30324-4 **I'VE GOT A CRUSH ON YOU** Carol Stanley
- ☐ MU32361-X **THE SEARCHING HEART** Barbara Steiner
- ☐ MU31710-5 **TOO YOUNG TO KNOW** Elisabeth Ogilvie
- ☐ MU32430-6 **WRITE EVERY DAY** Janet Quin-Harkin
- ☐ MU30956-0 **THE BEST OF FRIENDS** Jill Ross Klevin

Scholastic Inc.,
P.O. Box 7502, 2932 E. McCarty Street, Jefferson City, MO 65102

Please send me the books I have checked above. I am enclosing $_____
(please add $1.00 to cover shipping and handling). Send check or money order—
no cash or C.O.D.'s please.

Name _____

Address _____

City_____ State/Zip_____

Please allow four to six weeks for delivery.   9/83